D0092973

RECEIVED
JUL 03 2019
By

ALSO BY VIRGINIA REEVES

Work Like Any Other

The Behavior of Love

— A Novel —

Virginia Reeves

SCRIBNER
New York London Toronto Sydney New Delhi

Scribner
An Imprint of Simon & Schuster, Inc.
1230 Avenue of the Americas
New York, NY 10020

This book is a work of fiction. Any references to historical events, real people, or real places are used fictitiously. Other names, characters, places, and events are products of the author's imagination, and any resemblance to actual events or places or persons, living or dead, is entirely coincidental.

First Scribner hardcover edition May 2019

Interior design by Kyle Kabel

Manufactured in the United States of America

1 3 5 7 9 10 8 6 4 2

Library of Congress Cataloging-in-Publication Data

Names: Reeves, Virginia, author.
Title: The Behavior of Love : a novel / Virginia Reeves.
Description: First Scribner hardcover edition. | New York : Scribner, May 2019.
Identifiers: LCCN 2018023180| ISBN 9781501183508 (hardcover) |
ISBN 9781501183515 (trade paper) | ISBN 9781501183522 (ebook)
Subjects: LCSH: Therapist and patient—Fiction. | Psychological fiction.
Classification: LCC PS3618.E4458 B44 2018 | DDC 813/.6—dc23
LC record available at https://lccn.loc.gov/2018023180

ISBN 978-1-5011-8350-8
ISBN 978-1-5011-8352-2 (ebook)

To my love, Luke Muszkiewicz,
and the memory of his father, Mike

The bird would cease and be as other birds
But that he knows in singing not to sing.
The question that he frames in all but words
Is what to make of a diminished thing.

—Robert Frost

Boulder, Montana

—

APRIL–AUGUST 1971

Chapter 1

Ed's work keeps him late. Yesterday's pile of incomplete tasks awaits him in his office, and today's begins the moment he steps from his car. He never knows what the first thing will be, but it always meets him here in the dirt parking lot. Yesterday, it was Margaret wandering toward the Boulder River, whose waters have already drowned one patient. The day before, it was a six-year-old named Devin eating gravel. Today, it's a young man bursting out the front doors of Griffin Hall, a white plastic chair over his head, a denim-clad orderly close behind. The orderly's rubber club is raised. The boy drops to the ground and curls himself into a ball. The chair topples down the stairs and scatters a group of patients.

Orderlies are to use the clubs only if they feel physically endangered. Ed made this clear the day he became superintendent of the Boulder River School and Hospital. He's been there every day for over a year now, and the clubs are still there every day, too.

The orderly is dragging the boy to his feet, pulling him back toward the doors. Ed doesn't recognize either of them. He's been doing his best to learn everyone's names, but there are 750 patients in his care, and the staff turns over constantly.

Ed lights a cigarette and walks over. "I'll take the patient from here," he says.

The boy's face is averted, chin cast down toward his left shoulder, teeth mouthing tongue. He holds his hands in fists at his chest. Ed can see grime on the boy's neck, the stuff of weeks.

"All yours, Doc." The orderly drops the boy's arm. "If he runs again, you're chasing him."

The boy makes no move to run.

Ed should reprimand the orderly. He should get his name, at least, so he can write him up. But there are five cases in front of this one, all of them more severe, and the hospital is operating with only twenty-five percent of its needed staff. Plus, what with the regular turnover, Ed may never see this orderly again.

"The average tenure is seven weeks," Sheila told him his first day. She's one of the few long-term employees, a nurse who loves her patients. Single and dowdy and invested, Sheila doesn't seem to mind the poor pay or long hours or isolated location. She lives in a small apartment in Boulder's only brick apartment building, just up the road, wears bright red lipstick, styles her short hair into a feathered halo around her head. "What do I need extra money for?" she said. "It's just me and the cat."

Ed wants a hundred more Sheilas.

"Seven weeks?" he'd asked.

"Long enough to get 'em halfway trained."

Ed looks at the boy in front of him. He knows not to touch him; touch is associated with violence now, with punishment. Running and its accompanying freedom and joy are associated with that, too. This is what behaviorism is—equations. The boy is simple; his equations are simple. Running = beating.

"What's your name, son?"

The boy flinches but lifts his head. "George," he says, a two-syllable word in his deep voice. "Jor-Ja."

"It's nice to meet you, George. I'm Edmund. I like to shake people's hands when I meet them. You want to shake hands?"

George looks at Ed's extended hand, then back at his face. Down and up a couple times before shaking his head.

"That's fine. We'll try again later, all right?"

George unclenches one of his fists in a wave, open-closed, and Ed lets himself smile at the small success. None of his friends from med school understood why he wanted to work with the developmentally disabled as opposed to the mentally ill. "You've got no chance of fixing them, Malinowski," a pal once said. "No cure for those issues." But Ed has always been more taken with an example of progress like George's than with a decrease in psychoses. Maybe it's the innocence of mental disability, or the misunderstanding, but Ed would take this hospital over the mental institution at Warm Springs any day.

"You play outside, now," Ed says to George and leaves the boy on the steps.

Inside the building, the day disappears—the sun, the sky, mountains, trees, muddy play yard / parking lot. The confines of the building are the only reality, the edges and walls. All institutions share this in some way—a miniaturization of space, a shuttering of time—but Boulder's compact isolation feels stronger than that of any institution Ed has previously worked in. Chairs line the hallway, and he fights the urge to hold one over his own head and flee.

Through the windowed doors of the dining room, Ed sees patients at different stages of eating, in terms of both progress and ability. Some are nearly finished, the meal a mess covering their faces and hair, clothes and hands. Some are just starting, their focus intent on the spoon or fork, its slow, shaky rise to the mouth. Table etiquette is part of their therapy—table etiquette and toilet training and self-dressing and shoe tying.

The din of the room makes its way to Ed—restless as the ocean, swelling and receding. A man in his twenties drops a green bean into the pocket of his shirt. Why are they serving green beans for breakfast? A woman feeds toast to a man twice her age. A boy scoops porridge into the curled claw of his fingers and rubs it across the bald head of the man next to him. Ed sees only one aide for the whole room but nothing that needs his immediate attention.

The year before Ed came, the staff went on strike. The National Guard was called in to man the hospital until the state raised pay a token amount and agreed to extra compensation for overtime. It was enough to stop the strike but not the deterioration.

"Whatever you need to get us out of this mess," the director of institutions told Ed when he took the job. "Name it, and it's yours."

He should've known the word *money* wasn't one they wanted him to name.

He makes his way down the east hallway toward his office. He isn't one to believe in ghosts, but he always feels something both more and less than human as he walks these corridors, his shoes just another click and tap along the linoleum, mixing with the squeak of sneakers and clogs, the scuff of chairs pushed and repositioned. The hall is full of hapless patients, their voices mostly guttural, wide wordless sounds that nevertheless have a current tripping along underneath, a tendon of intellect.

"What're you hearing today, Dr. Ed?" Penelope asks. She sits in a chair, a journal in her lap. She is his favorite patient, one of the few bright spots in the entire hospital.

She was sitting in the same spot a year ago when he was interviewing for the position, and she caught him listening to the institution's sounds then, too. "You hear that?" she said. "It's like a song when you listen right." Ed had been taken by her voice first, its lucidity, and then the straightforward beauty of her face, her composed smile, her tall neck. "I try to write lyrics to it sometimes." She held out her hand and introduced herself.

"What brought you here?" he asked.

"Take the job and you'll find out."

He shouldn't have taken it. He works endless days and effects no change, not even for Penelope.

He sits down in the chair next to her. "I'm tired, Pen."

" 'If thus to sleep is sweeter than to wake, / To die were surely sweeter than to live.' "

"Just because I'm tired doesn't mean I want to die. That's the problem with all your poems. They lack logic."

"It's perfectly logical. Sleep is a lack of consciousness, and if that temporary lack of consciousness is sweet, then death—the permanent lack of consciousness—must be even sweeter. It's not the logic you have a problem with. It's the fact that you don't follow it."

"Quit showing off." He would like to stay next to her all day, listening to the hallway's sounds, but there's work waiting in his office. "See you this afternoon," he says.

Individual therapy isn't part of his job, but Ed makes an exception for Penelope. "It'll keep me from becoming all admin," he'd told his buddy Pete when he first started. "Keep me on the side of my staff."

Pete is one of the resident psychiatrists, and they'd been drinking at the Tavern, Boulder's one bar.

"Tell yourself what you want," Pete had said, raising his glass. "We survive this place however we can."

— —

In his office, Ed turns to the pile of paperwork on his desk: misconduct reports to write, phone calls to return, patients to follow up with in regard to the misconduct. He wants to work on the proposal more than any of it. The proposal is why he was hired. "Fix this place," the director said. "Hell, deinstitutionalize it if you have to. Just get us out of the hot seat."

Ed was on the deinstitutionalization team at Howell, and it was that work—much more than the psychiatric treatment of the residents—that made him pursue this position in the first place. He oversaw innumerable transfers to group homes and assisted living facilities, even a few independent apartments for higher-functioning individuals. For the vast majority of his patients, the institutional model has become irrelevant. Penelope is an obvious example, but many of her peers are as well—Chip and Dorothy, Frank and Gillie. Really, only the severely handicapped necessitate institutionalization—the nonambulatory and comatose. The rest should be part of their communities, as regular as senior citizens and children.

Of course, the proposal is the thing Ed has to prioritize last. He's been tasked with fixing the place at the procedural level, but the institution is such a damn mess on the ground that he can't step away long enough to rewrite the policy governing it.

He reaches into the pocket of his coat and rubs an arrowhead he found earlier in the week along the bank of the river. He's trying to get it smooth before he gives it to his wife, but the motion is about more than polishing now. He's grown accustomed to it—something to occupy the worry in his fingers.

Ed works through the morning and early afternoon, takes a late lunch in the cafeteria, where he polices more than he eats, then returns to his office to work through dusk. At six, Pete knocks on his door and drags him to the Tavern, where they drink themselves into a dull enough stupor to allow them both to climb into their cars and return to their wives in Helena, forty minutes away. Working in an institution requires distance, six cigarettes, several beers, and a decompression chamber called a car. Also, a drive that lasts long enough for thoughts to rise that haven't yet risen, for drowned thoughts to rise again, and for events to write themselves over. Like police officers and firemen and soldiers, state psychiatrists teach themselves to separate experiences—home versus hospital. The in-between times are for parsing.

Ed sips a beer from the six-pack he took to go. He cracks the window to ash his cigarette, and the lingering cold from the mountains chills his hand. Other than Pete's taillights up ahead, there are no cars on the road. Everything is quiet and grand. He reminds himself that—even with the trials of his work—he is in love with this place. When he came for the interview, he marveled at the mountains that rose up around him, the valleys sweeping out golden tan, the sky so big and blue he couldn't describe it. "Like Lake Michigan," he told Laura when he returned, "but greater, deeper."

"We can't move somewhere just for the sky."

"I married you for your eyes."

"No, you didn't."

— —

The kitchen is dark, and there are no leftovers to reheat. The counters are clean, the stove cold. Ed walks to the patch of light pouring from their bedroom and finds Laura in bed reading. He sits at her feet and loosens his tie.

"Did you have dinner?" he asks.

"I'm not hungry." She speaks without looking up.

"You have to eat." Ed rubs her leg through the covers, then pulls the arrowhead out of his coat. "I have something for you."

She sets her book down and cradles the rock in her right hand, inspecting its gray-green symmetry. She turns it and flips it, grasping the base in her fist, pressing her thumb into its point. "How hard do you think I'd need to push to draw blood?"

"Jesus, Laura."

She smiles and moves her thumb away. "It's lovely, Ed." She sets the stone and book on her nightstand, then slides down and turns out the light. In the dark of their room, she murmurs, "What are you going to do when you run out of pretty stones, Dr. Malinowski?"

He wants to tell her there is no end to the stones he can find. He has moved them to the Rocky Mountains, cliffs and peaks and riverbeds of stone. He'll gather every rock in Montana and lay each one at her feet in offering. His work is hard and encompassing now, but it will get easier. The stones are promises for a future he knows they'll have—big family dinners, the two of them surrounded by hordes of children. He wants to tell her the stones will last until then, and by then they won't need them.

But Laura's eyes are closed, and her back is turned, so Ed goes to the kitchen for another beer.

Chapter 2

Ed dreams about convincing Laura to come to Montana. Though wavy, like all dreams, it starts the same as it did in reality: lying in bed after lovemaking. They each have a glass of whiskey and a cigarette, and Ed builds the state with his words. He excavates a bowl in the middle of the mountains where Helena stands, and he draws the town's old buildings, mining the copper from its tunnels in Butte, digging granite out of the stone quarry just above Second Street. He fires the bricks at the Archie Bray, a manufacturer near Spring Meadow Lake; they're made from the state's own clay, dug from riverbanks, dried in huge honeycomb kilns.

The dream shifts, and Laura becomes Delilah, the woman he saw a couple times during his interview trip. The room is gaudy and loud—gold plates and fringed velvet lamp shades and burgundy wallpaper. She wears high-heeled slippers with pom-poms on the toes, baby-doll negligee, the hint of underwear. She tells him she was in the circus before she came west. "Acrobatics," she whispers. "You'll see."

Ed is half awake now, the dream sharpening into a memory. He was drunk but sober enough to know alcohol was no excuse. He visited Delilah's room because he was a man in need of a woman's physical pleasures—not Laura's voice on the phone and his own hand.

Ed was often accused of having no conscience back in college, in graduate school, in his various jobs. "Pursuing physical pleasure is not a soulless act," he argued, often going long on evolution's justification of sexual appetite. If he had any cerebral or emotional attachment to Delilah (or any of the others), he would be the first to welcome guilt. But Delilah satisfied a purely physical need—food to abet hunger, water to quench thirst. The need for sex is just as basic, just as necessary, and Ed needs it sometimes when Laura isn't available.

His occasional trysts have nothing to do with his marriage.

Laura is still asleep beside him.

Ed rises to make coffee.

He's brought home several of the old institutional reports from Boulder—a backlogged library he's slowly sifting through. He opens the one from 1912–13, a time when the institution was still called the Montana School for Deaf, Blind, and Backward Children. They'd just finished building Griffin Hall on the south side of the river to house the "backward" portion of the population, separating them from the deaf and blind students. Surrounded by cottages and dormitories now, Griffin Hall was alone in its fields back in 1912, four-storied and proud. Ed knows it as a three-story building; he has no idea where the fourth story went. He'll have to ask Sheila.

Further in, the director notes that a "spirit of kindness, contentment, and happiness reigns supreme among our pupils."

"Bullshit," Ed says, but he knows there is some truth in the report, that 1912 gave patients a better life than he probably can six decades later. There was hope then, at least, that the wayward population of Boulder could be "brought out and reclaimed," their downward course arrested. It was a true training school, a place for growth.

"You want to be a hero," Laura said when he first repeated Boulder's hardships, "but what's in it for me?"

"The money is good," he said, "and houses are cheap. You wouldn't have to work. We could start trying." He knew a child would ultimately be the deciding factor, a stone in his pocket even then.

"This is what you were waiting for?" Laura asked. "A superintendent's job in the mountains?" She'd been asking for children since their wedding night.

"I've been waiting for stability," he lied, and Laura believed him enough to come.

— —

"Shouldn't you be gone already?" She puts the kettle on the stove, lights the burner. "What are those?"

"Annual reports from Boulder." She's right, Ed should be at work, but he's still reading, and his reasoning is twofold: First, he needs the historical context; he needs to be a scholar when it comes to Boulder. Second, he needs a break—a day spent at home with Laura. Coffee in the morning, a couple pots' worth, turning to beer in the afternoon, sun filling the house through all its windows, perched there atop its hill on Chaucer Street.

"Chaucer?" Laura had asked before the move.

"That's right. Our house is on the corner of Third and Chaucer." The corner of threes and old tales. Ed had imagined himself a soothsayer, reading the signs: *There will be three chances and a host of strangers.* Jung saw three as something nearly complete—nearly, but not quite. A baby or two will complete them.

Laura drops a teabag in a mug, sun on her lean face.

"I'm playing hooky so I can stay home with my sexy wife," Ed says.

"I don't believe that for a minute, Dr. Malinowski." Still, she's smiling when she sits down at the table, and she flips open the cover of one of the reports, years 1922–23. Her eyes scan the pages as she feigns reading. She turns to a spread of photos showing the teachers' offices and sitting rooms. "Is that a taxidermied hawk?"

"Yes." It was the first thing he noticed, too, a hawk coming down from flight, wings wide over a piano. "Maybe it was meant to be motivating."

Laura laughs. "Is it still there?"

"I haven't found any taxidermy. And most of the buildings in this report are condemned or gone."

Laura reads with new interest. "Oh, God. The physician's report—poor John Holland. He died from drinking indelible ink." She turns the page. "The ranch produced eighty-three turkey eggs! And they had three geese. Look at all this—four hundred and ninety-two bunches of parsley? A *ton* of rutabagas? I didn't even think rutabagas were real."

"The ranch isn't there anymore."

"What about the choir?"

He shakes his head. The beading and painting and embroidery, the woodshops and metal-working—those activities are as absent as the farm and the ranch. Rooms that once were classrooms and studios now stand empty but for the residents. "It's ironic, really," he tells Laura. "The same ideological do-gooders who're attacking our current circumstances claimed the hospital was exploiting patient labor back then. It was easier to disband the programs than to pay the patients more, so they just did away with everything."

"But you knew that going in."

"I didn't know it was this bad." Ed flips back to the list of teachers in the Industrial Department. "Look at their subjects—carpentry, printing, sewing, basket and hammock weaving, broom making. My patients would love to have the opportunity to do just one of those things."

Laura runs her finger down the list. "They must be so bored."

"They are, and the state won't give me the money to hire teachers, so I'm thinking about putting some of the higher-functioning patients into leadership roles. Like Penelope. I could get her to do a reading group."

"Oh, good. You're going to get Penelope's help. Genius move, Doctor."

"Stop it, Laura."

"No, I mean, I'm impressed. Nearly twelve hours without mention of her name? You do realize you were able to lullaby me to sleep with just your native war weapon last night, right? No hospital tales featuring our favorite damsel in distress. And here you are in the kitchen of your own home at"—she turns and looks at the clock on the stove—"nine a.m., and you're just now bringing her up? I think it's a new record."

"She's my patient."

"She's more than that."

"She's *sixteen*. She's a kid, and she's a ward of the institution I run, and she's drawn the shortest fucking straw possible. Giving a shit doesn't make me a bastard."

Laura is quiet for a moment, and then she says, "I shouldn't be jealous of your patients, Ed. You have to recognize the truth in that, at least."

— —

An hour later, Ed knocks on the door of Laura's studio. She resisted using it at first, insisting it was the baby's room, but finally, she unpacked her canvases and easel and paints. Still, she painted the walls a child's creamy yellow, and she keeps her supplies much tidier than she did in their old apartment, ready always to move. "I'm just borrowing the space until the baby comes."

She doesn't respond to his knock, and Ed opens the door to see her sitting on the stool at her easel, clouding a sky. She paints mostly landscapes, which helped convince him that the natural beauty of Montana would quiet her initial reservations about the move. The room is full of paintings inspired by the local scenery—the Elkhorn Mountains covered in snow, Mount Helena rising up in the middle of town, Prickly Pear Creek and Ten Mile, their cottonwoods flaring yellow in the fall—but she swears she likes none of them. "Too clean," she says sometimes. "Too nice. They're nothing more than pretty pictures, and the view can do that by itself." She won't let him take any to his office, won't let him hang any in the house.

"Laura," he says quietly.

"Go to work, Ed."

He looks over her shoulder as the canvas's sky transforms from blue to gray. The blue is still there, but as part of thunderclouds now. He's always loved to watch her paint.

"I can't paint storms here," she says. "The blue always wants to come back." She tips her paintbrush with black, swirls it with white on her pallete, returns.

Ed knows better than to touch her when she's painting. "Would you stop for a minute?"

The sky grows darker, the thick anger of a summer storm, and then she raises her brush and drops it in a jar of turpentine. She turns to face him. There is blue paint in her hair, a tiny smudge on her right cheek.

Ed kneels in front of her. "I'm sorry I have to give the institution so much of my attention right now, and I know I've promised this before, but it won't always be this way. When we get the funding figured out and I can get my proposal together, it'll be better. I promise. And I have a solution in the meantime, a way for us to see each other more often and to put some of your worries to rest." He is nervous as he speaks, torn. What he's about to suggest may solve some of Laura's concerns, but it may open even more—not just with Laura but with his staff and his patients and himself. Still, he knows Laura needs to see him make a real sacrifice. She needs more than stones. "What would you say to coming out once a week and teaching an art class to a group of patients? You know they need activities."

She squints at him. "This feels like a trick, Dr. Malinowski."

"Well, clearly, I'm manipulating you with invisible behavioral techniques, but that doesn't mean it's not in your best interest."

She smiles. "I've never taught."

"You'll be a natural."

"I know you're just doing this to smooth things over. You're going to regret it tomorrow morning." He regrets it already. But she is standing and pulling him to his feet, wrapping her hand around the back of his neck, bringing her mouth to his. His desire supplants his misgivings, and he follows her to their bedroom, where they make love twice. He gives himself over to his family for the rest of the day—his wife and the child he's sure they're making. Like Laura said, regret waits until morning.

Chapter 3

— *Laura* —

I've taken a job at a little clothing store downtown. Just a couple of day shifts during the week. If the art class at Ed's institution actually happens, I can easily work around it.

He doesn't know I'm working, and I see no reason to tell him. He would see it as lowly, as he did my job at Sally's back home, and I don't want to have to defend what I love about working in a shop. I tried to explain it for two full years, and he never saw my work as anything more than a waste of time. "We don't need the money," he'd argue. "You should be home painting."

I tried to tell him it was about the people—something he should've understood—but he still saw those people as beneath me. Or else he saw me as beneath them. "It's not like you're friends with the customers, Laura. They see you as a glorified servant."

When he sold me on his new job in this place, he used the money as another bargaining chip: "You won't have to work." He said it again and again, as though work was the hardest part of my life.

"I want to work," I told him. "I like to work."

He is too prideful for jobs in the service industry, and I suppose I'm too prideful to sit at home painting all day. I haven't earned that life yet, and I am used to working. My mother worked through the beginning of her illness, and when both my parents were sick, they insisted it was a lesson for me in resilience and strength. "You'll provide for yourself, Laura," my father said. "Above all else." He died a year after my mother. I was sixteen.

Plus, it's lonely there, alone in that house.

I've opened my own checking account so Ed won't question the deposits. The money sits there untouched, waiting for something.

The owner of the shop is an ex-dancer named Miranda. Rows of bangles on her wrists announce her movements, and she is always layered in scarves, even in the summer. She has little in common with Sally back in Michigan, but she reminds me of her all the same. The air of prestige that all clothing store owners seem to share. The insistence on quality and aesthetics. They have different styles but the same expectations.

I bought one dress here before I took the job—a pale yellow shift to wear to dinner on Ed's and my anniversary. "You have good taste," Miranda said when I brought the dress to the counter, and then after just a few minutes of conversation: "Would you like to work here?"

I am often the recipient of random gifts and favors from strangers. Sally's offer came in a similar manner. I think I must wear my dead parents on my face, something forlorn and lost. I usually say no to the gifts and favors, but I take the job offers.

Miranda's store is downtown on Last Chance Gulch, a street I didn't believe existed until I saw the signs myself. This was a miners' town, the last chance for many. Old kilns still hunker in the hills, shafts and tailings. I'm trying to paint these scenes, but they feel flat and contrived, as though the paint knows I'm a stranger.

The shop is familiar, at least.

The bell over the door chimes, and I look up to see a young man in this women's clothing shop. He looks confused.

"May I help you?" I ask. *The pub is three doors down,* I imagine I'll say. *The sporting goods store is two blocks up, one over.* He is handsome, with giant brown eyes, a couple days' stubble, shaggy hair. Ed keeps everything tidy—hair and beard and body—and I've made myself forget that I once liked the stink and sloppiness of other men.

"My mother," he says. "Is dead?"

"Oh. I'm so sorry. What do you need?"

"Clothes," he says. "It's open-casket."

Sally taught me the questions to ask of customers, a different set for men than for women.

"What was her favorite color?"

"Blue."

"That's mine, too," though I prefer yellow. "Do you know her size?"

He shakes his head, terrified.

"Do you know how tall she is? About how much she weighs?"

"Five-two. Barely a hundred pounds. She was tiny," he says, holding a hand just below his shoulder. "Tiny."

I'm familiar with tiny dead mothers. Mine didn't have a casket.

I lead him to a rack of blue dresses halfway between matronly and sexy. I want his mother to be this way—laced around the edges yet slinky about the hips.

"Yes," he says when I pull out a small. "That'll fit her."

I get him panty hose and apologize that we don't carry shoes.

"They said her feet won't show." The feet are so important. How can we disregard them in death?

The shop feels cold, though the spring sun shines warm outside. I wrap this dead mother's items in tissue paper and slide them gently into a bag.

"How much?"

"It's on the house," I tell him. "I'm sorry for your loss."

"No," he says, "let me pay you."

I shake my head in refusal, and he lingers for a moment.

"It's all right," I say. "Really."

He thanks me quietly, a formality his mother likely taught him. *When someone offers to pay, try to protest, but give in easy.* Then the bell over the door is ringing, and he is gone.

I add up the purchase and circle the total on the receipt, write my name at the top. I get a twenty-five percent discount, and Miranda will take the money out of my next check. Buying a dead mother's dress is a good use of the income I'm making here, and I imagine telling Ed how meaningful the job can be. *I helped a man pick out his mother's burial dress today,* I would say. *And I bought it for him. I made one piece of this painful moment in his life more bearable.* I'd like to tell Ed. But I won't.

— —

A week later, the same man comes in. He's cleaned himself up, and the confusion is gone from his face.

I'm hanging new earrings on a rack. "Hello again."

"Oh, good," he says. "You're working." He walks straight to me, and I am suddenly nervous. His handsomeness is more pronounced today, and I can smell his aftershave, good and wholesome.

"I wanted to thank you for your help." He hands me an envelope and then holds out his hand. "I'm Tim."

"Laura."

His hand is rough and callused, like that of my old boyfriend Danny, the firefighter Ed stole me from. Kind and strong, doting and a bit dumb, Danny was no match for Ed's intellect and humor, his bravado and voice. Ed sang to me the first night we met, jumped onto the stage of the bar to sing with the band, *to me*. Poor Danny was gone in less than a week.

But I miss his hands sometimes.

"How are you holding up?" I ask Tim.

"All right," he says, then shakes his head. "I'm surprised how unprepared we were, you know? I mean, she was sick for a long time. We knew she was dying. But then when she actually died—we didn't know what to do." He starts playing with a pair of earrings. "Sorry. That was probably a rhetorical question. I can't answer those any-more, all the idle chatter and the *how are yous*. I actually answer now."

"That's probably good," I say, remembering the same honesty after my parents died, my inability to smile and say, *I'm fine. Thank you*. Sometimes I wish it'd stayed. "Your bullshitting skills will come back soon enough," I tell him. "Appreciate the honesty while you have it."

He looks ready to ask me how I know, and I am ready to tell him, but the door chimes and an older woman walks in.

"Thank you," he says again. "It was good to meet you, Laura."

I watch him walk out, and I welcome my new customer. She needs a gift for her granddaughter, and we walk together through the store. I show her sweaters and necklaces and scarves. A pale pink taffeta skirt. A peasant blouse. But I am thinking about Tim's face and hands and honesty.

Chapter 4

Penelope closes the door to Ed's office and takes her regular seat in the chair on the left across from his desk. She keeps her journal open and her pencil in her hand. Ed knows she'll take notes during their session, for use in all sorts of things—poems, songs, stories. "Do you ever just use them for yourself?" he asked her once.

"All the time, Dr. Ed. That's why I write them down. The other stuff is auxiliary."

"Most sixteen-year-olds don't use the word *auxiliary*."

"Most sixteen-year-olds don't live in institutions."

"Fair enough."

She is always reminding him that she is disabled, and he is always forgetting.

Ed met several epileptic patients before Penelope, but their epilepsy was part of a greater diagnosis. Coupled with Down's or severe retardation, seizures were just one more abnormal behavior in a life where abnormal was ordinary. But Penelope's only diagnosis is epilepsy. Save for her above-average IQ and her love of old poetry, she is a perfectly normal teenager.

For the first several months of their individual sessions, they focused exclusively on the physical and emotional factors that seemed to predict Penelope's seizures. Physical: dehydration, lack of sleep, caffeine. Emotional: anxiety, sadness, frustration. Of the physical, they'd tackled dehydration and caffeine—water in place of coffee and soda. She keeps a jug with her most of the time. Regarding sleep, there is nothing they can do. She sleeps in a dormitory with twenty other patients, all mid-to-high-functioning but still noisy and animated through the night. There are no private rooms in Boulder. Sleep deprivation is part of the package.

They've tried to work on the emotional pieces, but those are trickier. Penelope has some grasp of the patterns to her anxiety and frustration, but even with most of the stimuli identified, there is no guaranteed way to avoid it. Her parents are her biggest triggers, and packages arrive from them nearly every week. The packages cause anxiety, and their absence causes even more. The girl's sadness is mostly elusive, arriving and departing without warning. Penelope's seizures are as frequent as they were before Ed's arrival.

Today he'll push something new. Jack Sorenson, a former colleague back in Michigan, recently sent him a paper on a study done with a group of high-functioning epileptics at Howell. Sorenson had designed individual behavioral models that required each patient to engage in valued activities previously avoided due to seizure activity. One patient was prescribed daily bicycle rides (a fond memory from his youth); another was given a job in the institution's kitchen baking bread (something she'd done regularly for her family before the onset of epilepsy). Engagement in these activities supposedly gave patients the power to reframe and recontextualize their lives. "Nothing to put in the bank yet, but seizure activity is down in all but one case," Sorenson wrote in his accompanying letter. "Worth a shot on your girl. Let me know how it goes. Still can't believe you're way the hell out there in Montana."

Penelope looks around the office. Sun pours through the windows at Ed's back, touching her arms and shoulders. He watches her eyes drift from his overfilled bookshelves to the filing cabinets to the wall where he's hung three of Laura's earlier paintings, work she did back in Michigan. A portrait of his father painted from a photo: Fred stares just past the frame, his cheeks gone jowly, his blue eyes bounding out of his wrinkled face. A slightly abstract painting of Ed's mother at the stove in his childhood kitchen. The last is his favorite—the great oceanic shore of Lake Michigan where his family has a cabin. Simple lines focused more on the dunes and pebbles than the water. He grew up there, spent his summers wind-chapped and sunburned, hair bleached blond and arms sinewy as rope from all the swimming. He and Laura honeymooned there, too. Laura painted the shore for him as a wedding present.

"Who are the people in the paintings?" Penelope asked the first time she came for a session.

"My parents."

"And the ocean?"

"No, Lake Michigan. It looks like the ocean, though, doesn't it? Have you been?"

"I went to Washington a few times before the seizures started. After that, my parents deemed me unfit to travel. They still go out pretty regularly with Genevieve."

"Your sister. Tell me about her."

"She's the perfect one."

Ed wishes he could send Penelope to the ocean as part of her treatment. *Penelope needs to partake in activities that were a regular part of her life before epilepsy,* he'd tell her parents. *You must take her to the coast.*

He has tried to convince her parents to become an active part of her therapy, but they are quick to dismiss him on the phone, and his letters mostly go unanswered. When he does get one of her parents to talk, it's always: "You're the doctor. Whatever you think is best. We're swamped right now. Tell Penelope a package is on its way." He can't get them to visit, let alone take her to the ocean.

"What are some things you used to do before you started having seizures?"

Ed watches Penelope write the question in her journal. She stares at it for a while before she speaks. "I went to school. I played volleyball. I rode my bike. I walked to the library and checked out books. I ate lunch in my English teacher's room and talked to her about literature. I drove my dad's car once. I went roller-skating. There's more, but that's all I can think of right now. Why?"

"We're going to bring some of those back."

"Again: Why?"

"It's a new therapeutic model. It's supposed to interrupt your brain, confuse it into thinking it isn't epileptic." Penelope is the only patient of Ed's who can understand the explanations of her treatment. The others live in the concrete world of stimuli and response, little more.

"I like the idea of tricking my brain."

They both smile, and Ed looks at the list he's written down as Penelope talked. Much of it is impossible within the confines of the institution—school, libraries, cars, roller-skating—but he can get her a bike. That's easy enough. She needs something intellectual, too, something to feed the school piece she so clearly misses—not the peers but the coursework. She's walked into this perfectly, just as he thought she would.

"What about that reading group I suggested?" he asks. "For the higher-functioning patients? It'd get you talking about literature again. Granted, it wouldn't be with nerd friends, but it might be an even better trick on your brain if you became a teacher." His left hand worries a new stone in his pocket.

Penelope looks at her lap, and Ed sees her again in that first individual session, after they talked about the paintings and her perfect sister.

"Can you tell me about your first seizure?" he'd asked.

"I was thirteen, and we were all at our family cabin up on the Flathead. Gen and I slept on the sofa bed, my parents in the loft." She'd pointed to the lake painting. "Flathead isn't that big, but it's beautiful. Anyway, Gen woke up to my thrashing in the middle of the night and started shouting for Mom and Dad. They gathered around me. Supposedly, my mother said, 'Put a wooden spoon in her mouth or she'll bite off her tongue,' but the seizure passed before anyone did anything. They say I was awake for an hour before I was really awake. The first thing I remember is the blankets—how thick they felt. And then the wetness. I pulled the covers back to see that I'd pissed myself. I started stripping the bed. My mother tried to stop me, but I wouldn't let her, so Gen helped instead, and we got everything off, and my father hauled the mattress to the porch, where he hosed it down. I took a long bath, and then they loaded me in the car and took me to the hospital. And that's it—the day Penelope Gatson got sick."

"Not the word I'd choose."

"It doesn't matter what word you choose, Doctor. The definition is the same."

He expects her to show the same resignation now. Instead, she asks, "What would I teach them?"

"Shorter pieces, relatively simple. Other than that, whatever you want."

Ed imagines her paging through the library of her mind, all the titles and authors. He doesn't read the way she does, for pleasure and temporary transcendence. Words for him are simply tools to explain theories and studies and policy.

"Maybe I'll start with Keats," she says.

Skinner spoke of Keats, Ed remembers, quoting him in the discussion of "Reporting Things Felt." It's a nice omen, but Ed knows it doesn't matter where Penelope starts; it matters only that she does. The girl is on her fourth medication, and so far it's proving as ineffective as the first three. The existing behavioral modifications don't seem to be performing much better. And as much as Ed believes Penelope belongs outside the walls of the institution, he knows he can't deliver her there without marked improvement. Societal expectations fall on the side of her parents: Epileptics belong with the disabled.

These are the exact expectations he's trying to break down for the benefit of all his patients, but the injustice of institutionalization is especially pronounced in someone like Penelope, whose brain is brilliant whenever it isn't seizing.

"That's not what they see, though," she said to him once. "It doesn't matter how brilliant I can be. Once someone sees me fall on the ground and piss myself, I'm an imbecile, and once an imbecile . . ."

She had a seizure in the school library her freshman year of high school and has been at Boulder ever since.

He says, "How about you start next Monday? I'll supply the students. You provide the reading."

Penelope agrees, her face clouded with the same concentration she shows when she's writing lyrics for the hallways' sounds. Maybe just thinking about teaching a piece of literature to a group of disabled people will be enough to reorient her brain.

— —

After Penelope leaves, Ed calls Taylor Dean, the director of state institutions. He was the one who picked Ed up from the airport and first introduced him to Boulder. Ed remembers that drive clearly, how taken he'd been with the beauty outside the car's windows.

"You stop seeing it after a while," Dean said. "Here's the thing, Ed—all right if I call you Ed? Well, here's the thing. Boulder's up to its goddamned tits in negative PR right now. Don't know how much you've heard out there in Michigan, but it's a real mess. And my superintendent just walked out. You know that much, at least. That's why you're here. We need someone with your expertise, Ed. You're walking into a goddamned predicament, but it's one you can save. That's the thing—there's a place for heroics here, and if you're into that, then you're our guy. But heroes have to wade through shit, you know? So if you're squeamish around shit—and I'm talking both kinds here, the kind you deal with on paper and the kind you fucking step in—well, then this probably ain't gonna work."

Lots of shit.

Dean's secretary patches Ed through.

"Edmund! How's my favorite superintendent?"

"Not great, Taylor."

"Ah, come on, Ed. I know you're calling to complain. At least give me a moment to pretend otherwise. I know you have some good news for me somewhere."

"My wife is starting an art class, and one of our high-functioning patients is starting a reading group."

"There we go! See? That's the magic I hired you for."

"Really? I'm using a patient and my own wife to deliver services we should be paying professionals for. I need more staff, Dean. We're still at twenty-five percent."

"I'm working it from every angle, Ed, but I've got to tell you there's just no spare money. We'll try again next session, but for now we have to work with what we have."

"That's not what you promised when I took the job."

"Don't pretend you didn't know how government works, Ed. You took the job knowing damn well how full of shit I am."

Ed smiles. He both hates and loves Taylor Dean. The man is a bastard and full of bullshit that somehow mixes well with his candor. He laughed like a salesman that first day, willing to paint himself any color to get Ed to sign. But then in the next breath, he led Ed down to the former superintendent's office, talking about the staffing shortage. "Inadequate pay, long hours, remote location. Nothing to do about the location, but we're working on the other two. Every legislative session, we see another appropriations bill go through, and then we see it slashed by the governor. It's been tough to make the top of his list of priorities, but we have his ear now. Get enough bad press, and your demands finally get heard." Ed didn't know what he was talking about. "You haven't heard, then. Might as well get that piece done with." Dean pointed to a thick manila folder sitting on the desk. "Not enough to make national news, but we've been dragged across the state. This is what you're up against."

Ed read about the nine patients who had died at the Boulder River School and Hospital over the previous year. A thirteen-year-old boy prone to seizures had been left alone in a bathtub, where he drowned. Another woman had drowned in the Boulder River. A bedridden patient died in surgery after swallowing a spoon that another patient had shoved down her throat. The article quoted the former superintendent saying, "The woman was being fed by another patient because she might otherwise not have been fed at all."

A mute retarded boy was found hiding under one of the buildings after he'd been missing for over forty-eight hours. He'd survived, at least, but not without extreme trauma.

Stories reported the strikes Dean had mentioned. The National Guard had been called in to staff the hospital during one of them—using soldiers as aides made patients prisoners of a war they didn't understand.

Dean had known what he was doing. Even if Ed had gone directly to the airport, he'd have known Boulder's stories and taken them back with him to Howell, which felt utopic in contrast. He'd take the woman in the river and the boy in the bath, the patient on the surgical table, bleeding around a well-intentioned spoon. He'd sit in the dark with that mute boy, two days of hunger gnawing his stomach. He'd take them, and he'd want to save them.

Dean is a bastard and a bullshitter and also pretty damn smart.

"You've got to get me something, Dean. If you want to keep the current news trends, you better get me more money."

"Ooh, making threats now, Dr. Malinowski?"

"I'm not making threats, Dean. But I'm not making guarantees, either. I can't stop every potential accident myself."

"Fair enough. I'll see what I can do."

It's essentially the same conversation they have every time Ed calls. He likes to think Dean actually does something afterward—takes a meeting with the governor, writes a memo, contacts a few senators—but Ed knows he just hangs up, rubs his face, and gets back to work. Warm Springs is even worse off than Boulder. And the state prisons aren't much better. They're all under Dean's jurisdiction.

The Montana legislature meets every other year, and Ed missed the '71 meeting, too overwhelmed with his new world to make time for policy. But he'll be ready next time. He'll bring patients to testify. He'll produce success story after success story of former patients living healthy lives outside this institution, and he'll do what he was hired to do—fix this place. Change it.

Chapter 5

— *Laura* —

Summer is here, and Ed is finally taking me to Boulder.

He's been asking me to reconsider since he made the suggestion that I teach. He makes all kinds of excuses—no supplies, no aides, no experience—but I always refuse. He took me to dinner last night at Dorothy's. We sat in our regular spot, and he insisted I order a steak: an obvious bribe. We do burgers on weeknights.

"Reconsider?" he asked as I started eating.

"I didn't go back on my offer to move to Montana with you, even when I wanted to." That was my final argument, and here we are.

I don't even know if I want to teach art classes at Ed's institution, but I know I want to claim a piece of his workday. I want him to feel me in that place, to remember he has a wife.

"That's Strawberry Creek feeding in from the east there," he says, always a tour guide. He's still trying to sell me this state. "Strawberry Butte up above it—see? Dutchman Creek comes in right ahead. Most everything to the east is Forest Service. Miles and miles of trails. I've scouted some new camping spots for us."

The mountains and creeks and valleys don't comfort me like they do Ed. They're too big and grand, too empty of people, too wild. This landscape doesn't want us here.

We crest a mountain pass and look down into a great sweep of grasses, giant stones dotting the fields.

"You should paint this," Ed says, and I nod. I'm sure I will, even though the grasses will become one more flat canvas stacked in my studio. The room will be a nursery soon enough, and I will throw away everything I've painted of this state so far.

"You are with child," his mother would say in her thick accent every time we saw each other. A statement, never a question.

"Not yet, Mother." Ed would put his hand on my flat stomach, as though giving it his all, my damn womb simply refusing to do its job.

I'd say, "You realize I can't start making a grandchild for your mother if you insist I stay on the pill, right?"

We fought about it after every dinner with his parents, and he would say, "Baby, I'm not ready to share you," and I'd let him convince me I wasn't ready to share him, either.

He thinks we've been trying since the move, but I'm still on the pill. I needed time to settle in, and I knew he wouldn't give it to me. He was so adamant that it was time to have a child, so happy with his decision—always his decision, like the job and the move and the house. And then so damn naive sometimes. Even with his all-consuming schedule, we find a way to make love at least a couple times a week, and he hasn't once questioned the arrival of my period. "We'll just have to work harder," he says, or "It'll happen next month, I'm sure." He's so consumed by his work that he can't see anything I don't blatantly show him.

— —

We pull into a dirt parking lot.

Ed has warned me about what I'll encounter at his institution, but I'm not ready for the playground I see. There are patients everywhere. One boy pushes another's face against the ground. A girl slaps herself. Some stand in clumps. Many stand alone. They rock and moan, a great herd of sadness. It's more sickness than I've ever seen in one place, and of such a different kind. My mother suffered through stomach cancer that spread everywhere within months of diagnosis, its seeds blown into every corner. My father's cancer was in his lungs; he refused treatment, and every breath became a gasp. For them, death was a relief. But the people in front of me will never heal from their afflictions, and their afflictions won't kill them, either. They will simply remain.

In the distance, I see a girl riding a bicycle. She is such a contrast to the yard's disorder. And I'm starting to point her out, when Ed takes my hand and leads me into the main building.

Inside, he introduces me to his secretary, Martha, in the front office. We've spoken on the phone many times, and she gives me a hug instead of shaking my hand. "Thanks for sharing Edmund with us, dear. He's desperately needed out here, and we're tickled that we get to have you now, too."

"Once a week, Martha."

She smiles at me. "We'll take what we can get. You let me know if I can help with anything."

Martha is one of the few people on Ed's staff whom he talks about with respect. There's also Sheila, his favorite nurse, and then there are the boys—Pete and Gerald and Henry. We have regular dinners with them and their wives. Pete's wife, Bonnie, is the closest thing to a friend I have here.

Ed leads me up to a classroom on the third floor, again playing tour guide with his story about the 1963 fire that destroyed the fourth floor. "The damage was mostly contained, so the administration decided to shorten the building rather than tear it down. They rebuilt the roof and left the third floor as it was." We can see our footsteps in the floor's dust.

He unlocks a door and flips on the light. The tall windows need a cleaning, but they are south-facing. There are six wide tables, perfect for projects. Cupboards line one wall, over a counter and a sink.

"You're okay doing the cleaning yourself?" Ed points to a broom and dustpan in a corner. I nod. "I'll come back at lunch." He kisses me deeply, a kiss that feels wrong in this place.

I stand in the door and watch him disappear down the stairs. A breeze touches my arm. Skittering steps—mice, most likely—but maybe ghosts of those poor drowned patients Ed has told me about, slopping back and forth.

This shorn building with its soot and sadness is something to paint.

— —

When Ed comes to retrieve me at noon, I've gotten the floors swept and the cupboards cleaned out. For supplies, I have a stack of thin yellowed paper and a handful of pencils.

"I told you," Ed says.

"It's enough to get started. I can come up with the rest."

He takes me to the dining room, introducing me to patients and staff along the way, smiling broadly, his hand on my back.

Ruby is serving from the first two troughs of food; Stanley is at the next tray. "Pri. Tee. Lay. Dee," he says.

I thank him for the compliment.

The food looks wilted and old, but I accept everything they offer: corn, green beans, mashed potatoes, meat in a gray gravy, a small bowl of cherry cobbler. Ed does the same, and we carry our plates to a table by the windows.

"Is it strange that you haven't brought me here before?"

I can see Ed puzzling over the question, interrogating his options. "I didn't take you to Howell."

"You weren't the superintendent of Howell."

"No one else brings their wives to work."

I should know not to expect straight answers: *Yes, it's strange. No, it isn't.* He doesn't offer them because he doesn't know which one I want, but the problem is that he assumes there is one I want at all. Most times I have nothing specific in mind, so we both just stumble along blind and confused, making inconsequential remarks until we run up against something hard.

When I asked Danny the firefighter questions, he answered without thought. I think of his uncomplicated honesty, which makes me think of Tim with the dead mother, no longer able to answer rhetorical questions.

A yell breaks the chatter of the room, and I look toward the sound. A man and a woman appear to be fighting. The man has a shiny bald head and ears like trumpets, great curls of twisted horn.

He is exceptionally tall. His face blushes crimson, and his voice is heady and vicious. The woman's lips are off-centered by some kind of paralysis that's claimed half her features, but her frown is evident.

"That's Frank and Gillie," Ed whispers. "They're one of our few romances." He scoots closer to me. "They always have the same argument—she thinks he's flirting with someone else. We used to intervene, but now we're letting it run its course, trying to get them to new outcomes."

The woman is a full foot shorter than the man, wide in the hips and breasts. She moves close to him, her breasts level with his lower ribs, her face tilted toward his glowing head with its fantastic ears. I watch her raise her arm, and I'm afraid she's going to strike this giant boyfriend of hers, but instead, she rests her hand flat on his chest. Even though noise still floats through the room, her voice is loud enough for me to hear.

"You have broken my heart again," she says. Then she drags her hand away and limps from the room.

Ed is staring at Frank, who appears frozen in Gillie's absence.

"Was that a new outcome?" I whisper.

"It was." Ed looks fascinated. "She must have heard the line on television, but she applied it perfectly. It's the most astute verbal communication I've heard from her." His voice is gaining in volume and speed. "Just think about it—if Gillie can cross-apply words from fictional television characters to the reality of her relationship with Frank, then what else can she do? So many doors!" He is standing suddenly. "I'm sorry, love—are you all right here for a minute? I just have to grab Gillie and see if we can get some of this down. It's exactly the kind of example I need."

"Go do your work," I tell him, though it feels cruel for Ed to chase the woman down for an interview to fuel his theories. Her lover has disappointed her, and her heart is broken. What more does he hope to find?

— —

Back on the third floor, I raid a janitor's closet that's equipped with cleansers and rags, a mop and bucket. Though I usually hate to clean, I don't mind scrubbing this old classroom. I wipe down the tables and chairs and countertops, the shelves in the cupboards and along the walls. I clean the inside of the windows, still sooty from the fire a decade ago. The day comes in, and the room brightens. I dust the windowsills.

Ed did not come back to the dining room. He hasn't come upstairs.

At five-thirty, I go down and knock on his office door.

"Come in!"

Ed is at his desk with a girl who must be Penelope across from him. He doesn't have time to get his thoughts under control, and I have the rare opportunity to see him raw. He looks caught. It's clear he forgot I was here, and I wonder whether I disappeared the moment he left the dining room in pursuit of the brokenhearted woman, or whether I slipped away more gradually, fading completely only when Penelope walked into his office.

I asked him once if she was pretty, this girl he always talks about, and he said not that he'd noticed.

Penelope is impossibly pretty.

"Laura!" He shouts my name too loud and too late.

"Oh," the girl says, "Dr. Ed's wife."

Dr. Ed. Shared pet names.

I've never been in a fight, but images arrive in my mind—my fist busting her nose, my ring lacerating her cheek, a clump of her hair in my fingers. Disgusting. And satisfying. The girl is standing and making her way toward me, and I'm worried I'm going to slap her instead of greet her. Maybe I'll run. This must be what's meant by the notion of fight or flight. This exact moment. I've never felt it so pronounced before, and now I am angry, too. How dare this girl elicit such a response from me?

"This is Penelope." Ed is shouting. The room is small. It can't be taking her this long to cross to me.

I am shaking her hand.

I have not hit her.

"Hello," I say. "I've heard so much about you."

She looks at Ed. "I hate the thought of you talking about me. What have you said?"

"Only good things," I assure her, because I am an adult, and I do not need to be jealous of a sixteen-year-old patient of my husband's. Also because it is true—I hear only good things. All the time.

"I'm ready when you are," I tell Ed. Now I'm the one who's shouting. "Lovely to meet you, Penelope. *Dr. Ed,* I'll be waiting out front."

When I go, I accidentally slam the door, too jittery, but I don't want to reopen it to apologize. I walk away quickly, the fight overcome by flight. I want to be outside. Patients line the hall, and I dodge them to get to the front doors and out into the thick summer evening. I breathe in the air from the river, fresh and muddy over the hot-grass smell. I see my mother's sunken cheekbones, hear my father's shortened breaths. They always visit when I'm upset, these wasted ghost-parents of mine.

I sit on the top step and light a cigarette. I want Ed to come. I want him to apologize for abandoning me in this institution of his. I want to hear him say the girl is nothing, just a patient, one of many.

I keep my eyes on my watch.

Every minute that passes before he comes is time removed from the other side of us. I don't know in what increments—months, years—or when, but I feel it going.

Chapter 6

There's a half-ring of chairs in the common room, each holding a patient Ed barely recognizes—crossed legs, pensive expressions. Their heads are turned toward Penelope, who holds a book open for them to see. Others in the room stare, too, their hands quiet, the television low. Ed lingers in the doorway, spying from afar.

"Can anyone tell me what form of writing this is? The type? Yes, Chip?"

"Poetry." Chip slurs the word, his huge lips and tongue pummeling the sound.

"Good, Chip. Yes. *Poetry*. How do we know?"

"Lines," Delilah says. "Shorter. Big white." Delilah is a pretty woman with the mental acuity of a five-year-old. When Ed sees her, he can't help thinking of that other Delilah in her room over the saloon.

"That's right," Penelope says. "There is more white space on the page, isn't there? That's a good sign that it's poetry. I'll read it now." The room falls even quieter. Ed imagines the ghosts he semi-believes in, pausing in their haphazard flights, hovering near the ceiling, fixated as well. "The title is the same as the first line: 'Like the Train's Beat.'" Ed listens to the rhythm of the language, not dimpled and squashed like Chip's but fully bloomed, luminous as the first shoots of green in spring. The girl on the train is Polish, the *swinging and narrowing sun* lighting her eyelashes. She uses the ancient words of Ed's *babcia*, his mother's mother, tinged with ash and gray skies. His *babcia* often spoke in proverb: *Jak sobie poscielesz, tak sie wyspisz*. "You listen to that one, Eddy!" an uncle or aunt would shout. " 'How you make your bed, that is the way you will rest.' " *Kropla do kropli i bedzie morze*. "That's right! You hear that, Edmund? 'Drop after drop, there will be an ocean.' You have to keep at things." His *babcia*'s gnarled voice runs under Penelope's poem, an orchestra of blended consonants, burly and deep, then suddenly sharp as a snapped twig.

Penelope's voice stops, and the ghosts continue their movement, tripping along the corridors to hide away someone's file or take Pete's phone off the hook. A few of the nonparticipants initiate conversations in their corners, move pieces on game boards, set dominoes in serpentine lines. The faces Ed can see in the circle look scared and confused.

"I don't know what you said," Chip ventures.

Penelope laughs. "Poetry can be difficult. Let's start at the beginning." Ed listens to her explain each word, each line. She asks simple leading questions and celebrates each answer. "Yes, Nancy! That's exactly it. The speaker doesn't understand the language, just like he doesn't understand what birds are saying when they sing." Those bird notes, *a voice / Watering a stony place.*

"Let's look at that," Penelope says. "Describe a stony place for me." She's leaning forward in her chair, her whole body inviting feedback from her students.

They all start speaking at once.

"Hard."

"Dark."

"Not nice."

"Cold."

Gravelly, stern, frost-filled, dead. Penelope offers a few words, and the patients give others, all of them vivid and alive in the mouths of these people so often silent.

And then she asks the most important question Ed thinks they've ever been given, something he's never delivered so succinctly, eloquently, purely: "What are your stony places?"

"My dad," says Chip quickly. He seems scared to have admitted it.

"The bathroom in cottage fifteen."

"Venison. It's really deer meat."

"The shower."

"*Re. Gres. Sion*. Ug-ly. Word."

"When David takes my pillow."

Their answers are equally benign and poignant, and Ed has heard none of them before. Some he can solve; others he can at least introduce in one-on-one sessions. He can make sure Bill's counselor never says the word *regression*. He can talk to Chip about his father, follow up about the bathroom, identify the problems.

"Now," Penelope is saying, "if the bird's notes—and this woman's words—can't be understood, then what good are they?"

Chip bounces up and down in his chair, hand waving over his head. "Oh, Pen! Pen! Me!"

She smiles at him. "I see you, Chip, and I'll let you answer, but does anyone else have an idea? Maybe someone who's been quiet. Megan—maybe you want to tell us what you think?"

A sweet, slow thing in her mid-twenties, Megan chews the inside of her cheek. Ed has never heard her speak. Hers was not a name on the list of potential reading group members.

Penelope is nodding at her and smiling.

"Nice!" Megan blurts, bringing her hands into her lap, clasping them tightly. "They are nice to water the stony places. Nice to make the stony places soft."

"That's lovely, Megan. Yes. Chip, do you want to share your thoughts, too?"

Penelope successfully paused Chip—a near impossibility when dealing with most of the population at Boulder. To pause and then resume is an advanced skill, a difficult one to master. But Chip sat quietly, his bouncing nearly contained, while Megan found her words. Penelope is a natural.

Chip rattles on for a bit, and then Penelope closes the book and slaps her hands on her legs. Her charges copy her as though it's part of the program. *We talk about a poem, share our feelings, and then slap our legs*. And why not? It seems a fitting way to close things down.

"Should we do this again next week?" she asks.

"Yes!" A chorus, along with more leg-slapping. The regular din of the common room returns, and it comes so quickly Ed questions whether he actually witnessed what came before.

The group disbands, and Ed approaches.

"I saw you spying," Penelope says. He helps her move the chairs back to their respective tables. "You're not very good at it. I've been meaning to tell you for a while now."

"You've noticed me spying before?"

"You're spying all the time."

"I'm making observations," he says. It's what he tells himself, too. *I am simply observing my patient's behavior so I can document her routines and help find a pattern.* He hides because he doesn't want to alter her actions by introducing the oddity of his presence. He doesn't want to skew his data. Never mind that he often intervenes, unable to stop himself from rushing to her when she shows signs of an impending seizure. Sometimes he can get to her before she drops, and yes, there are times when he catches her in his arms before gently lowering her to the ground, where he turns her on her side and holds her jaw open to save her tongue, pressing his hand into her shoulder to keep her arm from sustaining new bruises. The girl is covered in purple swatches, blue and green-yellow.

"Professional spying," she says. "I see."

"That was incredible, Pen."

She looks ready to disagree but instead nods and smiles down at her feet.

"Will you keep doing it?" he asks.

She nods again, and they put away the last of the chairs.

"Will you make some copies for me before next time?" she asks. "I think it'd be good for them to be able to look at it themselves."

"Of course." He'll do anything to replicate what he just saw. He's building programs, and the reading group is a brilliant step forward for the institution. Proof of the work he's doing.

He wishes Laura could see that.

He can still hear her angry voice on the drive home that first day he brought her to Boulder. "Oh, so your meetings with *Pen* are for the greater population? You forgot about your wife on the burned-out third floor of this haunted building because you were busy talking about *programs*? And the conversation was so critical that it took you twenty minutes to wrap it up? I'm sorry to be the one to break it to you, Doctor, but you're not spending time with Pen for the sake of the institution."

"She's part of the institution."

"Too big a part."

They rode the rest of the way in silence, and she closed herself in her studio as soon as they got home.

"You ready for our session?" Penelope asks now.

He looks at his watch. He wasted time watching the reading group when he should've been doing paperwork, and now Penelope is right—it's time for their individual session.

— —

Ed and Penelope have recently started playing poker as part of her therapy. For bets, they use pistachios, a treat they both love. They respect the work it takes to eat one, the cracking and splitting, and agree that the scale is better than that of the sunflower seed. "Too small," Ed says.

"Right? All that work for such a tiny reward. Pistachios have heft."

They'd been walking the grounds during that exchange, Penelope joining him on one of his tours. Ed remembers her weighing out coconut-sized pistachios in her open hands.

"The work you do actually matters."

"Exactly."

They'd laughed, and Penelope had nudged him playfully.

Now she sits across from him in his office. "I see your four pistachios and raise you ten." Penelope drops the nuts slowly from her clasped hand one at a time, their shells rattling against Ed's desk. He resents the impulse he has to reach out and catch a pistachio as it falls from her fingers.

"Ten! That's nearly all I have left." Ed cracks a shell between his teeth, chews the green kernel inside. They always eat through their pots while they play, bankrupt by the end. He scoops a handful and drops them all on a pile in the center. "I'll hold. You're bluffing."

He's homed in on Penelope's bluffing face, and though the bluff itself won't help with her treatment, the extra time studying her behavior will. She loses all conscious control of her expression with the onset of a seizure, and by comparing her lucid face to those moments, Ed has been able to identify the specific tics that predict activity: asymmetrical blinking dominated by the left eye; tightening and thinning of the lips, often accompanied by a clicking of the tongue; low eyebrows; smooth forehead.

She shows none of that now and lays down a straight flush.

"Damn it!" Ed has two pairs, aces and queens.

"I'm watching you, too, Dr. Ed." She pulls her haul of pistachios to her side of the desk. "You sit much taller when you have a really good hand, and you always twist the right side of your mustache when you're bluffing." She starts to separate the pistachios, arranging them in lines. Her voice gets quieter. "Everyone has their patterns."

He watches her fingers move from shell to shell. "What's wrong, Pen?"

She remains silent, and he knows to let the silence grow. To let it swallow her so that she'll fight against its dark belly and emerge loud and clear. He passes her the handkerchief from his pocket—clean that morning—and watches her wipe her eyes, dab her nose. It's the first he's seen her cry, and he wants to lift the desk that separates them and throw it through the windows. He wants to kneel at her feet and tell her she's broken and perfect all at once.

She holds his handkerchief balled in her fist, her other hand on a pistachio—leader of a line, commander. "I'm not going to get better."

He lets himself rise and go to her side, turn the other chair to face her, and lower himself into it. He knocks the nut from her fingers as he takes her hand. "You're going to get better." He feels the dampness of his handkerchief. Their knees touch, and her nails bite into the backs of his fingers. "I really think the behavioral model is going to work—the reading group especially. And we'll try another drug if we have to. I promise we'll figure it out. I promise."

He knows he has no right to promise her a cure, but he has to believe that he can make her better. She is the one patient in the whole institution whom he can actually heal.

Laura's paintings hang on the wall behind Penelope's head.

"We'll try everything we can until something works. That's the process."

He watches Penelope's lips, chapped on the bottom, a couple flaps of dried skin. She whispers, "I want to believe you."

He can feel every point where their bodies touch—knees, hands, the underbellies of her forearms on the tops of his thighs—and when he pulls back and stands, he feels a severing, like a bandage ripped from skin. He drops her hands as quickly as he can and steps to the side of his chair, then back another few feet. Distance. They need distance between them.

"You all right, Dr. Ed?"

She smiles at him, and he's thankful for her ability to normalize, to shift back into their roles. Nothing happened. There was no impropriety. He merely comforted a sad patient.

He digs his hands into his pockets and returns to the safety behind his desk. His fingers close around the latest stone, smooth from all his worrying. He will be normal, too. "You all right?"

"I asked you first."

He laughs. Playful banter is part of their routine. Handholding isn't. "I'm just fine, Pen." He feigns a look at his watch. "Ah! Our time's up."

She looks at the wall clock opposite Laura's paintings. Then she stands and scoops up the pistachios, dissolving the lines as she stashes them in her pocket. She keeps one out, cracks it open. "Our time's been up for half an hour," she says.

— —

Laura is asleep again when Ed gets home. He's late but not asleep-already late: nine o'clock. He can still feel the touch of Penelope, and he tries to dispel it on his own in the shower. But it's still there when he's done, too strong.

He presses against Laura in bed. "Hey there, beautiful. I know you're not really asleep."

She mumbles, "Stop it, Ed," and scoots away.

The desire is too much—the need—and so he takes himself down the hill to the rooms over Dorothy's, where he's lucky enough to find Delilah between customers.

"I remember you," she says.

She is a professional, and she gives him exactly what he craves: simple pleasures and anonymity.

Afterward, Ed goes downstairs to the saloon for a beer and a shot—a good excuse, should Laura wake to find him gone. *Just needed some fresh air,* he'll tell her, *and a drink. Didn't want to wake you.* He'll give her the latest stone in his pocket, red-gold and flat as a coin.

Chapter 7

— *Laura* —

Ed has filled most of the summer with excuses for why I'm not ready for students, but the classroom is clean, the cupboards stocked. I even have a folder of lesson plans I've put together. The fall is coming, and he has finally folded.

"They're a handful," Ed repeats continuously. "Not like anyone you've ever worked with."

I've never worked with students of any kind, so there's nothing to compare.

I wish he were here to greet them with me, but he's away trying to put out the most recent fire. "Boulder River School and Hospital Hires Rapist" ran on the front page of the paper this morning. Ed swears he didn't hire the man, but the paper interviewed him as if he were responsible anyway.

"Why didn't you tell me about this?" I asked on the drive.

He was quiet, as he so often is. "It's hard," he finally said. "It's hard to talk about."

When we got here, he rushed to his office with only a hurried "Good luck" over his shoulder.

I can hear my students coming, their feet heavy on the stairs, their voices loud, an aide hushing them, angry. All the employees seem angry, all but Nurse Sheila.

"In here. *Eva, stop touching Jimmy*. Everyone, *STOP*."

The footsteps stop, but the babble continues, a few hollering voices. Then Penelope's face pops into the doorway. "You ready for us, Mrs. Dr. Ed?"

"Laura," I say through the shock. "Call me Laura."

Ed has put her in my class, so I'll be forced to stare at her pretty face for hours. I'm sure he thinks I'll become as smitten with her as he is. She'll become the daughter I never had, or some such bullshit, and I'll welcome her name at the dinner table.

He's an idiot.

"Penelope," the aide's voice hisses, ghosting in from the hall. "Get in line."

The girl ducks out, and another face replaces hers—this one gone to wrinkles before its time, pickled and salty, lips like leather. "This the art class?"

I nod, and the aide leads in her wards, ordering them to sit down. One boy has already wandered toward the windows. "Jimmy!" the aide shouts, reaching for the club in her belt.

"No, no." I cut her off, my hand to the boy's elbow, gentle like Ed taught me. "Jimmy, come with me." His head droops, and it seems to take considerable effort for him to raise it, but he brings his gaze level, giant brown eyes blinking in a fragile face. He makes an unintelligible noise, familiar only in tone—excitement—and lets me lead him to a chair at the front.

"All yours," the aide says. "Bring 'em to the yard when you're done."

There are seven of them, Penelope sitting alongside six others who are clearly not her intellectual peers. "I can tell you everyone's names," she volunteers. "I'm Penelope, in case you don't remember. This is Eva, and Janet. That's George. You've met Jimmy. Over there are Raymond and Lilly." At their names, each person perks up, smiles. Raymond waves and begins chanting, "Ray-mond. Ray-mond. Ray-mond."

"Hello, Raymond. It's nice to meet you." The repetition stops when I touch his hand, which is filthy. I resist the urge to wipe my fingers on my pants.

They vary in size and shape, in their faces, but they are all similar in their movements and temperament. They are clumsy and thick, even Jimmy, whose hands are long and graceful as a pianist's. Eva is clearly reluctant to unclench her fists. George drums his pinkies and thumbs on the table, teeter-tottering his hands. Raymond rocks in his chair. Janet has a piece of her hair in her mouth, sucking. Lilly flutters her lips, a buzz in the back of her mouth, a small motorboat. And then there is Penelope.

I hate that she'll be useful to me.

"Teach us some art, Mrs. Dr. Ed."

"Laura," I repeat. "My name is Laura. We are going to draw today."

Most of them nod. Many of them bounce in their seats.

The lesson is simple. I've arranged a still-life on the small table at the front of the room. An apple, an empty vase, a tied bunch of dry tufted grass. "Start with the outlines," I say, drawing an oversize apple on the chalkboard, then the vase, the straight lines of the grass. "Then we'll shade to add depth." I demonstrate on the apple, light and dark, its shape growing underneath my hand, rounding, realizing itself. My students clap, all but Penelope. "Your turn," I say, passing out wide, blunt pencils and thick paper. Raymond stops rocking, eyes pinched as he peers at the scene, deep concentration. Jimmy's long fingers wrap around his pencil as if he's holding a baseball bat. Lilly shifts the pencil from one hand to the other with no seeming preference. Their marks are hard and dark. Eva tears her paper and begins to cry, but I succeed in soothing her, replacing the paper, lifting her hand, setting it down, my own hand over hers, coaxing a softer line. "See? Don't push so hard."

"Do me!"

"Me!"

"Uh!"

They all want my hand on theirs. I dismiss the grime of their nails and the dirt on their skin, and I go from Eva to Janet to George to Jimmy to Raymond to Lilly, returning to Penelope, who says, "I've got it." She lifts her hand to show her progress, the stilled moment emerging in perfect proportion, an artist's sketch, as good as anything I could do.

"Have you had lessons?"

"Yeah, we get private art lessons out here all the time."

Eva elbows her. "Pen. Show. Off." The jab makes Penelope smile, and I try for a moment to soften toward her. What would it be like to face adolescence trapped in this place? I can feel those years, the weight of my body one I can conjure on command. I can feel the hairs on my arms rise when Robert Gault walks by, the most handsome boy I'd ever seen, the first I let touch the body I was so aware of—first under my shirt and months later, my pants, making him swear, promise on everything sacred, that he'd tell no one. And the Monday morning afterward, when he'd not only told but exaggerated. I feel that morning, those eyes on me in the halls, my virginity gone without the act to show for it.

There's no one here spreading rumors about Penelope, but I wonder if that is worse. Would it have been better to be isolated, away from all the Robert Gaults of the world, my body my own?

This is the closest I can come to compassion for this girl—grieving the lies she'll never have spread about her.

My students draw for an hour, Penelope on her one masterpiece, the others on many. George draws one item at a time—the apple, then the vase, then the grasses over and over, lines with seeds scattered at their ends. Some of their work is loose swoops and lines that somehow still convey form. Other marks are tight and controlled—all detail and precision. The range is extraordinary, and I am disappointed when our time is up.

"Write your names on your papers," I tell them. Most of them are able, and Penelope helps those who can't.

"J-A-N-E-T," she says. "Janet. That's right."

They are reluctant to give me their papers. "How about just one, then? I want to watch your progress." I don't think they understand. "It's all very pretty," I say instead. "I like your drawings."

This makes them smile, and Janet gives over all of hers, Eva and Jimmy, too. George gives his vase and apple and one of his grass pieces. Lilly gives two of her five, Raymond just one. Penelope hands over her single perfect drawing.

"You keep it," I say.

"What am I going to do with it?"

"Hang it in your room? Give it to one of your doctors?" I am acting like a petty teenager.

She takes the drawing back and gets in line with the others at the door. They are easy and compliant, nothing like Ed said. Penelope is at the rear, and I lead them through the dusty hallway, down the dark stairs, another hall, and then out the front doors into the devastating sunshine. The day is bright, and I watch my students move slowly into it, cautious, timid. Soon they are absorbed into other groups, and I feel as though I'll never see them again. They will all drown in rivers and bathtubs before I can return. Except Penelope. There is no doubt she will survive.

— —

It's dark already when we start the drive home.

"You sent me Penelope, huh?" I light a cigarette and look outside. Black cows stand stark against their golden grasses, the sky lit orange in the west, a great fire descending into the sea. I have never seen the ocean, but I have always yearned for it, and here I am—so close. I could be at the shore in twelve hours. There is an imagined town on the Oregon coast where I have always lived. I build fires in a wood stove when the storms knock out the power. I drink coffee in the clear mornings on my deck that overlooks the sea. I am an orphan, and I have chosen to marry no one.

"She needs the stimulation more than any of them."

"That's not why you sent her. She can get art lessons on her own from books."

"So that means she shouldn't get lessons in person? That doesn't seem fair."

I can't fight with him about this girl anymore. I pass him my cigarette to finish and lean my head against the window. "I won't have her in class, Ed."

"What the hell do you mean, you won't have her in class? You can't kick her out because you're jealous—which is ridiculous, Laura.

You're offering your services to this institution, and Penelope has just as much a right to participate as anyone else." He says more: I am acting petty and stupid and small. I am misguided. I am misreading. Finally, he says, "If you don't keep her in class, you can't teach."

It seems so easy for him to make this choice—patient over wife. I wonder how he'd respond if I had a Penelope of my own. Someone I spent every day with and mentioned at every meal. Someone I chose over him, again and again.

Wards

—

DECEMBER 1972–JUNE 1973

Chapter 8

Laura has been teaching at the institution for over a year, but her presence still feels new and foreign. Ed can't shake the feeling that she doesn't belong—too much mixing of his worlds, too many demands on his time. He can't focus on her when he's at work, can't make her his priority every Tuesday. He has the whole damn institution to run, patients to treat, staff to supervise, policy to write. The next legislative session is just around the corner, and he needs to be ready.

He bought her a car six months ago in an attempt to fix the situation. "This way you won't have to get up so early, and you won't have to wait around for me all day. You can just drive over for your class."

He was sure she'd stop coming. Laura hates to drive—avoids it whenever she can—but she has driven herself to the institution every week since he got the car, more resolved than he's ever seen her.

His last hope is pregnancy. She has to quit when she gets pregnant.

But she's not pregnant.

"Maybe you're too stressed," he said recently. "Maybe teaching is too much."

"You think I haven't gotten pregnant because I'm teaching two hours a week?"

"There's the drive, too—you hate to drive."

"If you think the once-a-week drive to Boulder is causing my body so much stress that it can't grow a baby, then maybe you should start giving me rides again."

He's dropped it for now. There's too much else to worry about, starting with a thing both simple and indomitable—Montana's seasons.

Winter is back, the institution's hardest months. The patients get anxious cooped up inside, their rhythms thrown off by the short days and long nights. There's a melancholy that takes hold, a new tone to the music of the hallways. Sad. Hopeless.

Ed remembers a photo from one of the old annual reports: a two-story Christmas tree in one of the former sitting rooms, a fire burning in the nearby hearth. He knows it's too grand, and ultimately probably meaningless compared to all the other things that need to be done, but he has to do something to brighten the place. Plus, he loves Christmas, loves it with the full weight of history and myth that holidays rightfully conjure. He is a lapsed Polish Catholic. He doesn't believe in God, but he damn well believes in celebrations.

"We're going Christmas-tree hunting," he tells his staff. "I'll lead the hike myself, and I'll take as many patients as I can handle."

"I'll go with you, Ed."

"Me, too."

"Hell, I could use some fresh air. Count me in."

They take thirty-eight residents, roughly ten each—Ed and Pete and Sheila and Donovan Brady O'Connor, a long-timer like Sheila and the only aide Ed has any respect for. Freckled and fair, he comes from old Irish stock in Butte. No one knows why he goes by all three of his names, but it's common practice by patients and staff alike. He's never just Donovan or O'Connor.

They bundle up the group, giving the more capable ones the task of buttoning the others.

"A Christmas-tree hunt, huh?" Penelope smiles.

"You don't approve?"

"If I didn't approve, I wouldn't be coming. You think we can handle it?"

"If I didn't think you could handle it, you wouldn't be going."

She laughs an easy laugh, which her fellow hikers mimic. Lilly grabs Penelope's arm. "Fun-ny Pen. So fun-ny." Penelope pats the girl's mittened hand. She is gentle and kind, and Ed curses the flash in his stomach.

The group sets off, Ed at the front with Penelope. Sheila and Pete are in the middle and Donovan Brady O'Connor at the end, shepherding the stragglers. They walk along the two-track lane cut through the snow by one of the school's trucks, feet kicking clumps of ice, pine cones, rocks. The pack lets out great whoops of joy, and Chip announces, "I love trees best of all that grows." Then he barks loudly, a seal in the sun, his face to the sky.

Penelope falls back, and Ed hears Dale sputtering: "Pen. Pen. Pen."

Penelope stands still as the others shuffle past. Her right hand opens and closes, her eyes gaze straight. She makes a rhythmic ticking noise between her tongue and teeth, a beat that matches the clenching and unclenching of her hand. A petit mal, her brain not completely shrouded. She isn't conscious, but she isn't entirely gone. Ed has brought her out of these before.

He grips her upper arms, squeezes hard, and shouts her name. Pete passes with a nod and takes over at the front of the line, corralling the residents who've started off on their own, a few wandering into the woods.

"Penelope!" Ed's job is to interrupt the interruption, jump-start her brain back to its regular rhythm. Or just keep her from falling. In reality, his actions might not be doing anything. Petit mals are short by nature.

She blinks, smiles. "Hey, Dr. Ed." Clear and bright. Unlike her all-encompassing grand mals, the small ones have no aftereffects. She is gone, and just as quickly, she is back. "Petit mal?"

"Real short. You okay to keep going?"

She is, but Ed makes sure to stay close to her.

"You're hovering," she chides.

"You could have a big one. They often follow."

"I'll know if one's coming." True about half the time. Penelope reports auras, both visual and olfactory—hazy light at the corners of her vision, "like a gold fog," she told him in one of their sessions, "coming from every direction, and the smell is awful—rotten ocean is all I can think to call it. Like a carcass washed up on shore."

But just as often, her seizing catches her off guard.

Up ahead, Chip hollers in his great baritone. Ed wants to reinstate the music program if only to hear Chip sing in the choir, his voice so rich and deep.

"Tree! Tree! Tree!" Chip's arms are wrapped around the trunk of a thick Douglas fir, the word *tree* spilling from his lips like praise. Pete stands with his hands on his hips. Sheila and Donovan Brady O'Connor direct the group into a misshapen circle, Chip and his prize at their center.

"It's a bit big," Pete says, big and flawed with a huge gap in the back, carved out like a cavity.

But Ed deems it perfect, and they all stand rapt as Donovan Brady O'Connor saws into the wood. Chip's hands hold the trunk over Donovan Brady O'Connor's head. Everyone shouts as the tree falls, their noise rising with the splintering of wood, the snap of branches, the slight *whump* of boughs landing in snow. Everyone crowds in to help haul the tree back. Penelope hangs behind with Ed.

"You don't want to get in there?" he asks her.

She shakes her head. "They remind me of a litter of kittens, fighting for a spot to nurse."

Ed likes the comparison. "You shouldn't be here, you know."

"You keep saying that, Dr. Ed, and yet"—she holds out her arms—"here I am."

Ed watches the group disappear around a turn in the road, then starts walking slowly. He likes the feeling of Penelope at his side, just the two of them out there in the woods. He knows it's this feeling of his that drives Laura's jealousy, try as he does to mask it. Desire is slippery, showing itself in disguise without permission, as with the yelling fit he threw in the car when Laura refused to have Penelope in her art class. He'd known it was stupid, but he couldn't stop the words that poured out, on and on in Penelope's defense. He's tried to convince himself he'd have argued as vehemently for any patient, but he knows it isn't true. Laura does, too. "You really know how to put my mind at ease, Ed," she said when they got home. "I feel like such a fool for thinking you care too much about her."

He feels Penelope's arm link through his. "How's the reading group going?" he asks.

"You know exactly how it's going. You spy on every session."

"True. But that's my perspective. I'm curious how *you* think it's going."

"Aha." She laughs and tucks in closer to his body. "I really love it, and I don't want to get too hopeful, but I think it's actually helping, like you thought it would. It and the art classes, maybe. There might not be a connection, but I've only had one grand mal a week for almost ten months now. And the only things that are different are the reading group and Laura's class."

He'd been right to insist that Laura keep her. "Fine," she finally said after those first days of arguing. "It'll be two hours of the week I know she's not with you, at least."

"You're enjoying the class?" Ed asks Penelope.

"As much as I can. Your wife clearly hates me, but the instruction is good."

"She doesn't hate you."

"She won't even look at me. And she collects everyone else's work but refuses to take any of mine. But it's fine. I'm there to learn about art, not to make friends."

Ed's anger with Laura reignites. Penelope is seventeen now, and she's acting far more mature than his thirty-year-old wife. Laura is the adult. She is the one with more wisdom and experience. It's her responsibility to set aside her unwarranted emotions in order to serve this disadvantaged child. Isn't it?

As if reading his mind, Penelope says, "Don't worry, Dr. Ed. Laura and I are fine."

His and Penelope's thoughts are aligning more often these days, a sign that they're spending too much time together. He should change that. He should gently remove her arm from his and quicken their pace to catch up with the group. He should reduce their individual sessions, maybe eliminate them entirely. He should start the conversation about her discharge. She's the poster child for deinstitutionalization, after all, a high-functioning patient showing marked improvement who would benefit immensely from the normalcy of society. He'll talk about her with legislators starting next month, when the session convenes. He'll have to be away from the institution, selling his ideas to the men who can make them realities. The distance from her will be built in, and he'll get her discharge started.

For now he keeps her arm where it is.

— —

The tree is up in the common room. They'll start decorating it tomorrow. Sheila has convinced some of the less surly aides to help supervise the stringing of popcorn garlands. At Penelope's suggestion, Ed will talk to Laura about making some ornaments in her art class.

He and Pete drive to the Tavern. Though it's been a good day, they still need to shed their institutional stink and suit back up into manhood, rich with smoke and whiskey.

"To Christmas trees!" Ed toasts.

Pete lifts his glass. "Polishing the brass, my friend."

Pete's honesty is blunt and merciless. Unlike Ed, he doesn't believe progress is possible. "Things break bad enough, and there's no going back," he said early on. "Let's say you stepped in a pile of dog shit in your running shoes. You can wipe it off to your heart's content, even get out the hose, but *there will always be a little shit left*. Got to start over with a new pair of shoes. And who's going to spring for those?"

"We can get all the shit off."

"Feasibly impossible."

"The institution isn't going down like the *Titanic,*" Ed says now. "We'll stop up the leaks before then."

Pete laughs. "I love your optimism, Doctor."

"I've got to take it where I can. A Christmas tree today. Another string of bullshit tomorrow. Dean just told me about some bastard up in Great Falls who's launching an investigation into the institution's deaths."

"Jack Haller. I know that son of a bitch." To the bartender, Pete circles a hand over his head—one more round, just one more, and then they'll be on their way to their wives. "The guy's making a run for governor and just wants to get his name in the papers. He's not even in the business. Jesus. What's he going to investigate?"

"Dean says he's lobbying to get the bodies exhumed and autopsied."

"Exhumed?" Pete snorts. "No way. He can lobby his fucking heart out. No one's digging up the bodies of those patients. Can you imagine that media hell storm? 'As if gross negligence weren't enough, the Boulder River School and Hospital is now digging up the remains of the poor bastards it killed.' "

"The institution didn't kill them."

"It didn't save them, either."

Ed shoots the new whiskey in front of him, gulps his beer. How many was that—two? He isn't ready to go yet. "One more round," he says to the bartender, "just beer this time."

Pete slaps his back. "You're not doing me any favors with my old lady, you know."

Ed doesn't care. What do favors with Bonnie matter when Jack Haller wants to dig up the hospital's dead patients? Or at least open an investigation, come sniffing into the mess Ed inherited. What did he think he'd do? Sail in on his gallant belief system and right this sinking ship, save the beautiful maiden walking the gangplank? *Pen.* His head swims.

Right after Dean mentioned the investigation, he told Ed they were out of funds for the year—no new money for staff or supplies.

The beer tastes good.

"You're making progress," Pete says loudly, the booze heavy in his mouth. "I know I'm a naysayer, but you're doing good work, Ed. More than any superintendent I've seen, and I've watched three come and go. You've gotten more patients released in the past six months than in the past six years combined." He raises his glass, hits Ed's. "Plenty to celebrate, brother."

Laura will be asleep again when he gets home.

"Pete." He wants to talk to him about it—Laura's jealousy and Penelope. "I have this situation." He gets the start of Penelope's name out, and Pete cuts him off.

"Like I said before, we survive this job however we can. But there are lines even I can't overlook. Just keep your dick in your pants."

"Jesus, Pete. I'm not a fucking rapist."

"Never said you were. But you're a man, and the last time I checked, it's pretty damn hard to turn down a pretty girl who's more than willing to give her all to the doctor who's singled her out for special treatment."

"I'm not giving her special—"

"Bullshit. Why do you think none of us were giving her individual therapy when you arrived, huh? 'Cause we're fucking men, and we know better than to trust ourselves with that much temptation."

Pete stands and slips on his coat. "Listen, I'd hate to see all the good work you're doing pissed on by the epic shit storm that'll rain down if you get caught fucking an underage patient." He throws a few bills on the counter. "Sooner you get Penelope out of here, the better. See you tomorrow."

Ed listens to the door open and close.

He needs to go home.

Chapter 9

He told Laura he'd be home for dinner tonight, but it's seven already, and the men at his table are *listening*. He can't leave.

He's spent most of the past two months wooing senators, either at the capitol or at Dorothy's. He's rarely in Boulder, more rarely home. But the session is almost over. It will all be different soon.

He motions to the waitress for another round. The chatter of the restaurant reminds him of the din of the institution, and he worries about his patients, about the whole place, languishing in its river valley without his oversight. But through the work Ed is doing here, the state will fix what's broken, provide what's needed. Group homes will spring up in every community, burgeoning like spring wheat and chokecherry blossoms, like tiny bunches of larch needles, greening up those empty boughs. Patients will live in homes. They'll learn to cook for themselves and do their own laundry; they'll sit together in living rooms and fall asleep in their own bedrooms. They'll no longer be *patients*. They'll be individuals, members of a community.

Lynn brings their drinks. Another round of beers, another round of Jameson.

He raises his shot to the legislators at his table and starts another story. "Take Belinda, for example. She was institutionalized for ten years, but she's living independently now—in her own apartment near the capitol complex. She's working as a janitor in the Mitchell Building."

Stewart Thiessen, a legislator from the highline, starts talking, his mustache frothed with beer. "These are all great stories, Ed, but they're clearly exceptions. We can't just set all your wards free."

"That's the thing, Stew—we can. Not all of them, of course. But most."

"That's a stretch, Ed." This from Wiley Dussault, a sleek-faced weasel of a man. Though Ed despises him, his voice is loud and his reach far. Everyone says Ed needs Dussault if he wants the bill to get any traction. "What kinds of jobs are we going to give these people? State-sponsored loiterer? Face-slapper?"

The men all laugh. Ed wants to grab Wiley Dussault's beer and toss it in his face, or grab the back of his neck and slam that thin-lipped mouth into the table, scattering plates, blood, and ketchup. God, he should be home, eating dinner at his own table, talking to his wife.

He starts again. This time with George, the boy with the chair over his head that one day. George's parents are the opposite of Penelope's. They institutionalized their son because they believed the doctors would do more for him than they could. They loved him and they missed him. Their visits to Boulder saddened them, but they hadn't known he could come home.

"It seemed so permanent when we signed those papers," his mother told Ed the day George was discharged. "I feel so negligent."

Ed assured her she wasn't. He assured her of George's growth and improvement during his time at the school, all truths. George had learned life skills that his parents hadn't been able to teach him. He'd excelled in occupational therapy. He was an expert at bagging groceries—one of the activities used to teach order and recognition, heavy items on the bottom, tender fruits on the top—and his parents had already secured a position for him at Thriftway, the local supermarket. They brought his apron and name tag when they came to pick him up.

George donned both proudly. "Doc-tor. Ed." He'd pointed at the tag. "Me. Jor-Ja."

"That's right, George. I'm going to come visit you at the grocery store, all right?"

Ed tells these men about sweet, successful George bagging groceries at Thriftway. George, who smiles enormously whenever

Laura comes through his line. "You should stop in and say hello," Laura tells Ed, relaying George's hellos and hollers and grins. "He always asks about you." But Ed doesn't have time to stop by a grocery store.

Wiley Dussault interrupts. "Listen, Ed. I appreciate what you're doing. Really, I do. But you're asking for too much money. We all want to help the less fortunate, but we have a state to run and only so much money to run it with. I can't speak for these fellows, but I know for damn sure my own constituents didn't put me in office to hike up their taxes in order to build homes for retarded folks."

Face smashed onto the table, maybe a tooth knocked loose, something permanently broken. Ed takes a breath. He conjures his calm doctor self, the one who walks families through the discharge process, the one who can get even reluctant parents on board. "I imagine your constituents put you in office to do what's best for the state's citizens."

The man laughs and motions for another round of drinks. "Actually, they didn't. Individuals don't care about the collective, Ed. They care about themselves. As long as there are more nonretarded voting folks than retarded ones, we're not going to be able to wrest money away from existing services. Get yourself some liberals in here and you might stand a chance. No way you're getting my backing, though."

Ed rubs his temples and reminds himself that he is *laying roads*. He might not have success this session, but his whiskey will sit in these bastards' bellies, and his words will seep into their brains, and when the legislation comes up again, they'll remember the great feeling of whiskey in their guts, and that whiskey will be tied to funds for the state's developmentally disabled, and if they do what those words say, they'll find themselves with more whiskey in their hands. Associative behaviors. Indicators and receptors. Ed is conditioning them. He knows better than anyone that conditioning takes time.

When the next round comes, he asks Lynn to bring him the check. The men at the table don't even pretend to fight over it. This is a perk of the job—free drinks late into the night. If the rooms upstairs hadn't been shut down recently, Ed would be buying them whores, too. The dividends from those associative behaviors would pay for years.

"Training is part of the process, gentlemen. There are innumerable jobs that would be perfect for the developmentally disabled and retarded—fabrication, janitorial work, stocking, bagging—anything that's simple and repetitive."

Lynn comes for the money. "Need change?"

"The rest is for you."

Wiley Dussault slaps her ass as she walks away, and she slaps his hand in return. "No touching," she says, scolding him like a child in a store, reaching for everything delicious. "Thanks, Ed," she says, looking his way, and then adds, her eyes back on Dussault, "Dick."

Everyone at the table laughs but Wiley Dussault. "I'll touch what I damn well want to."

"Calm down," Ed says. "She's feisty, has a kid at home she's raising on her own." He knocks back his new shot.

Tiny Dan Hutter from out east breaks in, a peacekeeper, quiet until needed. Ed likes him, not only for his ability to pacify Wiley Dussault and the other arrogant bastards like him, but for his thoughtfulness. He's always paying attention, watching, listening, his questions finely polished and astute when he asks them. "If we're giving our disabled population all these jobs, aren't we going to be driving able-bodied people out of work?"

Ed expects Dussault to jump in with an addition, callow and stupid, but his eyes are trailing after Lynn. Ed will have to wait until Lynn's done with her shift and walk her to her car. Or he can tell Jason, the bartender, protective of all his waitresses.

"Great question, Dan, but it really won't have that much of an effect. We're not talking about that many people—just the able ones. And what's more, we'll be creating new jobs. The group homes and community service organizations will need unskilled staff, too."

Dussault's attention is back. "So we take a retard out of the institution, put him to work in the community, and then make the poor bastard whose job he stole work at the retard's group home?"

"Enough, Wiley." Stewart Thiessen tips back the last of his beer. "Come on. I'll drive you back to your hotel."

Dussault looks ready to argue, a grumpy child whose dessert has been withheld.

"Time for me to hit the road, too." Tiny Dan Hutter is standing, reaching a hand out to Ed. "Thanks for the drinks, buddy. I think you're doing great work."

Stewart Thiessen shakes Ed's hand, too, then heaves Dussault to standing. The man sways once he's on his feet, drunker than Ed realized, sloppy enough not to be dangerous.

"Don't have my vote," he mumbles, his speech gone slurry.

Thiessen shrugs apologetically. "Come on, Wiley. Out we go." Dussault stumbles along next to him, eyes hanging on Lynn at the bar, then back ahead of him, too drunk to walk without oversight, more disabled than many of Ed's patients. He'll probably piss himself on the way to his room and sleep in his clothes and wake bleary-eyed and heavy in the morning. Ed has no tolerance for men who can't hold their liquor.

He walks to the bar and asks for one more shot. Lynn slides down next to him, off shift, a beer in front of her. "You know, some people judge a man by the company he keeps."

Ed laughs. "Sorry about that, kid. My work requires it."

She scoots closer, close enough for him to smell her—perfume and shampoo and food, maybe some sweat under it all. Though she's not really his type, he can appreciate her looks. Tall and blond, rounded in the right places, big bright eyes. As classic an American beauty as they come, knocked up in high school and now waiting tables and fending off letches like Wiley Dussault. This close, he can see the lines working at the corners of her eyes, threads of age and exhaustion. She can't be older than twenty-five.

"Just don't let him rub off on you," she says. "You're too good a guy." Her leg nudges his.

She's flirting with him, but the idea of Lynn taking him somewhere offers no allure. He doesn't need this lovely young thing, though he's sure sex with Lynn would be nice—more than nice. Still, he doesn't have time, not even for a quick fuck in the bathroom.

"You don't have to worry about me becoming anything like that sonofabitch." He shoots his drink, leaves a couple bills on the bar, kisses Lynn on the cheek, and stands. "Have Jason walk you to your car, all right? Just in case that asshole didn't head straight to his hotel."

"See what I'm saying? Too good a guy."

His gentle rejection is probably a relief to her, or at least a validation in some way. *Not all men are dogs.*

Ed waves to Jason and pushes himself outside. He's parked in the back lot, level with the second story of the building, and he takes the stairs along the side, treacherous with ice. The sky is clear, which will make for a colder night, but the stars are thick and gleaming, so brilliant he stands next to his car for a moment, head back, staring. He's been so busy that he quit noticing the place around him, just like Dean said he would. He'll take tomorrow off, he tells himself, let someone else buy those guys their drinks. He'll tell Laura to dress warm and wear thick socks and hiking boots, and they'll take to the south hills behind their home, climbing and climbing until they reach the top of Mount Ascension, and they'll stand there and look out over the white-dusted fields of the Helena valley, the tall mountains ringing it, the creeks burbling past the ice shelves along their banks.

Chapter 10

— *Laura* —

I've taken to looping hair elastics through the buttonholes of my pants, an extra inch of waistband. I'm wearing the baby low and inward, a secret I cradle.

Ed curves his body against mine when he comes to bed, his bearded mouth against my neck. "It's going to happen soon, love," he says. Since the legislature ended, he's been home a bit earlier—not every night, but a few of them, at least. He's attentive and tender and quieter than usual.

But he still hasn't noticed.

It's a teaching day, and my car is in the shop, so Ed is driving me. Our cigarettes are lit, the radio on, a good excuse not to talk. He likes quiet in the morning.

If we speak at all, we speak of insignificance in its many forms—how ready we are for summer, the camping trips we'll take, the upcoming dinner with Pete and Bonnie.

Ed kisses me in the parking lot, barely brushing my lips, and tries to rush off. But I grab hold of him. "Walk me to my classroom?"

"Laura, you know how busy I am. Come on."

"Please," I say. "I just want a little more time with you." I can see how much he wants to say no. "Just a few more minutes?"

He recognizes something in his brain, and his face warms—bright eyes and that winning Edmund Malinowski smile that gets him nearly anything he wants. What tool has he found in there? What psychological detail? *Small bits of attention can outweigh years of neglect.*

He holds my hand as we climb the stairs, and at the door of my classroom, he kisses me the way he does in our bedroom.

"I'm part of this place now," I whisper against his mouth. "I don't disappear just because we're here."

"Laura."

I need him to acknowledge me. I need him to hold me and want me—more than he does this place. I pull him inside, close and bolt the door behind us. The glass pane is frosted, the exterior windows high. No one can see us. I will steal his attention back from this institution. I will transcend the lines he's drawn, muddy his boundaries. He wants me in our shared bed, in our shared home, and I will make him want me here, too. I will cloud out my competition.

I push him against the closest table, hands on his belt, button, then fly. His admonishments are a weak match for his body's reaction. Always so easy, my Edmund. My mouth quiets him, but he is quick to take control, his hands turning me around, bending my body before him, pausing only briefly and inattentively at the improvised fastener. His fingers are sharp enough to leave red behind, tiny bruises in this new form I've taken. One part growing while the rest wastes away. I have no appetite, and the weight keeps going off. Ed presses against me. I can taste paint under my mouth. My belly grazes the table.

I've been to the doctor once. He insisted I should eat more and assured me sex was fine. "Comforting to the baby, in fact."

Ed stays frozen afterward, his stomach against my back. Frozen save for the hand he brings to my belly, a question in its fingers.

"Yes," I say.

It has taken him fucking me in my classroom in his filthy institution to notice I am pregnant.

Can you see me now, Edmund?

"Love." He wraps himself against me. "Oh, love." He turns me around. Our pants are still open. "How long?"

"Four months."

The compassion in his face shifts to anger. "Why the hell did you keep it from me for so long?"

I've practiced this moment, recited it in the mirror, his line nearly identical to the one in the script I've written. Sometimes I'm indignant, flashy and bold. Other times I'm timid, shy, sorry. Faced with the real Ed, with words from his own mouth rather than mine, I can only meet his anger. "Why the hell did it take you so long to notice?"

In my imaginings, he stayed angry, and I gave him other lines. *You didn't notice that I'm off food? Or that I'm throwing up in the morning? Or that I'm carrying around this fucking belly?*

In my imaginings, I stayed angry, too.

But here, Ed is crestfallen. He kneels and presses his cheek against my belly. "I'm so sorry."

I'd expected injured pride to win over remorse. It has in the past, and if Ed has taught me anything about human behavior, it's that we repeat what we have previously done. "And if someone changes their behavior," he told me once, "it's because they've been forced to. Something has happened to make them alter their habits, and whatever it is, it's big. Great loss, usually, or the threat of great loss."

Can he feel the threat?

He's still kneeling, like the little boy in all those photos his mother once showed me. "Here is Edmund—castle-building, is that how you say it? Here is Edmund with sand. Here is Edmund—tree-climbing, you say? And there"—her rough hand pointing to a smiling boy version of Ed, shirtless, a wide smile just about to spill into laughter, hands raised over his head in triumph—"how do you say, race-winning? Against his cousins. Always fast, my boy." I can imagine her chiding him now: *Slow boy. How could you not—what is the word—perceive?*

The Ed at my feet has only the troubles he's sought out, a career helping broken people and broken places—broken things that do not include him. He has always been on the outside of suffering. He has surrounded himself with it, but he hasn't internalized it.

The Ed at my feet doesn't know what to do with grief that's his own.

I run my hands through his thick hair. He is a child, and I will comfort him. We have played these roles before. Ed's shoulders shake just the slightest bit, and I feel damp against the skin of my stomach. Tears. I am more delighted than sad.

I pull him to standing and button his pants, then my own. I tuck in his shirt, smooth out the wrinkles. I straighten his collar.

He wipes his eyes. "I'm just so happy, Laura," he says, and then I'm angry again. *My wife has been pregnant for four months and didn't tell me? Hooray! My wife has been pregnant for four months and I didn't notice? How about that!*

"So happy," he says.

It's all I'll get now, this elated version of Ed. Where has the weeping boy gone? Elated Ed is still talking, filling the room with his chatter, and I look over his shoulder to my students' artwork on the wall. Chip's sketch of Griffin Hall, Karen's horse in full gallop, George's grasses. It's wonderful to see George at the grocery store, but I miss him in class.

Ed is still talking: ". . . can't wait to tell my parents. And Pete and Bonnie! They'll be so thrilled!"

I interrupt him. "I need to get ready for class."

"Right, of course." Ed cups my belly again, smiles grandly, a king proudly claiming his domain. *No, not that bad. A proud father? Maybe that's all.* "Oh, Laura, it's just so—"

"Exciting, I know."

He pauses. "You okay?"

"Really, Ed? You're asking that? It's been four months—we're nearly halfway through."

He looks devastated again, and I nearly want to take it back. But I don't.

"Just go, all right? I need to get set up. My students will be here soon." I kiss him so he'll stop looking so damn wounded. "We'll talk about it on the ride home."

"We'll celebrate tonight." He kisses me back, and I want it to be enough to heal us, to make these last few years go away and leave only the future before us, wide as these godforsaken meadows Ed so desperately wants me to love.

He heads toward the door. He is Dr. Malinowski again, ready to lead, nothing broken but his institution. No more tears. Of course not. What is there to be sad about? All that matters is the baby. *A baby is coming—his baby! Hurrah!*

He turns at the door and waves. "I'm so happy, Laura."

"Me, too."

Protection is an innate behavior as well. If lies will protect us, we won't hesitate to use them.

He's gone. But his scent lingers, that aftershave rubbed into my skin. The hint of sex, too, and I'm worried for a moment about my students. But they won't know. Penelope might, but I'd welcome that. *Smell that, you little bitch? That's sex I just had with my husband.* If the others sense anything, they won't know to ask, and if they do, I can easily lie. *That? That's just the smell of our new paints.*

I prepare each student's place. They'll paint a stormy ocean scene today, inspired by Gustave Courbet's *The Wave*. I'll show them the print I've brought from home, talking them through the textures of the great storm clouds, gray and plump and—of course—foreboding.

Chapter 11

The day after Ed finds out Laura is pregnant, he brings home a dozen roses and a bottle of champagne. Laura puts the roses in water and allows him to fill a glass for her, but she won't raise it with him. "I don't need roses and champagne, Ed." She takes her glass to her studio.

— —

The next day, Ed gets home at five and tells her to put on a fancy dress. He takes her to Dorothy's and insists she order the most expensive steak on the menu. "You're growing a baby! You need all the protein and iron you can get." He orders an expensive red and tries again to toast their fortune.

But she keeps her glass on the table, her fingers wrapped around the stem.

"What's your plan, Ed?" she asks.

"To treat you like a queen while you grow our son."

"Son?"

"Of course."

She smiles a bit, at least.

— —

Three days later, Ed arrives home at six-thirty, but he brings soup and sandwiches from their favorite sandwich shop.

"I have a doctor's appointment next Thursday at nine. Can you make it?"

"Of course!" Ed makes a point of writing it in his calendar for Laura to see. "Maybe I'll take the whole day off. We could go see a matinee and take in an early dinner."

Laura smiles. "That'd be great, Ed."

— —

A week later, he goes drinking with Pete and the boys. Pete's son, Hank, is three and they're trying for a second. Henry has two girls. Gerald has a five-year-old boy.

"To reproduction!" they shout.

Ed gets home around nine and finds Laura sewing.

He rubs her shoulders and whispers, "Come have a drink with me."

"Maybe," she says.

He builds a fire in the woodstove to ward off the last of spring's chill and opens a beer. He hears the electric chugging of Laura's sewing machine, a tiny train gaining steam and then letting off. He's high on the dream of his son, and he pulls his guitar off its stand, playing the songs he'll sing to the baby. He sings "Lemon Tree" and "If I Had a Hammer." He sings "April Come She Will," one of Laura's favorites. It will bring her out, he is sure. *May, she will stay / Resting in my arms again*. He sings, and she doesn't come.

— —

There is an emergency at the institution the morning of Laura's doctor's appointment. Ed is out of the house before she even wakes, a rushed letter left behind on the table. *So sorry, love. Emergency in Boulder. Will make up for it tonight.*

But he's late getting home, and Laura is asleep, a note in her handwriting next to his. *I am seventeen weeks pregnant. The baby's heartbeat is strong.*

Chapter 12

There is plenty about the institution Ed isn't proud of, but he's at least been able to boast that there've been no accidental deaths under his watch. That's over now.

Last night, a twenty-six-year-old man named Phillip choked to death on a green bean. His mangled gargling alerted no orderlies because there was only one staff person for both floors of cottage 3, and that one person had been dealing with a tiresome patient on the first floor who refused to get into bed. Phillip was ambulatory but low-functioning. The man in the bed next to his said Phillip always took green beans from the dining hall to eat through the night—something no one had addressed. By the time another patient alerted the orderly downstairs, Phillip was gone.

Ed remembers telling Dean he'd make no guarantees. "Not a threat, but I can't protect them all on my own." The words haunt him. What haunts him even more is the insidious hope he feels. Like Dean said at the beginning, get enough bad press, and the state has to start making changes.

But the problems don't stop with Phillip, and they're not all capable of being fixed by funding.

Jack Haller, the damn gubernatorial hopeful in Great Falls, is again demanding a full investigation into the institution, and the man has found a handful of former patients to talk to the press about their mistreatment at Boulder. A man from Billings is claiming he was given massive overdoses of Thorazine the entire time he was institutionalized; a higher-functioning Missoula woman claims she was "manhandled" constantly; and an eighteen-year-old girl's parents are saying the hospital coerced her into a sterilization operation as a condition of her release. Worse still, Nurse Sheila recently informed Ed that a nonambulatory woman in the custodial care ward is pregnant.

"How long has she been here?"

"Eight years. The—well, the *act,* so to speak—it happened on our watch, Ed."

Ed went to see the poor bed-bound woman, Caroline, embarrassed that he'd not been to her ward since the fall. Her belly is noticeable in her small body. Her eyes stare blankly, comatose. She has no speech, no understanding. No ability to give consent. The *act,* as Sheila called it, was rape. Ed alerted the sheriff. The rapist whom the hospital mistakenly employed and intentionally fired was questioned and released.

"He's got a sound alibi, Ed."

"How? The man's a convicted rapist, and he was working here when this woman was impregnated."

"He didn't work with the woman, never set foot in that ward. I know we don't have specific dates, but it seems he was let go before the woman was—" The sheriff couldn't finish.

"Jesus Christ."

"It's a damn shame, Ed. That's for sure. You let me know if you need me."

The case is closed as far as the sheriff's office is concerned, and there's little Ed can do at the hospital. They've questioned the higher-functioning patients, but no one saw or heard anything. It could've been one of the staff or one of the patients, impossible to know.

The hospital's physician has taken the woman into his care. She's due in about four months, close to Ed's own child.

He thinks he should quit. Move back to Michigan with Laura, get his job back at Howell. Raise their son near his parents.

But then he comes to the common room, where Penelope is just wrapping up her reading group, and his hope returns. Penelope makes him hopeful. She will be his greatest poster child—healed and strong out there in the world—and they'll take these recent tragedies and use them to their advantage.

Ed approaches. "Did you hear what Chip said about Yeats's 'Long-Legged Fly'?" Penelope asks. " 'We are all long-legged flies.' "

"He did not."

"He did! I thought you were spying to *learn* something. Sheesh." Together, they put the chairs away.

"Is Caesar the fly?" Ed asks.

"You're hopeless. His *mind* is the fly, moving upon silence."

"Take a walk with me?"

She smiles. "Of course."

Outside, they find twenty patients in the yard and no aides. Margaret and Barbara are headed toward the river. Those two, always seeking their deaths.

"Jesus."

"I'll get the ladies," Penelope says. "Maybe you could deal with Karen?"

Karen is hitting her head against one of the poles of the swing set, methodical and hard. She stops as soon as Ed touches her shoulder, her smile as big as the sky. She skips toward a group of her friends, so quickly redirected.

Ed then coaxes a twelve-year-old named Gregory off the top of the swing set and breaks up a slapping match between two thirty-year-olds. He watches Penelope corral Margaret and Barbara, shepherding them back to the pack.

An aide comes out, some new young man whose name Ed hasn't learned yet. Ed waves him over. "You need to stay out here with these patients until they go inside, do you understand? They can't be out here unattended."

"Sure thing, Doctor."

Ed feels Penelope's arm slip through his, sees the aide's eyes take it in. Lets him look.

"No one's left alone outside. Got it?" His voice is more forceful than necessary. He's posturing, proving his authority. He is the superintendent. He is running the damn place. He can link arms with whomever he chooses.

"Yes, sir."

They walk past the convalescent cottage, and Ed can't help but think about Caroline in there, pregnant and motionless in her bed. He shakes his head and makes himself think of his successes: He's moved twenty-five patients from institutional to residential living—ten to their families, eleven to group homes, four to apartments of their own. He thinks of George at Thriftway. Belinda in the halls of the Mitchell Building.

Ed and Penelope walk on. The cottages are empty, as they should be, patients in therapy and group time. He sees one of his therapists with a group of patients sitting in a circle in the grass, practicing speech patterns. The day is warm, not too hot. The sun comes and goes between white clouds. It feels like one of Laura's paintings.

They head toward the river, the welcoming sound of water. They are far from the others, out of sight down the slope of a hill.

"I'm exhausted, Pen."

She touches his back, low near the waist. "You're doing great work, Dr. Ed. You're helping so many people." He feels her hand slide along his body as she moves in front of him, but he isn't registering her proximity, the intimacy. His mind is with Caroline and Phillip, real people he's failed. And then Penelope's face is before his, her hands on his neck, and he returns, sharply, immediately, all senses alive, a great firing of information—wind and sun, river noise and grass, Penelope's face just inches from his own, her fingers digging into his neck at the base of his jaw, her mouth coming level with his, no words, and—*no*—her lips against his, the softest things he's ever felt.

"No!" He pushes her away so forcefully she stumbles.

She comes back, her hands grabbing for the buttons on his shirt, the belt on his pants. He pushes them away, and they return, persistent flies, and then her hand slips inside his shorts, his excitement so obvious she laughs, and her mouth is against his neck, whispering, "It's okay. I want to."

He has never turned away from the touch of a woman, and he gives himself a breath, a moment to bask in the manifestation of his yearnings. They could go to their knees in the grass. He could pull her pants from her hips, slip her underwear past her feet, yank her against him, take and take, until they're both full and healed. One breath. One imagined moment.

And then he is removing himself from her grip, the noise he emits not human, a gut-shot elk, running for the hope of cover, trailing its intestines, death ahead—slow and painful. He is far from her—five feet, six—shoving his shirt back in his pants, fastening those, cinching his belt.

"Ed."

"Not that, Pen. Never that. I'm sorry I let it get this far."

Penelope stands where he left her, fists at her sides, chest proud. "You love me," she says.

"I love my wife, Pen. I love Laura."

"You love me, too."

He did this. He's such an idiot.

"Not like that," he says.

She walks past him, and he can't chase after her, can't make them into that spectacle. He forces himself to count to sixty before slowly walking back toward Griffin Hall.

A young man named Leonard squats against the building, stabbing ants with a stick. He waves. "Hi. Doc. Tor. Ed."

"Hi, Leonard." Ed enters through the side door, walks down the hall to his office, closes himself inside, slides to the ground, back against the door, head in his hands.

The fear comes then. A young woman in his care put her hand in his pants, and he allowed it, if only for a moment. A good case could be made that he asked for it. His career is over, his marriage, his would-be family. He wants that life, the one he's imagined for himself and Laura on Third Street, the smell of Laura's paints, the chaos of children. He's been imagining that life since he first saw her face. He leaped over a table for her, and when she ignored him, he leaped onto the stage of the bar to sing "Girl from the North Country." She'd turned around and shouted, "How did you know?"

It was her favorite song.

He can't lose her.

But he is so afraid, and the fear conjures his *babcia,* that shriveled scarf-covered kernel of a woman with all her proverbs. There was a severity to her touch that established itself permanently as Ed's first fear, her fingers like the dead frog he once found in the park—on its way toward tanned leather but still meaty and bony underneath. As a boy, Ed had become convinced that his *babcia* was indeed dead, forcing them all to share in her slow disintegration. Death seemed gradual, a sloughing off, a tapering out, its start hard to determine. The frog in the park was certainly dead—no longer breathing, its heart no longer pumping its cold amphibian blood through its desiccated body—but its death, Ed thought, had likely started long before he found it. It may have been swimming through the park's pond, its webbed feet pushing against algae and weeds. It may have been sitting on the bank, catching bugs. It may have been ballooning its inflatable chest to attract a mate. The important thing, Ed insisted in his child's mind, was that death was not diagnosable at its onset. The frog was dead, even while it had appeared alive. *Babcia* was dead, but no one cared. Edmund Malinowski is dead, but he is still sitting on the floor of his office, breathing.

He stays there until the day goes away. He ignores Martha's calls and knocks. He declines Pete's shouts through the door for a beer. The institution hunkers around him, settling into its form of sleep.

— —

A week later, Ed calls Penelope's parents.

"Mr. Gatson?"

"Speaking." The man is skilled in the art of the ungreeting.

"This is Dr. Malinowski, Penelope's doctor out in Boulder. I was hoping you and Mrs. Gatson could come out for a visit. Penelope would love to see you, and I would love to sit down with you in person to discuss her discharge." He won't let the man refuse. "I insist we do this in person. I'm patching you through to my secretary to schedule the meeting." Ed buzzes Martha and places Mr. Gatson on hold. Done.

Next he has Martha retrieve Penelope.

She sits down opposite him, the safety of the desk between them. She won't look at him. They haven't had an individual session since the incident by the river.

But he's figured out how to fix it—an outcome that will be good for them both, one he should've pursued months ago.

"It's time for you to go home," he says.

"You're afraid what happened between us will happen again."

He was hoping she'd go the route he was—one of silence and forgetting. But he prepared himself for this response, too.

"What happened was a mistake, Pen. On both our parts. I shouldn't have let us get so close—"

"You don't believe that."

"Would you listen, please?"

She scowls at him, and he's scared of her anger. He believes Penelope cares about him, that she doesn't want to harm him, but the devastation of jilted love—was it really love?—can overpower the strongest intentions. He doesn't know what she might do in retaliation.

He doesn't want to push her there.

But she has to go.

"You're well enough to live outside this institution, Pen. You've been well enough for a while now. It's been selfish and stupid of me to keep you here this long."

"See? You kept me. You."

"I should've insisted you leave sooner."

"But you kept me because you wanted to."

"Maybe so, but it's out of my hands now."

"What do you mean?"

"As part of the deinstitutionalization process we're starting, all high-functioning patients are being returned to their communities. And even more—the state is no longer recognizing epilepsy as an indicator for institutionalization. Which is good. You and I both know you're not among peers here."

He doesn't tell her that he authored these changes himself just last week. The most recent draft of his proposal takes extra care to describe patient indicators for deinstitutionalization, and Penelope possesses every one of them. She is high-functioning and high-achieving. She is capable and able-bodied. And epilepsy should've been removed from the list long ago.

Ed tells himself he's simply writing good policy. If the policy aids this troublesome situation he's gotten into, so be it.

He watches Penelope sit with the news.

"I could talk, you know," she says.

He prepared for this, too, though he'd hoped she wouldn't play this card. He doesn't want to have to play his.

"Pen."

"I could tell everyone what happened between us. I could expose you."

Ed looks at Laura's paintings on the wall, then at the framed photo of Laura he recently put on his desk. He lays his hands flat on the leather blotter before him. "And what would you say? That you stuck your hand in my pants and I pushed you away? You'd look like a lovesick fool, and I'd look like a doctor who was the unfortunate recipient of a patient's misguided emotions." He hates what he's saying. Hates the way Penelope's face is changing, the anger turning to disgust turning to sadness. But he has to do it. "If you said it was anything more than that, no one would believe you."

She looks away, and her voice is quiet again when she speaks. "This isn't you, Ed. Pretend all you want, but I know better." She's standing now, her body growing with her voice, loud and tall. "I am better because of our time together. And you are, too." She comes toward him, her hand catching his before he can get away.

Just one more moment, he thinks, *and then she'll go. What's one more moment going to hurt?* He can see it clearly—his hands on her face and then her shirt, stripping her quickly, that perfect body exposed for him to cover and consume. *Laura,* a piece of his brain says. *Laura and*

the baby and the house. Your career, another part whispers. Another: *Prison.* He hears his grandmother murmur, *Co cialo lubi, to dusze zgubi.* "Remember, Eddy, what likes the body will lose the soul."

You are in control, he tells himself. *Take your hand away. Step back*

He does these things and tells her, "Your parents are coming next week."

Penelope steps past him, swift steps to the door.

Chapter 13

— *Laura* —

The baby rounds out of my belly like a giant stone. His limbs are sharp, and I picture him like one of Ed's arrowheads, the point pressing into my stomach.

Miranda loves it. "Customers always buy things from pregnant women. Just wait. Your sales are going to go way up."

And she is right. Everyone buys something, even the browsers who usually touch everything but leave empty-handed. Still, the day shifts are naturally slow, and I spend more time steaming and tagging clothes than I do selling them.

I am in the back when the bell chimes. "Hello!" I call. "I'll be right out!"

A familiar male voice returns, "Hello!"

It's Tim with the dead mother. I have his thank-you card in my studio, and I have memorized the words inside. *My mother always believed in the kindness of strangers. People were always doing things for her. But I never experienced any meaningful stranger moments before our meeting the other day. And now I know what she meant. Thank you.* And then, at the bottom, in even smaller print: *I hope I can buy you a drink sometime.*

I reread the card daily now. His handwriting is small and blocky, where Ed's is loose and illegible.

Tim is the tidy version of himself again. This version matches his handwriting, but I might prefer the disheveled one I first met.

"You're working," he says.

"I am."

It's been at least a year since his mother's death, and I have been working here longer than two.

Ed still has no idea.

"I walk by all the time, but I can never see you through the window, and I can't get the nerve to come in."

I have an armful of dresses to hang. "Are you in need of women's clothing?"

He laughs. "No."

I haven't been able to recognize flirtation since Ed brazenly wooed me away from Danny, but this must be it. The card. Walking by all the time. Steeling his nerve to come inside.

I'm flattered.

And then I turn to him, the dresses all hung, and he sees my belly.

"Oh!" he shouts, and I can't help but smile.

"Not what you expected?"

"No. I mean, I wasn't expecting anything. I mean, I was hoping—" His discomfort is consuming him, poor man, but then he swallows and stares at me. "I was hoping I could buy you that drink. But that's probably not appropriate given your—situation."

"The doctor says drinking is just fine, so long as I keep it under a six-pack a day." I am being ridiculous and unkind. He probably wants to turn and run, and here I am flirting back. I put my hands on my belly and say, "Listen, Tim. It's sweet of you to follow through on your offer, but I'm sure you weren't expecting to find me six months pregnant, so you're off the hook, all right?"

He looks relieved, but then he shakes his head and takes a couple steps toward me. "It's not a date," he says. "It's a belated thank-you for your help."

I'm confused. Is he really that nice a guy to buy a woman a drink with no hope of getting laid? And am I that woman?

I'm quiet too long, and he starts into nervous rambling again. "I'm so sorry if I made you uncomfortable. I was just so taken with your kindness, and I just wanted to thank you—really. Just a thank-you. But I completely understand if it's a bad idea. I'll just leave you alone and—"

"I'd love to have a drink with you, Tim. I'm done here at five."

"Great!" he shouts, clearly terrified.

— —

We talk for hours, like old friends. My belly is gone, my marriage. I am only a woman at a bar with a man. We talk about our dead parents, his brokenhearted father, childhood, high school, work. He's an architect and a builder.

"I did construction in college and realized how much I missed it once I started spending my days at a desk. So now I do the designs and the building both."

I tell him about painting. I tell him how much I love working at the store. I don't tell him about my art classes in Boulder because I don't want to talk about Ed. My ring is obvious enough on my finger.

It's eight-thirty when I leave the bar, assuring Tim I'm fine to drive. I only had three glasses of wine. I drive myself home in the stupid car Ed bought me, "practically brand-new and yellow—your favorite color. And it's an automatic. I know clutches make you nervous." He was so proud of the gift that he nearly convinced me his motivations were noble—a present for his wife, nothing more. But I know he bought the car to free himself of me, to regain his Tuesday drives to and from Boulder. "You like it?" he asked.

"Yes," I lied. "It's lovely."

The whole house is lit when I get home, and I'm not even out of the car before Ed is there shouting. "Jesus, Laura! Are you all right? Where the hell have you been? I've been knocking on the neighbors' doors. Pete and Bonnie are out looking for you. I was just about to call the police."

I laugh. It's all I can do in the face of such irony. I laugh and laugh until it turns into a bitter finger pointed at Ed's chest. "You were just about to call the police? Because I'm home at eight-thirty? Because I missed dinner? Oh, God! Clearly, something must be horribly, terribly wrong for me to stay away from home so late. There must have been an accident. Or a tragedy. Maybe my parents were killed.

Oh, but they're already dead. Maybe I was murdered! Kidnapped. The possibilities are endless. Right, Ed? I mean, why would someone stay away so late if not for an emergency?"

He is trying to talk over me, trying to calm me. "Okay, Laura. I see what you're doing. But I have responsibilities outside the house, and you—"

"Responsibilities that require you to go to the bar nearly every day with the boys? Well, maybe I have those responsibilities now, too."

"What the hell does that mean?"

We are shouting too loudly for the street. I don't want to be here. I want to be back at the bar with Tim, talking about the life I thought I'd have. Some critic picking my work out of the undergraduate showcase, hanging it in her New York gallery, spreading my name across the globe. Fame and maybe a little fortune. A marriage full of laughter and food and drink. Travel. Children with the expectation that I keep working.

"Doesn't sound so impossible," Tim said.

"Yeah, but the critic didn't pick me. She picked Tabitha Howser, who was nothing but a Georgia O'Keeffe knockoff, all vagina flowers. Tabitha's doing well, just had another opening in New York, and here I am in Helena, Montana."

"I know I haven't seen your work, but I guarantee it's better than vagina flowers." He raised his glass.

"What are we toasting?"

"Your career."

I can't remember the last time I talked about my career with Ed.

"Are you at least going to tell me where you've been?" he asks.

"No," I say, and head inside.

— —

Ed is home early the following night, with wine and TV dinners he insists on heating up himself. I don't move from my spot at the window, waiting for our pair of Clark's nutcrackers to return after

Ed's car startled them off. We feed them peanuts in a flat feeder. They're loud birds, big and black and gray. We've named them both Lewis.

"The Lewises?" he asks, and I nod.

"I think they're gone for the day."

"They'll be back," he says, pouring me a glass of wine. "Here you go, beautiful."

I hate this version of him, the attentive ass-kiss. I prefer the angry asshole, or the sloppy drunk, or the absent doctor. At least those Eds are real.

The timer goes off, and Ed brings over our steaming meals. Meat loaf and mashed potatoes, green beans and gravy. We used to laugh about our shared love of TV dinners, how our mothers would cringe if they knew.

He raises his glass, as though if we toast enough, all our problems will vanish.

"To the baby again?" I ask, and think of my drinks with Tim. A toast to my work.

"Something else," Ed says. "I wanted to tell you the other night when you went missing." He pauses for effect, and I wait. I will give him no explanation about my absence. "Okay—not taking the bait. Well, here's the toast, then: Penelope is getting discharged!" He delivers it with a flourish, chiming his glass against mine, his face all smile and pride. Like my childhood dog who brought me a dead squirrel once, laying it at my feet with the utmost care. He sat back on his haunches and smiled up at me, tongue lolling, so proud. I didn't have the heart to refuse the gift, so I petted his head and told him he was good, and because my parents were sick, I had to scoop the squirrel into a bag and deposit it in the trash when my dog was distracted by his dinner.

Ed wants to be petted and told he's good. But he is more misguided than my dog, whose only mistake was thinking a human would appreciate the same thing a dog would. Ed's mistake is greater, the gift he's laid at my feet dirtier. If Penelope's departure is worth toasting, then her presence was worth worrying about. By toasting her, he is acknowledging my fears and suspicions. He is giving them life and blood.

He is such a fool.

And I am too tired to fight.

So I raise my glass with him, and I toast the end of what I now know was an affair. Whether or not it was physical, the relationship he had with her was a betrayal.

I think about Tim. I try on the word *betrayal.*

Ed is eating his meat loaf, and I am back on those steps of his institution my first day, waiting for him to finish his meeting with Penelope. I am counting the minutes he is with her.

Chapter 14

Penelope's parents stand before him, a couple of feet behind the chair their daughter occupies during her sessions. Ed can see her in their faces, nearly a perfect blend of the two. On their own, their features are nearly comical, especially when compared—the father tall and thin, the mother short and round. They need Penelope to complete them, to make them relevant to each other. Ed finds it alarming, if not offensive, to see Penelope's vivid eyes behind her father's spectacles, her thick hair falling around her mother's shoulders. Her nose sits above her father's thick, salty mustache; the tiny shells of her ears tuck themselves against her mother's skull. It's a puzzle, a hidden-picture hunt. He wants to study them for hours, ticking off the replications. Mother's forehead, father's chin, mother's hands, father's legs. The pieces are perfect in Penelope and disconcerting in her parents, thieves stealing a piece of her at a time.

Penelope hasn't spoken to him since she last left his office.

"Thank you for coming in today." Ed introduces himself and shakes their hands. Father: firm and angry. Mother: flaccid and weak. "Have a seat." The father sits in Penelope's chair.

"Why do you always sit there?" Ed asked her once.

"It's farthest from the hall," she said, "which means more steps to take, should someone come to snatch me away. If I'm here, you have time to jump in and save me."

"Would I tackle the intruder to the ground?"

She laughed her bell-ringing laugh.

The mother now sniffs and rummages in her purse for a handkerchief.

The father says, "I'm going to be blunt, Dr. Mali— What was it?" He remains tall even when seated, and his voice is too high for his height.

"Malinowski." They've heard his name innumerable times, seen it in the regular correspondence he sends to their home. It's odd and long but not impossible.

"Dr. Malinowski, right." Mr. Gatson sets his hand on his wife's arm, clad in a flowered blouse that seems forlorn, its flowers readying to wilt. "We have no idea why you're pursuing this route."

The mother brings the handkerchief away from her nose to shout, "Penelope is diagnosed with epilepsy and psychotic episodes! And you want to put her back into our home!"

"Calm down, Hattie." The father pats her.

Ed looks at the Lake Michigan painting. He sees Laura in her bikini, waist-deep in the surf, sun on her skin, bright eyes turned in his direction. "Come in!" he hears her shout. "It's wonderful!"

"Mr. and Mrs. Gatson." He draws out their names like dinner entrées, elaborate specials. "Diagnoses simply describe what has been observed in a patient. Here." He slides a copy of Penelope's recent expanded diagnosis across the desk, a formula he put into place within weeks of his arrival. "We have a much broader picture of Penelope now."

Penelope's father takes the paper in his hands, holding it at both sides as though it might blow away.

"What does it say, Lionel?"

Mr. Gatson begins to read aloud, an odd lullaby Ed has already memorized. "'Social diagnosis: a seventeen-year-old Caucasian female with one sister (Genevieve, five years older), who performs well (A's and B's) in school, writes and reads extensively, and has healthy developmental relationships with peers (so much as can be determined in the institutional setting).' Healthy! Hah! Maybe out here with a bunch of retards, but she sure as hell doesn't maintain healthy relationships with the kids at school. They're terrified of her!"

It's the wife's turn to play pacifier. "It's all right, Lionel. Calm down."

"Would you like me to expand on the diagnosis?" Ed asks.

They look at him as though he's offered to take his pants off, a ludicrous and irrelevant suggestion.

"That's not necessary, Doctor." Mr. Gatson goes back to his reading, the words strange in his mouth, devoid of meaning, just a series of sounds like the grunts and squeals in the hallways, the mewling and barking. " 'Medical diagnosis: isolated occurrences of petit and grand mal seizures. Responds well to medication. Psychiatric diagnosis: developmentally normal.' "

Huff. Stomp. Pat. Slap. Noise untethered from comprehension, rafts floating on the rolling waters of a lake, no connection to the shore.

Mrs. Gatson stares at Ed with her squinty eyes. Penelope is lucky to have avoided that genetic inheritance. "This doesn't even talk about her psychotic episodes!"

"I have no evidence of psychosis in Penelope. We feel strongly that that was a false diagnosis."

"Well, you're an idiot, then." The woman pokes at the paper in her husband's hand. "And what does it mean by 'developmentally normal'? She has *fits*. And this whole 'slow to anger' part is ridiculous as well. She's a monster after one of her episodes."

Ed finds his tact slipping. Idiot? His diplomas and medical license are framed on the wall. He could direct her attention there, then to the books on his shelves. He could show her his résumé, all the time he's spent in institutions, all the patients he's overseen. *Idiot, you say? I'm sorry, where did you go to college?* He knows the answer. It's in Penelope's case history. Her mother hasn't set foot on a college campus.

No. Shame doesn't work on shameless people. Shame doesn't work on anyone.

And you are *an idiot, remember,* a voice says, maybe his mother's. *She is right, Eddy. You are a stupid man.*

He takes a deep breath and re-tents his hands. "I understand your hesitancy, Mrs. Gatson." He pauses, listens to a truck rumble off on its errands. What is it doing? The grounds are a mess. "However, Penelope has been at the hospital over three years, and she has shown marked improvement with new medication and changes in her routine. She has an above-average IQ and is not among developmental or intellectual peers. We simply can't justify keeping her here."

"But you can justify releasing her into the world?" Mr. Gatson jumps in again. *Lionel,* what a pissy weak name, all soft and loose on the tongue. The man's mustache bounces as he speaks, a pet there on his face, something to stroke and tend, yet no time for his daughter. "Have you stopped to think that maybe she's doing so well *because* she's here? That your diagnoses have changed because of the environment?"

Ed hears Penelope say, *I'm better because of you.*

He says, "One of the concerns with keeping Penelope—or any patient—longer than necessary is the effect that institutionalization has on the patient's identity. Penelope already identifies herself as someone ill enough for institutionalization. The longer she remains, the more she internalizes that identity. Keeping her here past the time of need will likely elaborate her illness in her own mind. She will get worse." Ed is surprised not to be interrupted yet—no yelps from Mrs. Gatson. "Right now, Penelope is strong and capable, but she won't continue in that direction without intellectual stimulation beyond what we can give her." He decides to stand, a signal to them that he is in charge and their time is nearly up. He is telling them what they need to know. That will have to be enough. "When a diagnosis no longer fits, we have to abandon it and return to the person in front of us. Who we are as individuals is constantly redetermined and redefined. Penelope's needs are different now."

This part of the script he has memorized. He's made it to dozens of families: *People are malleable, as are their behaviors, and behavior is really the only thing of interest and import. When behaviors meet societal norms, people need to reenter society*. Some of the families are receptive, some combative, like Penelope's. He had one set of grandparents—a highly functioning boy's only relatives—claim that their grandson couldn't be released because "he'd wind up impregnating another retard and bring more dummies into the world." Ed wanted to point out that their grandson's chances of impregnating a disabled woman were much higher in an institution whose population was solely the disabled than it was in a community of able-bodied citizens. "Very unlikely," he said instead, and ushered them out. He is still searching for a group home for that particular boy.

"What if she gets worse again?"

"We are here to support your family," Ed promises them, "and there are safety measures we put in place right away. Penelope will be required to see a psychologist once a week, or twice if you think it would benefit her. She'll be continuing her medication. We're sending you with recommendations for her diet. Seizures are often brought on by dehydration and malnutrition, so it's important that she remain physically healthy."

The Gatsons stand before him in their odd little pairing. "I hope you're right about this, Doctor," Mr. Gatson says.

"I'm very confident."

They leave his office in silence, only their steps making noise on the stairs, the din of the first-floor hall muted by yard time—everyone outside. He leads them back to the waiting area by Martha's desk and goes to collect Penelope from her room.

— —

Ed finds her packing the few personal items she owns—books, the paint set and sketch pad Laura gave each of her students (an expense out of her own pocket, which was out of *his* pocket; he didn't have the energy to complain), journals, one full, one filling, the clothes her parents supplied. She could've had plenty more, but it's dangerous to own things as a patient, hard to keep them safe. Penelope told him often about the items that would go missing. Sometimes she'd find them again—a pair of her pants smashed into the dirt of the yard, one of her books in the dining room with large sections removed—but mostly, the things just disappeared. Once she caught a woman wearing one of her sweaters, but she'd stayed quiet. "She doesn't know what stealing is," Penelope said when she reported the story. "She saw a pretty sweater, prettier than the hospital-issued clothes she's been wearing her whole life, and she put it on." All of this would be easier if Penelope weren't so damn kind.

The dormitory is dim, even with the bright day outside, the beds rumpled. Penelope is about halfway down, standing by a bed on the right, her back to him, miscellaneous bits of her institution life spread on the mattress before her. He walks to her slowly, conscious of his echoing footsteps, the heaves and moans of the building, the rustle of Penelope's packing.

She has to hear him, but she makes no indication.

They are alone, and this is their goodbye. Her life is moving outside this place, far from him, to the other side of a great chasm he tries to maintain in his imaginings. Too often, though, he finds himself thinking of her proximity back there in her parents' home in Helena: truthfully, just on the other side of downtown. He's memorized the address. He can't unlearn it. Still—a chasm. Enough that if he should run into her around town, he'd merely remark on her great health and then continue on his way.

Their goodbye, though—he has to have one.

He is behind her, a foot away, too close. He reaches for her shoulder. He expects her to turn at his touch, but she keeps facing the bed, a book in her hands. He's never touched this particular spot on her body. His hand spans from collarbone to shoulder blade, all those sharp pieces of her. She is probably too thin, though meat clings to the right parts—the perfect ass, the round breasts. He's looked too often, cursing himself, forbidding himself to look again. But here he is, looking one more time.

"Are they here?" she asks.

He can't move his hand. "They're waiting with Martha."

"How'd they take it?"

He can't stand the defeat in her tone, all the rich color she's showered on him and the other patients—gone, bleached away. He tugs on her, a slight pull. "Turn around, Pen."

She turns and dives against him, forcing his hand off her shoulder, dropping it to her lower back. Humans are wired to return an embrace, to hold each other; they instinctively look for a body to

press against, warmth to garner and distribute. If someone recoils, it has been bred into them through trauma, and Ed has no such scars. He has other, more immediate reasons not to return her embrace, but he wraps his arms around her anyway, and he holds her without thinking, aware only of her body against his, her cheek against his chest, her breasts against his ribs—he is so much taller than she is—down to the bony bend of her right knee, where it digs into his calf. He would absorb her if he could.

She says, "Please don't make me go."

His hand finds her hair, strokes it. "It'll be all right. They're not perfect, but I believe they love you in their own way, and they'll give you what you need—a house, food, rides to school and therapy, reminders about your medicine. Plus, you'll be with Genevieve, so how bad can it be? And—you're going to turn eighteen in a few months. A bona fide adult. You and Genevieve could get your own place."

She doesn't loosen her grip. Her hands are holding fistfuls of his shirt, and she doesn't move her body away from his, but she tilts her head back. "I know you don't want me to go."

He has to extricate himself. He creates a set of instructions, like those he'd give a patient, every step detailed clearly as to avoid confusion. *Remove your hand from her hair. Remove your other hand from her back. Step away. Take another step. The distance between you should equal three feet.* He removes his hand. She grabs it. He steps back. She stays with him.

"Tell me you don't want me to go."

"You're well, Pen. You need to be out in the world."

"Not that. *You*. What do *you* want?"

He wants to throw her on the bed.

Her face is so close, mouth partly open, inviting.

But behind her is a row of dirty beds. They hold patients he is responsible for. And he is responsible for more than just patients. His wife. And now his son.

He is stronger than Penelope, and it is easy to remove her hands from his shirt. He keeps hold of them, but out in the open, a barrier between them. "You're going to be all right, Pen."

She pulls away and turns, shoving the last of her things into her backpack.

"Pen."

"Stop it! Stop talking!"

"All right."

They carry out the remainder of their duties in silence, Ed lifting her small suitcase, Penelope shouldering her backpack. They walk back across the yard and into Griffin Hall, where he gives her suitcase to her father.

She doesn't respond when he says goodbye.

Dependents

—

SEPTEMBER–DECEMBER 1973

Chapter 15

— *Laura* —

Ed swore he'd make it to this appointment, but again he calls, saying, "Laura, I'm so sorry."

I don't let him explain the crisis that will keep him in Boulder, whatever it is—another no-show orderly, or a pervert his former boss hired, or simply a patient in the throes of a breakdown, no one but Ed there to comfort the poor soul. I don't care. Ed staying won't fix the problem. One more afternoon can't fix anything, no matter what Ed claims. There will be other crises.

"There will be other doctor appointments," he said after missing the last one.

"Not for long."

He's made it to one so far.

It's nearly snowing, cold rain and sleet that sting my face. The streets are slick under the new moisture, and I drive slower than usual. It's more than clutches that unnerve me; the entire driving experience shakes my resolve. Moving these huge hunks of metal around, four round tires the only contact with earth, so many moving parts—it feels foolish.

An angry man passes me on Winne Street, a residential neighborhood. He flips me off, honks his horn. I wave. *Kill them with kindness,* my mother used to say. I want her next to me in this car, driving to my doctor's appointment to check on the child in my belly. My mother would've made Ed's absence acceptable somehow.

I should've asked Bonnie to come, but Bonnie has come to the last two appointments, and it's starting to feel like she's the other parent.

Still, she defends Ed's absences. "You're fine," she tells me. "What do you need Ed here for, anyway?"

"Attention," I told her once. "Like the kind he gave his precious Penelope."

Bonnie has always tried to hush those concerns, too. When Penelope was discharged, she said, "See? If there'd been something going on, Ed never would've sent her away."

I think we both knew she was lying.

I light a cigarette, crack the window. At the doctor's encouragement, I've cut back during the pregnancy, but it's impossible to quit entirely. Besides, the doctor is suspicious about the health risks: "Low birth weight is the only thing they've hit upon, and you're a tiny woman. A smaller baby means an easier delivery for you."

Drops dot in from outside, freckling my hand. Wood smoke hangs in the air, a scent that will last until spring. I'll build up the fire in the woodstove when I get home. Ed loves that I know how to build a fire.

The baby moves in my stomach, a dive and roll.

"Hey, there, little man." I sing: " 'Hush a-bye, don't you cry, go to sleep, my little baby.' "

At the office, I'm weighed and measured—blood pressure, belly growth. "You should be gaining more weight," the nurse says, snide and plump.

"I'm trying," I tell her, though I'm probably not trying hard enough. The nausea of early pregnancy didn't stop at the fourth month, as promised, and food has become a necessary annoyance I have little patience for. Everything makes me sick. Everything sounds disgusting. Only beer tastes good, wine. I force down soda crackers, homemade broth, mashed potatoes, tasteless porridge.

The nurse listens to the baby's heartbeat, a whale's whooshing, something for underwater caves. "Very strong," she says, a new kindness in her voice for this skinny woman with a strong-hearted baby inside her. *See? I can grow a strong child, even with little nourishment. He will feed off me, and that's enough.*

The doctor comes and presses his fingers against my rounded stomach, slides them inside me. He keeps his eyes over my head. He takes his hands away and a step back before speaking. "Everything looks perfect. You're the model case, Laura. Wish every pregnancy were so easy."

I ask my list of questions, tallied in the notebook I keep in my purse. *Breasts ever stop hurting? Okay to eat only white food and liquid? Sex still okay?*

"That baby is in the safest place possible, Laura. You and your husband can have sex right up to the delivery date. Your breasts are going to hurt even more when the milk comes in, so just get used to that one. And you know, I hate to say it because of what it means for you, but babies are parasites. They take everything they need from the mother, so the only person who's going to suffer from a white-foods-and-liquid diet is you. Eat what you can and don't worry. You're doing the Lamaze class?"

"Yes."

"And how's your husband?"

"Fine."

The doctor smiles and writes in my chart. I could say, *My husband is a disgusting louse,* and the man wouldn't hear it. His patients have husbands, and it's his job to ask after them. No more, no less. How the husband is doesn't matter.

"One more appointment and then we'll be meeting at the hospital." He walks out, talking over his shoulder.

The nurse leaves, too, and I dress slowly, playing the sound of the baby's heartbeat back in my mind, so different from my own. His conjures rain and waves, a great coastal storm I imagine hitting the Pacific coast, the baby and me tucked safe in a cottage as water pelts the windows and pounds the sand below us. I want to tell Ed: *Our baby's heart is a storm, a great show of power and strength. He is stronger than we are.*

At home, I start a new painting. A body, hips to neck, with a huge belly and transparent skin. Inside, a baby. The baby's body opens to the storm it carries in its chest, a great ocean breaking against rocks, rain clouds in the sky.

— —

My students love my belly, and I give it over to their hands willingly. Even the clumsiest of them become elegant when they touch me, fingers suddenly fluid and controlled.

Chip screamed the first time he felt a kick. "Lau-ra tum-mee a-tack." He pulled his hand away as though it'd touched flame.

"Sometimes he'll push a foot against my belly so hard you can see the outline of it."

My students' eyes go round with the magic of it—a foot inside my belly. Pregnancy is a gift the institution doesn't often receive.

"How get out?" Lilly asks.

"Through. The. Hoo-ha!" Eva shouts.

Everyone laughs, and I smile. Why had I assumed they wouldn't know about sex? They are delayed and disabled but still physically whole. Still women and men.

My due date is only a month away. Ed continues to pressure me to quit teaching, and I continue to refuse. I started teaching to try to regain Ed, but it has nothing to do with him now. I come every week because I love my students. I love watching their skills improve and their subjects expand. I know it's far easier than everything Ed must do for them, but I believe the art class has improved their lives in ways Ed's other programs can't.

It's nice to beat him at something. Especially this thing.

Some teaching mornings, I say, "Fine. I'll stay," just to get him out the door. And then I call Sheila and Martha to assure them that—contrary to what Ed is likely to tell them—the art class will be happening as planned, and would they please help get the students up to the classroom?

This morning is one of those.

"He's not too quick, is he?" Martha says, laughing. "I mean, he just walked in and told me you were staying put today, to call off the class. Not recognizing the patterns, huh?"

"He believes what he wants to believe."

There have been at least two Tuesdays I've slipped in and out of the institution without his notice, the infraction brought up later only after he saw evidence of new art or had a conversation with one of my students.

"Dale said you were there yesterday," he shouted at me last week.

"I was."

Anger rose thick in his face. "There are so many pieces of this that aren't all right, Laura. First, you lied to me in the morning. Second, you're driving that dangerous road without anyone knowing. Third—"

"People know."

"Third, you don't even say hello to me when you're there?" He heard my response only after he finished his own speech. "Who knows you're going?"

"I always tell Bonnie. And I call Boulder. Martha and Sheila know to expect me."

"They're my staff!"

"I'm one of your volunteers. It's your staff's job to support me." I picture the baby loaning me some of his stormy blood.

Ed always backs down, cupping my belly with his hands—his plea. *Stay home for the baby.* Not for me, not for him, but for the baby.

"I'm going to keep teaching until the baby comes," I tell him. "If you want to fight every Tuesday, we can, and I'll lie, and I'll go."

I love, in a deeply pitted part of me, that he can't alter my behavior. This behaviorist, with all his training—I've outsmarted him, slipped his reins.

We left it at that, and I lied again this morning. "Fine. I'll stay."

"Are you lying?"

"No."

"Can I trust you to tell me the truth, Laura? Will you please stay home? You're putting the baby in danger every time you drive that road."

"I'll stay."

To Martha on the phone, "Class is on."

"Of course it is."

What would Ed say of his own behavior? His need to create the fiction even when he knows it won't come true?

Today, my students are starting new paintings. They've built the frames themselves, stretched and stapled the canvas—skills they can take with them. In one of the morning arguments with Ed, I used this project as an example of why my class is important. "I'm giving them vocational training, Ed. This isn't just creative expression. We're *building things,* like the school used to, like you're pushing for."

"You're not a vocational therapist, Laura."

My students are already in the classroom when I arrive, an hour early, a surprise. Sheila is there with them, attending, no surly orderly to shout commands and pull clubs. I can hear their voices from the hall, a din of excitement, and I spy from the doorway for a minute.

It's a baby shower of sorts, each of my students tending to his or her gift—artwork I'll hang in the nursery. They've made more canvases, working outside of class, organizing themselves somehow, getting access to the tools and supplies. Raymond's piece is enormous, nearly the size of the table, great swirls of greens and yellows. Janet's piece is large, too, paint and collage—a technique they all love—the images taken from *National Geographic,* lions and elephants in a savannah she's painted, arid trees, pale sky. Eva has painted one glorious apple.

I turn my voice to singsong. "What do we have here?"

They scream and act as though they've been caught in the worst and best of indiscretions. They all want to be the one to take my hand and lead me to their offerings, and I allow them each a place around me, their fingers on my arms and shoulders, swooping me toward the tables. Sheila has a camera. "Surprise!" she calls.

Raymond insists on his first. "Beautiful," I say, squeezing him. "It's perfect, Raymond." I go clockwise from there, each artist bursting with the excitement of the day. I hug them all, welcome their wandering hands to my stomach. "Beautiful," I keep saying. "They're all so beautiful."

I come to a small canvas last, eight-by-ten, with no one next to it. "From. Pen," Chip says. My husband's adulteress, back to haunt me. It is a portrait of Ed, and it is all I can do not to smash it to pieces.

I leave it where it is and thank my students again. "These are all wonderful. I'm going to hang them in the baby's room."

"In your tum-mee?" Chip asks. "No fit."

Janet squeals at the thought of it—*paintings in Laura's belly!*

"My tummy is only his room for another month, Chip, and then he'll come out and live outside me, and he'll have his own room in our house. The paintings will be in there for him to see."

Chip squints, unsure.

Janet chants, "Belly house. Belly house. Belly house."

"Let's get to work," I say.

Sheila helps move the gifts to the side of the room. "Give me your keys and I'll load these in your car. Raymond, will you help?"

Raymond comes eagerly. I have found that they all love jobs, work to do.

I settle the rest of the class into their seats and pass out canvases with their subjects already sketched in pencil. A road, a large triangle that might be a mountain, more grasses, a long stretch of beds. Janet hands out palettes for me, and I squeeze blobs of acrylic onto each—black, white, red, yellow, blue. Simple colors they've learned to use well, mixing and blending into original shades and hues.

They've been so focused lately that I've started practicing with them. I return to my own canvas on the front table, my own simple paint palette. I am painting a house I've never seen, thick-walled and brick-sided, strong and indestructible.

Raymond returns with my keys and sits at his spot. He's working on new grasses, taking over where George left off.

We paint together for over an hour, stopping only when an aide bellows from the hallway, "You're missing occupational!"

My students look panicked. "It's all right," I assure them. "You're not in trouble. Head to your groups and I'll clean up. I'll see you next week. Thank you again for the artwork."

This brightens their faces—they respond so well to praise.

I am sad to see them go, and I stay to work on my own piece longer than I should, as my students' paints go hard on the palettes, their brushes stiff. Evening is coming, and I realize I am waiting for Ed, waiting for him to acknowledge that I'm here—my car in the lot filled with his patients' artwork, my body in this room filled with his child. I will wait until he comes. I will sit here at this stained table, painting this house, until he shows up in the doorway.

My love, I imagine him saying. *Why are you still here?*

My love, it's so good to see you painting. What are you working on?

My love, let's go get dinner.

The sun sets, and dark sweeps in from the east, pocked with stars. The building quiets around me as patients finish their dinners and go off to their cottages.

Ed is not coming.

I scrape the palettes, set the brushes in soapy water to soak, leave the paintings where they lie. The hall is dark, only my classroom casting light, but I can't leave the lights on—a waste of electricity Ed would use against me—and so I flip the switch and stand in the doorway waiting for my eyes to adjust. I feel no fear. The ghosts here are like my students—kind and gentle. They will guide me down this darkened hallway, these dark stairs, another flight, and here to the side door. I stand outside in the grass. The entire institution is quieter than I've ever heard it, battened down. The lot holds only the skeletal night shift's cars, and mine stands alone in its row. Ed's car is gone. It would've been nearly impossible for him not to notice mine as he left.

"Good night, Boulder," I say, keys in hand.

Chapter 16

Ed is in his office, a rare quiet moment at his desk, working on the revised proposal he's going to take to the next legislative session, when Martha buzzes in.

"Ed, Mr. Gatson's on the phone. He's upset. Can I patch him through?"

Penelope has been out of the institution for over a month, nearly two. Ed has called to check in a couple times but gotten only brief, cold responses from her parents when they pick up. More often, he gets the answering machine, and they never return his calls.

"Mr. Gatson? How can I help you?"

"You son of a bitch. You said she was *well*. You said she was *ready for society*. You promised us this was the right thing. You want to know where Penelope is now? Up in the hospital in Great Falls. The doctors at St. Pete's were shocked to hear that she'd been discharged from Boulder, and they sent her to the specialists up there."

"Why was she in the hospital at all?"

"Nonstop seizures. Her mother and I didn't know what to do. It's never been this bad."

"Is she taking her medications? And following the behavioral plan?"

"She said she was, but we can't watch her every second of every day." The man breathes heavily, an angry bull. "Listen, I have no interest in discussing this with you. Her doctors in Great Falls want to confer, so I said I'd let you know they'd be calling. Someone named Wang or something. You can be sure we'll take no more advice from you."

The man hangs up.

Ed knows exactly who Penelope's doctor is in Great Falls—Anthony Wong, a friend and colleague. Ed has talked to him several times about Penelope's case over the years. He leaves a message for Anthony and looks back down at the papers on his desk. He'd been so sure he was making progress. Caroline, the pregnant woman, had given birth to a healthy, developmentally normal baby girl. A piece of information Ed could use to dispel the lingering fear that developmentally disabled citizens beget more of their own. Boulder perpetuated the fear early on, the institution's own literature claiming that if patients were released, *the boys will become criminals or victims of the criminally inclined, and the girls will become outcasts in society and bring more of their kind into existence.*

Caroline's parents have adopted the baby. Yes, they're in the process of bringing suit against the state of Montana and the institution itself, but still, the baby is healthy and safe.

He's placed three more patients in community facilities.

He's making it home in time for dinner at least three nights a week, and Laura is softening. Just last night, they bundled up against the early winter cold and sang together on the front porch. And they had too much wine, which led them to their bed for the first time in months, and the sex was the best it's ever been, the reality of Laura's belly proving that the act was out of desire and in the pursuit of pleasure, procreation be damned. There is no biological reason to have sex with a pregnant woman.

And he reveled in it all, knowing that Penelope was doing well out there in the world. He let himself imagine her in the last year of high school, chatting with friends in the hallways, maybe even flirting with boys. That's where she belongs.

But she isn't there. She's in the hospital in Great Falls.

The phone rings again, and Martha patches through Anthony Wong.

"Sorry we're catching up over these circumstances," he says. "I wish I had better news about your girl, but she's been seizing uncontrollably for extended periods of time since she got here. We're able to get the seizures under control with injections of diazepam, but she goes right back into another the minute the drug clears her system. We've reintroduced the Tegretol, but it's not kicking in yet."

"She was already on Tegretol."

"It's not showing up in her blood work. It looks like she must have stopped taking her meds at some point."

How had Ed not thought of that possibility? He'd simply assumed she'd follow her discharge instructions: daily medication, lots of water, no caffeine, healthy foods, exercise, mental stimulation in the form of school or coursework. He'd assumed her parents would help, but they probably left her alone, frustrated by the burden of their sick child.

She hadn't wanted to go, so she sabotaged herself in order to get back.

"I'm leaving now." Ed hangs up, grabs Penelope's file from the cabinet, tells Martha there's an emergency, and rushes to the parking lot. Laura's car is there, and he realizes—faintly, briefly, a wisp of cottonwood seed on the breeze—that she's teaching up in her classroom. There isn't time to tell her he's leaving.

— —

He drives too fast through the canyon.

Anthony meets him in the hallway of the hospital, and Ed gives him the thick folder of Penelope's history at Boulder. They agree to grab a drink when Anthony's done with his rounds. And then Ed goes to Penelope's room.

A nurse is tending to her IV. "Family?" she asks over her shoulder.

"Yes."

"Poor thing. She's had a rough go." The nurse hangs a new saline bag, taps the line, makes a note on her clipboard, then bustles past Ed toward the door. He closes it after her and walks to the bed.

Penelope's head is covered with sensors. Wires run to machines.

Ed listens to her heartbeat through the beeping of the monitor. He takes comfort in the green blips on the screen.

"I'm here," he says. "Pen, I'm here." They are alone in the room, and he lets himself take one of her hands. "What the hell were you thinking?" He wants to be angry with her, but he is angry only at himself. He knew Penelope's willfulness and determination. He should've predicted this possibility, should've put safeguards in place. But he was too fixated on his own salvation.

He lets go of her hand and pulls up a chair. The nurse brings him a cup of coffee, and he starts talking, telling Penelope any story he can think of. Anything to keep his voice in the air for her to hear. He talks about his mother and father, his brothers, his grandparents. "My mother was always old. My oldest brother is dead. My second oldest brother is thinking about becoming a priest." His mouth talks, and his mind rambles, and his mother stands before him, asking, *What are you doing, Edmund?*

Trying to wake her up.

She is not yours to wake.

He has always needed the stern comfort of his Polish mother, a strong woman with a wizened face dug by lines. Even in the photos from her childhood, a wooden pull-horse crafted by her grandfather trailing behind her, she wore an expression of worry. She appeared immune to the joys of childhood, in both her own life and her children's. Ed can feel the quick silencing that his mother elicits. He can feel it there in the hospital room. He is a boy again, laughing wildly with his brothers, pretend cowboys in their yard with cap guns and holsters, fearless and loud until their mother appears behind the screen door on the back porch. They could all sense her before she spoke, hands clasped at her waist, mouth a thin line, eyes squinting against the day. As soon as she said the word *dinner,* holsters and guns were immediately dropped in the bin on the porch, shoes plucked off and lined up neatly on the mat, and single-file, they'd walk to the bathroom, where they waited in birth order for a turn at the tap—water so hot it pinked their hands, soap so thick it took a full minute to wash away.

"I am a religious hand-washer," he tells Penelope. He stares at the leather restraints cutting lines into her wrists.

You're being sentimental, he hears his mother say. *You're doing no good.*

But that voice has to be wrong. Ed stays and talks.

At eight, Wong comes, and they drive together to the Sip 'n' Dip, where ladies in seashell bras swim in a huge tank of water behind the bar. Ed has been to several bachelor parties at the Dip, including Wong's own. They order shots of whiskey and pints of beer.

"There's some good news," Wong ventures.

"Oh?"

"We're starting to be able to pinpoint the exact origin of seizures in the brains of epileptics. You've probably seen some of the recent literature. If we can identify the problem area, we can go in and remove it. There are complications, of course, and it's brain surgery, so we're exploring it only in the most severe cases."

"You want to remove part of her brain?"

"If it's a part she can live without, yes." Wong shoots his whiskey. "Listen, Ed, I've performed both the tests and the surgery on three patients so far, and they've all shown a complete elimination of seizures. There's a significant recovery period, but I swear to you, their lives are far better now than they were before."

The field knows so little about the brain in relation to the rest of the body. Who was to say the part they identified wasn't necessary? What if it was the part that made her write lyrics to the muffled sounds of Boulder's hallways? Or the part that loved poetry?

"She's a brilliant kid, Anthony."

"She'll still be brilliant," Wong says. "The tests we've done so far suggest the seizures are originating in the left temporal lobe. We're going to back those up with an intracranial EEG that'll monitor her brain over a series of days, and if we get the results we're hoping for, we'll just go ahead and whisk her right into surgery."

"Her parents okayed this?"

"Are you kidding me? They didn't even let me finish my spiel. 'Wait—you're saying she can have a surgery that will fix her? Where do we sign?' "

Fix her. As though she were a broken toy, a car with a flat tire, a chipped plate.

Ed shouldn't be surprised. Her parents are interested only in eradicating her seizures. If part of their daughter is permanently erased in the process, it would be worth it.

He wants to go back to that day by the river. He wants to follow every craving and let the consequences come.

Or he wants never to take the walk in the first place, never to suggest she leave. He wants to go back to his office and play a hand of poker with pistachios as chips and talk about the great work she's doing with the reading group. Watch her continued improvement, see fewer seizures every week. And when it was time for her to leave the institution, they would both agree it was for the best. She'd go directly to college—live in a dormitory with other young people and attend fascinating classes—and she wouldn't have anything to do with her parents. She would be an adult, and the Gatsons would have no say in the treatment of her brain.

"It's all set, then?"

"We'll start the intracranial EEG tomorrow," Wong says. "You're welcome to stay and observe."

Ed watches a blond mermaid press against the glass, then turn to the surface for a breath. He tells himself he wants to scoop her out of the water and take her to the cheap hotel next door. The fantasy won't hold, though. Not even a sexy wet woman in a seashell bra can take his mind off Penelope.

"I'll go sit with her tonight," he tells Wong, "and then see about tomorrow."

They say their goodbyes, and Ed uses the payphone in the back to call Laura. She doesn't pick up, and Ed leaves a message. "I'm so sorry, love. There was an emergency with one of my patients, and he was transferred to the hospital in Great Falls. I'm up here working with the doctors. I'll probably be home tomorrow, but I'll call in the morning to check in. Hope you're sleeping soundly. Pat that belly for me. Love you."

He should've been lying about Penelope from the start. Maybe if he hadn't talked about her so much when they first moved, Laura wouldn't have developed her suspicions, and the whole situation could've remained benign.

Back at the hospital, he pours himself a cup of coffee and returns to Penelope's bedside, where he tells her more stories in the quiet spells and helps the nurses hold her down during the bouts of seizing that overtake her three different times.

All her progress is gone.

And tomorrow, Anthony Wong will cut open her skull.

— —

Ed is staring at the wires pouring from the opening in Penelope's head when a nurse comes into the room. "Edmund Malinowski?"

He wipes his eyes, blurry and fatigued, in order to focus on the nurse's face. He's been in Great Falls over forty-eight hours, and he knows he needs to go home, but he's terrified to leave Penelope's side. It's irrational, but part of him believes he can protect her. That if he stays, the girl he knows can't disappear.

He hopes the tests will be inconclusive—no point of origin—so her brain will be left alone.

The nurse has a piece of paper in her hand, notes to read. He doesn't understand her hesitation. "A friend of yours called—someone named Peter? He wanted to get you a message."

"Yes?"

Ed's imagination isn't working. There is only the present—this room with Penelope, her health, her recovery. Pete will be telling him to get back to Boulder. That's all.

The nurse swallows and blinks. She looks at the paper as she speaks. "Boy. Six pounds, two ounces."

Penelope whimpers in her bed.

The nurse congratulates him and leaves the room.

It takes Ed a minute to understand.

He hears his *babcia* say, *Co było, nie wróci,* and then his mother: "What was, won't come back. You hear me, Eddy? You cannot take again what has already been taken."

The baby is early.

He is a father, father to a son, like his own father and grandfather before him. Their surname means *dweller by raspberries,* which Ed's father perpetuated, planting the barbed plants around his home, as his mother had, and his *babcia,* and his *babcia-babcia,* and on and on until the beginning of time.

Why is the baby early?

Penelope's eyes open, but she isn't fully conscious.

"Hey there, Pen. The baby came, and I need to go." He thinks he can see a faint smile on her lips. "I'll be back as soon as I can." He kisses her on the cheek.

— —

Once he leaves Penelope's room, Ed can't move fast enough. The hospital corridors are too full, the parking lot too big, his car too slow. He speeds through the canyon like he did on his drive up, but even the quick curves seem long and unending. He feels days slipping by, maybe even years.

Helena's hospital parking lot is much smaller than the one in Great Falls, and sparsely filled. Ed is quick to get inside. Still, he is too late. The receptionist tells him Laura and the baby checked out earlier in the day. "Lucky to go home so soon," she says.

He is sure Laura will never forgive him, and he thinks about heading back to Great Falls. He could pull up that chair next to Penelope and pretend there is no other life. No wife and baby. No house on Third Street. Penelope is eighteen now, and she is no longer directly under his care. Their relationship wouldn't be celebrated, but it wouldn't be illegal, either.

He thinks of her hands on him, her mouth.

But he drives to the store for flowers and champagne.

— —

Through the back French doors, Ed can see Laura sitting in the rocking chair, the baby in her arms. She should look tired, but she looks radiant, more awake than he's ever seen her. The fantasy of Penelope vanishes. This is where he belongs, here in this house with Laura and their son. There are holes in the perfect life he envisioned for them, but he can patch them. He can be the husband Laura needs him to be—present and attentive. He can be a father to this boy, a great father. And they will have more children, and Laura will look at him again like she did early on, when she believed he was the greatest man she'd ever known.

He walks in.

"Who was it?" she demands the moment he closes the door. "Who had the emergency?"

He crosses through the kitchen and into the living room, where he kneels in front of her. "Is he okay? He was early."

She pulls the baby closer to her chest. "Who was it?"

Ed can see the baby's ear, a tiny shell, his nose, his lips. Thick black hair like Ed's own.

"One of our low-functioning patients," he says, setting his hand on the baby's head. "You don't know her."

Laura scoffs. "Really, Ed?" She pushes him aside and walks to the answering machine, already adept at moving with a baby in her arms. How has she learned so quickly? She pushes a button and Ed's voice speaks to them loudly. "I'm so sorry, love. There was an emergency with one of my patients, and he was transferred to the hospital in Great Falls." Laura pushes pause, then rewind. Play. "I'm so sorry, love. There was an emergency with one of my patients, and he was transferred to the hospital in Great Falls."

She looks at him. "*He* was transferred to Great Falls. So, let me ask again: Who's the patient?"

So many mistakes, and the one to ruin him a misplaced pronoun. Laughably small. He knows better than anyone that the best lies are those closest to the truth. He should've made the fake patient a woman. "You know who it is."

Laura nods. It's so hard to look at her with their baby in her arms. He doesn't even know the child's name.

"Am I still a fool for thinking your relationship with her was inappropriate?"

He sees Penelope in her bed in Great Falls, all those wires.

He sent her away so he could save his marriage. And here she is, ruining it again.

Ed imagines saying, *I promise never to see her again.*

She is nothing to me.

But he knows Laura won't believe him any more than he does.

"She got worse, Laura. I discharged her, and she got worse, and now a neurologist in Great Falls is going to cut part of her brain out, and she may never recover."

The baby whimpers and Laura bounces him gently in her arms. Ed wouldn't know to calm him that way, and he wonders whether Laura's skills as a parent are innate or whether they came with the baby, Laura a day ahead. Either way, Ed recognizes his disadvantage. He is afraid he'll never catch up.

Laura moves back to the rocking chair, and Ed watches her settle the baby onto her breast. "I have tried to have compassion for her, Ed. I know her life is unfair. I know it's tragic. But ultimately, I don't care. I don't care if her brain gets cut into and she never recovers. I don't care if her parents are awful. I don't care if her seizures get worse." She repositions the baby's mouth. "You made her my rival, Ed. This child. This patient of yours. And I don't know what all has happened between you two, but I know it's more than you've said, and now we have a baby, and I don't know what to do." She looks at him. "What should I do, Ed?"

"You should let me fix things."

"I've tried that, too."

"Once more." He kneels down again, his hands on the arms of the rocking chair. "I will be here for you and our son, Laura. I promise."

"What was that quote you loved so much, Ed? That one by Skinner, maybe. Or Watson. One of your great fathers of behaviorism. 'Words fail. Only actions matter.' Was that it, Doctor?" She has never looked at him more coldly, but it lasts only a moment.

Then her eyes are back on their son.

Chapter 17

— *Laura* —

Ed has brought me a puppy. A tiny thing, black and soft with enormous ears. Ed swears it's a pure black Labrador, but I suspect there's some hound mixed in.

He brings it home in a box, along with a collar and leash, a bed, dog food, toys. When he walks in, I'm cooking dinner, a box of noodles and a jar of red sauce. He leaves the box on the table, and I don't even notice it at first. My brain doesn't work these days.

The baby begins to whine from the bassinet in the dining room. I named him Benjamin at the hospital and agreed to give him Edmund's name in the middle because of its family history. Benjamin Edmund Malinowski. I'm calling him Benjy.

"I'll get him," Ed says.

I hear more whimpering and ask, "What's that noise?"

"What noise?" I hear Ed talking to our son: "It's all right, little guy. Nothing to be sad about." He returns to the kitchen with Benjy against his shoulder, and I see the box now.

"Oh!" I lift the little dog out and hold it eye-level. "Hello there." I cradle it in my arms and look at Ed. "Pretty low, Doctor."

"At least you're looking at me."

I look away.

Benjy's nearly two months old, and Ed has been getting home in time for dinner nearly every night. He takes the baby for walks so I can rest. Most of the time, I go directly to bed, but just yesterday, when Ed took Benjy, I went to my easel instead.

"You're painting again," Ed said, coming to stand behind me. The canvas was small, the image simple at first glance—dried seeds on the branch of a box elder tree, crisp gold and bean-shaped. The lines were intricate and precise, not like anything I've painted before.

"Laura, I love it."

"Thank you" was all I volunteered in response, but over dinner, I admitted how I'm drawn to the tidiness of detail work right now, order, every line and color in its place. "Life with a newborn is all chaos and mess. Benjy and I are dirty and smelly and covered in shit or milk or piss or all three, given the right moment. It's nice to make something clean."

This all feels like progress, but I still don't know what I'm going to do.

Now I hold the dog away from me, its tiny hind legs dangling in the air, its naked belly exposed. I turn it one way, then the other, inspecting. "You're disgusting," I say. "Ugly and disgusting, but I suppose you can stay. Add to the mess." I bring the little beast to my chest, snuggling its face against my neck like I do with Benjy. Over its silky head, I say, "I wanted a dog when the house was empty." I put it back in its box so I can finish with dinner.

"Anything I can do to help?"

"One thing at a time, Ed. You can't walk in the door one night, suddenly the perfect man." I give him a smile, though, and our dinner feels nearly perfect—me there nursing the baby, Ed cutting my food and feeding it to me, our new dog asleep in his box—nearly the life I imagined us having.

— —

I do not sleep. There is Benjy, always hungry, and now there is the puppy. I'm calling him Beau because it's a sound Benjy almost makes, a near-consonant-vowel combination, a near-word. When I get up at night to nurse the baby, I step in a puddle of dog piss, sometimes a pile of shit. Ed, meanwhile, can sleep through anything.

I wanted a dog back when I was alone all day in Michigan, working at the shop. But Ed refused—too much work, too much mess, too much need. He chooses this moment to change his mind? He's trying to distract me, a magic trick, a sleight of hand: *Look over here! Ta-da! The rabbit that was just in my hat is gone!*

I am trying to feel something, but nothing comes. Instead, I am objective, a scientist studying a subject. My subject is Edmund Malinowski, age thirty-six, behavioral psychiatrist, superintendent of the Boulder River School and Hospital. He is a man devoted to his work. He can listen with great focus. He can shine the light of his whole mind and heart on any given recipient at any given time, and that person glows under the power of his gaze. He does not share his own life. He does not engage in intimacy. The flow is one-way. He absorbs, and he feeds back what he's taken in, but he does not offer up his own thoughts, his own reflections. This makes him a brilliant doctor, and it might make him a brilliant father. But it makes him a terrible husband.

I think of a line Bonnie said the other day, the two of us talking about our men out there in Boulder, all those drinks at the Tavern after work, all those late nights home. I told her how Ed had been getting home earlier for a few days. "In time for dinner, even."

"No."

"And he takes the baby and helps me cook."

Bonnie laughed and said, "All I can say is enjoy it while it lasts. Because it's damn hard for men to change. They pretend to. They try. But it's like asking a dog to walk like a cat—it's just not in their nature."

Like asking a dog to walk like a cat. Who would ask that?

But maybe that's what I've been asking of Ed, to walk like a husband when he's really a bachelor.

Bonnie seems to have accepted Pete for the dog he is. "They're good men," she reminds me.

"He missed his son's birth because he was with another woman," I remind her back.

— —

Miranda says my job at the store is there whenever I'm ready to come back, but I can't justify getting a babysitter. It's amazing to me that I've now worked and left a job with Ed never knowing. The bank account sits there quietly, too.

Bonnie watches Benjy on Tuesdays for my class out in Boulder, and now on Wednesdays so I can go for long runs in the mountains.

"You don't need to lose any more weight," Bonnie says.

"I'm not trying."

"Are you eating?"

"Some."

Bonnie pours us each a tall glass of wine; Benjy and Hank are both napping. "How's sex?"

I laugh through my shudder. "We haven't had sex since before Benjy was born." I think about telling her I'm pretty sure we're done, Ed and I, that I'm just an observer and he's just a man to be observed. I say, "Benjy's touching me all day, touching and nursing, and it's wonderful, but I'm so damn tired of being touched." This is what women say after they have babies.

I am just about to tell her about Tim, whom I've had a couple more drinks with, when she says, "You have to have sex with Ed. Tonight. I won't watch Benjy again until you do."

"Jesus, Bonnie."

She shrugs and knocks back her wine, refills. "You've got to break the dry spell. It'll be easier after that. You want to keep teaching your class and getting your workouts in, you better report some good news Tuesday morning."

I am a scientist. Scientists conduct experiments.

I finish my wine and accept another pour. If I am drunk enough, maybe I can do it. If I am drunk enough and Ed is home before I'm asleep. It will be part of my study of him. *How does the bachelor react when asked to sleep with his wife?* I will take notes, add them to the file in my head marked *Malinowski, Edmund.*

— —

Ed is late but not atrociously. Dinner is still on the stove, lukewarm. I've eaten a bit, nursed Benjy, and put him to bed in his nursery, surrounded by all those paintings by my students. It's a rarity for him to spend the night in there. Mostly, he sleeps next to me in bed or in the cradle in our room.

I've finished off a bottle of wine, and I find myself a sloppy mess that throws herself at Ed as soon as he walks in, briefcase falling from his hand. His body responds immediately to mine. He lifts me easily, my legs surrounding his waist, and he walks blind toward our bedroom, stumbling against the counter, the doorframe, the footboard of the bed. It is hungry and primal, and we tear the clothes from each other, even my bra. My milk is depleted, my breasts just breasts again if only for the little while it takes them to refill.

"Oh, baby." Ed's face presses against my flat belly, and there is pain like the first time, that very first time so long ago in high school with Tommy Baxter (when did I last think of him?) in his basement room while his parents were gone. Not the pain of childbirth but of capture.

I force my way on top, my fingers digging into Ed's chest, the catch of his breath loud in my ears. "Tell me you see me," I whisper, the bones of my hips sharp and piercing, his fingers tight.

"Oh, baby." A gasp of words, gutted.

"Tell me I'm real."

He pulls me against him, presses back, his thumbs digging into skin, muscle, bone, pushing it away. All-consuming and all-consumed, he is here alone, and I am writing my notes. *Sex with wife is just sex, all physical, as one would expect from a bachelor. Wife is invisible. Wife disappears.*

— —

Afterward, we smoke together in bed, my head on his chest, his hand in my hair, and I think about adding a footnote, but there is nothing really to add. A head on a chest is not intimacy.

"Goddamn, baby. That was perfect."

It was good. Sex with Ed is always good.

I rise for the shower. Moments after I get in, Ed's face appears around the curtain. "Room in there for two?"

"Give me a minute in the water." I kiss him, payment for a little more time alone.

Change

—

NOVEMBER 1974–JUNE 1975

Chapter 18

Time has sped up since Benjamin's birth—something everyone said would happen, but Ed couldn't understand until he felt the days moving so quickly. Benjamin is somehow a year old now, and Bonnie has delivered her and Pete's second son.

Ed and Laura arrive at the hospital in separate cars—Ed coming from the institution, Laura from home. Bonnie has given birth to an enormous baby, eleven pounds, four ounces. "See?" she crows. "That weight wasn't all going to my ass."

They name him Justin Edmund Pearson, in honor of Ed, and so their boys can share a name. "Like brothers," Pete says, his arm slung around Ed's shoulder. They raise shots of whiskey around the hospital bed, and Bonnie shoots hers while the infant nurses. Benjamin sits at her feet, jangling Laura's keys; Hank plays with his action figures in a corner.

"Good job, Mama," Ed says. He fits his arm around Laura's waist, his mouth in her ear: "We better get to work on our second one."

She leans her head against his chest but says nothing.

Ed's sure they're knitting themselves back together, that their intimacy has remained strong ever since that night she ambushed him. He isn't getting home as early as he promised, but he makes it back before dinner at least once a week—in time to put Benjamin to bed in his own room, to have a drink or two, and to go to their own bed together. Sometimes she's still awake when he arrives home late, propped up in bed reading, or sitting out on the sofa, or painting at her easel, and they lie together those nights, too, all the anxiety of his day fleeing. Penelope surfaces in his thoughts occasionally—he's heard that she's made a full recovery—but he pushes her away quickly. He is focused on Laura. And Benjamin. His family.

Pete and Bonnie are still in their own world, eyes only for each other and the new baby.

"Bonnie won't be able to watch Ben for a while," Ed whispers to Laura. "Think it might be time to take a break from the art class?"

He feels her stiffen. "Fine," she says. "You win. You can finally get rid of me."

"It's nothing like that," he says, though he feels a wash of relief. To separate Laura from Boulder seems like the final piece of this repair. "You should be painting your own masterpieces," he says. "Not helping my patients."

"Of course you know what I should be doing."

He hears his own mother say: "I am deeply suspicious of the word *should*." Ed and his brothers learned never to use it in their reasoning or explanations. "There is nothing that *should* be done, Eddy. There is only what *is*." She has the same rhythm and tone of his grandmother, just a different set of words.

"Sweetheart." He squeezes her hip, noting her newly sharpened edges, bones jutting out where there used to be flesh. "You've got to stop running so much. If you don't, you're going to disappear completely."

He can't place the look she gives him. "You can see it?" she asks.

"See what?" Bonnie hollers, attention back on the greater room, eyes on them. "What are we looking at?"

"How skinny Laura is." Ed knows it's the wrong thing to say, just as he knows his gesture is the wrong thing to do—hand out like a game show host, up and down Laura's body as though indicating a prize—and yet he doesn't stop. "All skin and bones these days, don't you think? Always off running." *Stop talking. Reroute. Redirect.* "That's just what we need, right? A health nut on our hands. Next thing we know, she'll be telling us to stop drinking." He reaches for the bottle in an effort to deflect, holds it high as evidence of—what? He doesn't know. Evidence of the life they *should* have? Whiskey and babies and curvy bodies?

"Are you kidding?" Bonnie laughs. "The Laura I know would never quit drinking, isn't that right, lady?"

Ed looks at Laura's face, stuck somewhere between sadness and disgust. He watches it transform itself into levity for her friend—for Bonnie, not for him. "Never." She smiles and refills everyone's glasses, shooting her own quickly and refilling even quicker.

He should know how to fix this.

There shouldn't be anything to fix.

Ed looks at their son there at Bonnie's feet. The boy stares at the keys in his hands, his inquisitive eyes boring into them. Ed tries to bring Laura back, but she dodges his touch, slips away to the bed, perches on its side. She lifts and rattles the keys, and Benjamin smiles at the noise, makes a noise like the word *keys*.

The new babe has fallen asleep, mouth lolling under Bonnie's exposed breast. God, they're beautiful, women—especially when they transform into mothers, the full breasts, the ferocious strength, the powerful sense of protection. It shouldn't be sexy, but it is, and Ed is suddenly viciously aroused.

"Could you guys watch Ben a minute?" he asks, grabbing Laura's hand, his hold too hard for her to escape. "I just need to talk to my wife for a minute."

"Stop it, Ed. We'll talk later."

"Real quick," he presses, pulling her up.

"Go," Pete says. "Take your time. We've got the little guy."

Laura is a dull weight behind him, but he drags her from the room, out into the stark hospital hallway, eerily abandoned in its cold light. There are voices from the nurses' station, the beep of monitors, the squeak of shoes somewhere nearby. The bathrooms are to the right. He remembers seeing them—private rooms with toilets and sinks and showers for the new mothers, a place to clean themselves after the mess of birthing children. He barely hears Laura's voice, resisting: "Ed, come on. Let me go."

He ducks into the first open door, pulls Laura in behind him, closes them in.

"Ed, what are you doing?"

He takes her face in his hands and kisses her like a starving man. He can feel her refusal at first, but he moves a hand down to her collarbone and then her waist, fingers tugging at the button of her pants, finding a way inside—a flash of Penelope, quick and then gone—and Laura loosens under him. He pulls the pants from her hips, turns her around, presses her against the sink, both hands on her breasts now. He removes none of his clothing, and when he presses inside her, she gasps.

He can see them both in the mirror, hair falling in Laura's face, her eyes closed. She is every lover he could want—mysterious stranger, trashy whore, stunning waitress. *Beautiful patient?* He closes his eyes to the fantasy rising in his mind. Penelope in the grass by the river, Penelope against his desk, Penelope here under his hands, whispered breaths growing deeper, the two of them finishing together.

Laura is looking at him in the mirror when he opens his eyes. She returns his smile, but he sees the suspicion behind it, and he fears what she might have seen before he returned to her, the details of his mind writing themselves across his face. *She would've seen only your passion for her.* But still, he feels the breach, and he feels Laura feeling it, too.

Laura extricates herself, tugging tissues from the box to wipe herself clean. She buttons her pants, smooths her clothes and hair in the mirror. He's still behind her, and he makes himself start the same motions, tucking away what happened with the tails of his shirt, fastening his belt. He meets Laura's eyes in the mirror again. She says, "You're a good lover, Edmund Malinowski. I'll give you that."

He turns her and kisses her, gently this time, an attentive husband's kiss.

She pulls away and pats his cheek like a child. "You're making love to yourself, though. You know that, right?"

She closes the door behind her, forbidding him a response.

You're making love to yourself. What did she see in his face? What did she feel? He wants to assure her that she's the spark that starts his desire. Her beauty drives him, every way she wears it, the different shapes—artist, drinker, wife. Everyone's thoughts stray. Humans are primal, carnal beings. She knows that. And the thoughts are a quick picture show across his mind. She is real, and no fantasy can compete with that.

Thoughts are covert behaviors.

He believes this in the world of his patients and work, but he can't apply it now. His actions, his visible behaviors—those are what matter. Yes, he's slept with prostitutes when he couldn't have Laura, but those actions aren't betrayals; they're fulfillments of physical need. It's the emotional connection with Penelope that would make physical connection with her so dangerous to his marriage, but except for one momentary lapse (that could be argued away; he didn't return her advances, after all), he is clean. He has kept his thoughts covert.

He will take Laura to dinner, focus all his attention on her, ask about her latest paintings, about her lessons in Boulder. He'll insist she keep teaching. A stupid idea for her to stop.

He smooths his beard and hair, checks his teeth as though he's just eaten, practices a winning smile. They will be fine, he and Laura. All is well. He makes sure his shirt is fully tucked, his fly zipped. In the hallway, he smiles broadly at a sweet young nurse, who smiles back nervously. He can make all kinds of women smile, can please all kinds of women, but he is focused on Laura. Only Laura. This strong, brilliant woman he convinced to be his wife, funny and sharp and talented. Biting. *You're making love to yourself.* He laughs at the words now, in love again with Laura's honesty. She's never fawned over him.

"Dinner!" he shouts as he enters Bonnie's room.

He's met by Pete's voice. "You buying?"

He hears Bonnie laugh. "I don't think I'm getting out of here tonight. You boys go grab a bite, though. Take Hank and Benjy. I'll join this guy in his nap." She's staring down at the baby, still asleep in her arms.

Ed scans the room—Hank playing quietly in the corner, Benjamin fascinated by the keys, Pete standing next to the bed, Bonnie and the baby. "Where's Laura?"

He watches the look exchanged between his friends. He's supposed to know where she is. Their faces make that clear.

Uncomfortably, Pete says, "She popped in to say goodbye. Said you were going to give her a little break to get some painting done."

"That's right," Ed says after another moment's hesitation. "I thought we were going to meet back in here real quick to exchange car keys, since Ben's seat is in her car."

Bonnie perks up. "Already done! Laura fished yours out of your coat pocket." She points at Benjy. "And those are her keys."

Bonnie and Pete smile at each other, calm again, focused on their new son, not their wayward friends.

Ed feels fear rising, a nervous energy in his stomach. He pictures Laura's face as she walked out of the bathroom—resolved—and he realizes she could leave him. She really could. He's feared it often, but he's never actually believed it. They could fail. The fantasy could never materialize. Is this how she'll do it? Pat his cheek, tell him he's making love to himself, and then disappear? He sees her racing to their house, throwing clothes into a bag, grabbing a few toiletries, her box easel and paints. Will she take the dog? *Beau, come on, buddy. Load up.* She is driving west, his car carrying her up MacDonald Pass, then down into Elliston and Avon, Garrison, and the interstate that will take her all the way to the Pacific Ocean.

He picks up Benjamin, holds him to his chest. *She could never leave her baby.* This is his solace, his only comfort, and he won't let himself read behind it, the words that float just out of focus. *She could leave you, though.*

Chapter 19

— *Laura* —

I dream about climbing a rickety staircase that spills me into a large room—a cross between an arcade and a gym, machine/game hybrids. A young woman rows a boat that tips and capsizes over a simulated pond—an exercise in balance. A man heaves a basketball into a net over his head, his feet constantly jumping, the ground burning hot. His is an exercise in motivation. I walk to an enormous fish, knowing it's for me. I lie down and slide my legs into its open mouth. My body disappears from the hips down as its lips close tight around my stomach. An attendant ties my hands over my head with rope and flips a switch. The fish flicks and shakes, its mouth squeezing. My exercise is in escape.

All morning I feel the ropes on my wrists, those wet fish lips around my waist. *Too pointed,* I think. *Too obvious*. My subconscious bubbles right at the surface.

Ed is at a conference in DC.

In the evening, I drop Benjy at Bonnie's and meet Tim for a drink.

I seem to do nothing but compare the two of them—Ed and Tim. They are so physically different, Tim slight where Ed is broad, each body better suited to the other's work. But Tim is attentive, where Ed is preoccupied. I am all Tim sees when we are together. The bartender could shatter a tray full of glasses and Tim wouldn't move his eyes from my face.

After two drinks, I get in Tim's car, and he drives us to his house.

"This place is too nice for a single guy," I say. Wood floors, cathedral ceilings, a huge fireplace, leather sofas.

"Did you forget what I do for a living?"

He is a builder. He built this house himself.

There are twelve boxes of Girl Scout cookies on his coffee table.

"Those?" I ask.

"The Baker girls," he says. "Tireless little bloodsuckers. Worst thing about the neighborhood. You'll have to watch out if you start coming around more often."

Not a subtle invitation.

The thumbnail on his left hand is black.

He drove us here, but I am the one to cross the few feet between us and press my mouth to his. He pulls away briefly to ask, "Are you sure, Laura?"

I answer with my hands on his body, and he leads me to a high four-poster bed he sheepishly admits he also made.

I am having an affair, but it is quiet and gentle. Nothing like Ed in the bathroom at the hospital or the time in my classroom in Boulder. There's no desperation. Tim removes each piece of my clothing with care, inspecting as he goes. He touches my shoulder as though it's precious, his fingers running the length of my collarbone. "I've wanted this since I met you," he whispers, his mouth against my neck.

"You were mourning your mother when you met me."

"And feeling guilty about how much I wanted you."

I expect my own guilt to rise at some point. I expect to see Ed, to feel the weight of him pressing against me. But I am only right here, focused and consumed. And Tim is, too.

"I don't have any expectations," Tim says afterward. "You don't have to leave your husband if you don't want."

I hate the word *husband* in his mouth.

"I think I do." We are facing each other in bed, and I wonder if it will continue, this thing with Tim. I have always been with older men, but Tim is four years younger than I am. He is smarter than my firefighter but nowhere near Ed. His hands are rough, his body lean and muscled. He has good tastes and can build things, big things like houses.

I imagine Ed saying, *I am rebuilding an entire institution. What's a house compared to that?*

But I want the house, now. I want the tangible thing, here in front of me.

I have no use for aspirations anymore.

Tim drives me back to my car, and we kiss like teenagers behind foggy windows for much too long.

When I finally break away and open my door, he says, "Please don't disappear, Laura."

I know he means from his life, but I hear his words only in relation to the greater disappearance I've been facing. Already more in tune than Ed, he is asking me to stay, to fill myself back in.

— —

Something has started. I feel it. When I pick up Benjy, I can tell Bonnie feels it, too.

"You all right?" she asks.

"I am."

She looks suspicious. "You'll tell me what's going on, I hope?"

"Soon," I promise.

Benjy raises his arms into the air. "Mama?"

He has many sounds but has been slow to acquire words. "Mama" and "Beau" are his regulars. No "Dada" yet.

I lift him up and settle him on my hip. He's getting big, this baby of mine.

Bonnie offers me a glass of wine before I go, and I turn her down, anxious to leave. I want to know if it feels different to be alone with Benjy now. Just the two of us.

"Something's going on," Bonnie says again.

"I'm fine," I tell her.

When Benjy and I get back to the Third Street house, it feels temporary. I walk through the rooms, touching things, and so few of them are mine. My easel and paints, my clothes, a few books, my students' artwork.

— —

A couple days later, I go for a walk with Benjy and Beau. The streets are mucky with spring runoff, littered with gravel. We wander down the hill, across State and Highland, pausing for the traffic on Broadway and then down farther, past Breckenridge, another worded street interrupting the numbers. We turn east on Sixth. Benjy is asleep in his stroller. Beau trots dutifully at my side, holding part of his leash in his mouth. I can still taste Tim's breath, feel his hands.

The leaves are budding overhead, grass greening in yards, and here on my right, at the corner of Sixth and Beattie, is a little green house with a sweet front porch and window boxes newly planted with annuals, a "For Rent" sign in the yard.

In Ed's book about dreams, six is a symbol of completeness. My grandmother's name was Beattie; it means *bringer of joy*. I do not believe in omens, but I write down the number on the sign. I hustle home, half-running up the hill, pushing the stroller, Beau galloping at my side.

A deep-voiced man answers on the first ring. "I can show it to you right now, if you're interested," and I say, "Yes, yes, yes. Please."

Chapter 20

Ed is home in time for dinner. He walks in the back door as Laura pulls takeout from a bag, the white boxes from On Broadway, their special-occasion place.

He puts his hands on her hips, kisses her neck. "Anything I can do to help?" he asks.

"Sit with Benjy," she says. "Get yourself a beer."

A perfect answer.

Ed shrugs out of his jacket and pulls off his tie, pops the cap off a beer from the fridge. "You need one?" he asks Laura, and she nods to the glass of wine on the counter, standing next to its half-empty bottle. "Thatta girl."

Benjamin sits in his high chair, tiny fingers pinching peas and bits of meat, deliberate as a crane, and Ed sits down next to him, pushing food into the center of the tray.

"This boy's getting so big," he says. "We're going to have to give him a little brother or sister one of these days." He's been saying this since Pete and Bonnie's second son was born, pushing it whenever he can, but Laura's birth control pills stay in the medicine cabinet.

She doesn't respond.

They eat at the table in the kitchen, Laura plating their meals as nicely as the restaurant would if they were there—steaks and garlic potatoes and sautéed mushrooms. Benjamin remains fixated on his own food, taking the bits of potato Laura gives him, the tiny bites of steak. She gives him a piece of mushroom, and he chews it for a few seconds before scowling and swiping it from his mouth. They both laugh. Ed tells her about his day, how much he enjoys his patients, how Chip is going to move in with his uncle and start working as a janitor at the nearby elementary, a great success.

Ed continues. "It's nice to treat ourselves. We'll have to go out soon. Get this little guy a sitter."

After dinner, they put Benjamin in his playpen and go to the front porch, Ed with another beer, Laura with a full glass of wine. They can look through the big living room window to see Benjamin sitting in his little cage, analyzing his toys. He doesn't seem to play with them, only inspect. They leave the front door open so they can hear him if he cries.

Ed lights them each a cigarette.

The evening is warm, and the lilacs just off the front steps are starting to leaf out. Ed can nearly smell the blossoms. Lilacs are his favorite. So many favorites in one night.

Laura says, "I need to talk to you about something."

His thoughts are still light and airy. Maybe she is pregnant—a missed pill and another baby on the way, a wonderful surprise, great news. Maybe she's sold a painting and her art career is on the verge of exploding, a brilliant artist discovered in this small mountain town.

He reaches for her hand, laces his fingers through hers, seeks her ring that he regularly plays with. It isn't there, and still—still!—nothing sounds in his brain to signal concern, no alarms, no bells. She must have taken it off to paint. She does that sometimes.

He has time to think all these things.

Laura takes a drag of her cigarette, and he's just about to tell her how damn sexy she is when she says, "I signed a lease on a house today."

Ed is confused. They own their home. There's no need to lease.

"It's down on Sixth Street—corner of Sixth and Beattie. That was my grandmother's name, you remember? It's close, which will be nice for Benjy."

Ed isn't making sense of the words. She's talking about her grandmother, for some reason—probably dinner. Wasn't her grandmother a great cook? But was there something about a house? Her grandmother's house?

"I'm going to start moving my things tomorrow."

That sentence is perfectly clear. The ignorance breaks, a thick-shelled egg cracked open.

Benjamin is whimpering in his playpen.

"What can I do?" Ed crushes out his cigarette and Laura's, covers her hands with his own. "Anything, love. Tell me."

Benjamin's noise grows louder. A word comes through. "Mama!"

She shakes her head.

"Mama!"

"No, Laura. You don't just end it."

"Mama!" A fierce wailing.

"Coming, Benjy." Laura slides her hands from under his. She leaves a warm place next to him on the bench where she was sitting.

Ed knows the limits of his profession—all the ways he can fail his patients. He knows the need for change and redirection. When one model doesn't work, he tries another. And then another. But he failed to cross-apply that principle to his own marriage. He even noted the changes in his marriage's behavior, but he didn't rewrite its treatment. He simply continued, blindly believing it was healing itself.

— —

Ed doesn't know how long he's been sitting outside. It's grown dark, and he hopes it's some future spring, all this behind them, everything repaired.

Inside, Laura lies on the sofa, eyes closed, though he knows she's not asleep. He sits on the floor and leans his head against one of the seat cushions. "Please," he says. "I can change. I'm a behaviorist. If I can change other people, I can change myself." He feels her hand come to his hair, her long fingers running through the strands, soothing him like she soothes their son when he scrapes his knees or touches something hot or sharp. "Please." He'll say the word until she says yes. "Please. Please."

"No, Ed." Her voice is as soft and gentle as her hand in his hair.

He stands up and grabs her, pulling her against him, her arms and legs loose as a doll's. "Please."

"Put me down, Ed."

He doesn't. "Please, Laura." She can't leave him if he keeps her in his arms.

"Put me down."

He waits a moment more.

"Now, Ed."

He sets her down, and they sit next to each other on the sofa.

"Come to bed."

"No, Ed."

He begins to weep. It's a deep, ragged sadness he's never known, and he holds his face in his hands. Laura's fingers are on his back, tracing circles. *Hush,* her touch says. *It'll be all right. Everything heals.*

But he doesn't want the injury, not this one.

Please. He doesn't know if he's saying the word aloud anymore, but it's all he hears, all he feels, an urgent, unyielding request.

Like the time on the porch, this time in the living room stretches into nontime. They have always been there, and they have never been there.

— —

He's lying on the sofa when he wakes to Benjamin's morning whimpers. His head is still in Laura's lap. He feels her slip out from under him, one of her hands cradling his head and easing it down gently onto the pillow she tucks in to replace her. He keeps his eyes closed and listens to her soft voice with their cranky son.

"Hello there, my love. Oh, there's nothing to cry about. Let's get you changed and have some breakfast. Does that sound good?" The whimpering dies down, replaced with giggles, small chirps of pleasure, and the loud shout of "Mama!" He hears the scrabble of Beau's nails on the floor, raising himself from his bed near the stove, the jangle of his tags as he shakes the sleep from his body. Laura's voice again: "Should we let Beau outside?" And Benjamin shouting, "Beau!" Then the slap-stomp of Benjamin's feet on the floor, trotting out from his room as though it's any other day. Slap-stomp to the back door alongside Laura's gentle footsteps, the creak of the floorboards, the open-and-close, the click of the latch, Beau barking at someone walking by. Ed hears Laura lift Benjamin into his high chair, fasten on the tray, shake out Cheerios for him to start with. She lets the dog in, and Ed listens to the rattle of food in Beau's metal bowl. "Sit," Laura says. "Stay. That's a good boy. Here you go." Why has he never listened to all this before? These sounds of his family.

Maybe you dreamed it.

He returns to that first trip. Dean wooing him, mountains and rivers, the sweet downtown, this house, everything perfectly aligning itself for their lives in Montana. But what if he was wrong to bring them here? He flies back to their old apartment in Michigan, Laura's easel in the nook off the living room. He brings her a puppy the first time she asks, agrees to children right away. The apartment grows thick with bodies until they're forced to find a new house of their own that they shop for together.

Would they still be finding themselves in this place?

Maybe they would, and that scares him more than the possibility of being wrong about the move. Their demise more inherent—destined, no matter where he took them.

He sits up and Laura brings him a cup of coffee. "You should get going or you'll be late."

"I'm not going in today."

"You have to. You have that meeting, remember? You told me about it during dinner, a big meeting, something important." She forces a smile. "You should go, Ed."

He lets her pull him up and turn him gently. Lets her propel him toward the bathroom, where he somehow showers and trims his beard. Then he walks himself to his closet and selects clothes that he somehow knows how to put on, a tie he knows how to knot, a jacket he knows to fill with his wallet and his cigarettes, his lighter and keys. When he returns to the kitchen, Laura is sitting at the table with Benjamin, a cup of coffee held in both hands as though to warm her, a tiny fire. Benjamin looks up at him and shouts, "Dada!"

"That's right, Benjy." Laura looks at Ed. "Dada."

She stands and walks him to the door. *Stay,* his mind says. *Take off your work clothes. Put on jeans. Take your family into the mountains. Hike to the top of Mount Ascension like you've planned so many times.*

He sets a hand on the side of her face, stares at the composition, trying to memorize every bit, so he can conjure it at will and bring her back. "Stay?"

"No."

He brings his other hand to her face and presses his mouth to hers, grateful when he feels her respond. They remain wrapped together until Benjamin calls them apart, banging on his tray for more food and hollering out his nonsense words. Laura holds her hand in front of her mouth, lips to fingers.

Ed cups her face once more. "I'm sorry," he says.

"Me, too."

Stay.

But he doesn't, and she's gone when he returns.

Chapter 21

They agree to tell Bonnie and Pete together, meeting them at the Third Street house. Benjamin is asleep in his playpen, Justin asleep in his car seat, Hank entertained by the television in the living room. The adults sit around the kitchen table, two six-packs of beer in front of them that Ed doesn't think are enough.

"No whiskey," Laura said. "Please."

"But how can I get you so drunk you'll forget this whole thing and come to bed with me?" He was trying levity, the wit and humor he originally wooed her with.

"No whiskey."

It's been a week since she left. Laura doesn't believe he hasn't told Pete already, but he hasn't. He can't. He doesn't know if he can even now.

"You sure you want to do this?" he's asked her each of those seven days. "There's still time to back out." He'll reach for her, and she'll back away. He hasn't touched her since that last morning, though he's tried every time he comes to her new house to take Benjamin and the dog for a walk. "Join us?" he'll ask. Another shake of her head. He'll reach for her when he brings them back, and she'll shake her head again.

He tells himself it's just a separation. He's agreed to tell Bonnie and Pete only because he thinks they'll take his side.

They each open a beer, and Pete says, "You guys are way too serious. What the hell is going on?"

"We're getting a divorce," Laura says.

"No," Ed says. "That's extreme. We're separating for a bit. Laura's taking some space." He gulps down his beer, reaches for another.

Bonnie and Pete are silent, staring.

Finally, Bonnie says, "I don't like it."

They all laugh nervously.

"I don't, either," Ed says. "Help me talk her out of it, won't you?"

But the laughter is gone because Bonnie is looking at Laura, and Laura is crying and starting to speak words that aren't quite words yet, until they suddenly are, and Ed is listening to a version of the life he thought he was living, cast in a light that makes it foreign and ugly. "And I was so lonely," she's saying, "lonely and trapped and so angry and then so sad, and he couldn't see that I was disappearing, that I needed him. I was so tired of competing with his patients, with Penelope. I needed him to make me believe I was real and important and part of something, and the few times it came, it left so quickly, which was nearly worse than it never coming at all. And I just want to be whole again." Her voice is breaking, but it smooths out here. "I need to be whole again."

Ed tries to pull her against him, to comfort her, to make her feel safe and whole. He can do that. But she struggles away, lurching to her feet, toppling the chair behind her, and shouting, "*Goddamn it,* Ed. You don't get it. I needed your arm around me years ago. I needed to be your fucking *wife*. Not another patient you could solve. And Jesus, if I was going to be a patient, I needed you to at least do a better fucking job with my treatment."

She rights the chair and grabs her sweater from the hook by the door, and then she's gone.

How many times will he have to watch her leave?

Bonnie and Pete both pound their beers and open new ones.

"I'm sorry, brother," Pete says.

Ed looks at them, his two friends across the table, a great couple. "How do you do it?" he demands, nearly angry. "Pete works the same damn hours I do, and he drinks the same after-work drinks. Why the hell are you still around?" He glares at Bonnie as though this is her fault.

She lays her hands flat on the table, a gesture Ed recognizes in the back of his mind as a pacifying move, as well as a powerful one. He hears Hank laugh at something on the TV.

"Are you sure you want an answer to that question?" she asks.

No. "Yes."

"I'm still around because Pete's never fucked around with one of his patients."

"Jesus, Bonnie." Ed glares at Pete. "Did you tell her that?"

"Those weren't my exact words."

"Come on, Pete," Bonnie says. "What are you protecting yourself from now? Laura's gone." She gives Ed her own glare. "Pete told me about your relations with Penelope, Ed, but you know who else did? Your fucking wife. And I did my best to defend you, but it got pretty damn hard when you missed Benjy's birth. So you go right ahead and call your attention to that girl whatever you want, but we all saw it as something else. And I can say for damn sure that if I ever had an inkling of suspicion on that front in regard to Pete, he'd be out the fucking door."

"Calm down, Bonnie."

"Shut up, Pete."

Ed has rarely seen them argue. "I was Penelope's doctor. I went to Great Falls because she needed my expertise."

Bonnie scoffs. "Just like she needed individual therapy sessions with you back in Boulder?"

"Jesus, do you guys have a running file on me? And who the fuck are you to judge me, anyway? What the hell are you doing with your life, Bonnie? Drinking yourself drunk and hoping your kids don't hurt themselves while you're passed out? And Pete—you're just putting in your goddamned time out there, going through the paces. You don't care if we fix the system. You probably don't even give a shit if we help anyone."

"I swore to Laura you weren't an asshole deep down, Ed. Don't make me doubt that, too."

"Fuck you, Bonnie."

Pete and Bonnie both shake their heads, and Ed hates that they can reunite over their disappointment in him. Hates that they can reunite at all. Pete's no better a man than Ed is. And Bonnie's sure as hell no better a woman than Laura.

They keep quiet as they collect their boys.

At the door, Pete says, "You know Bonnie's surly, but we're here for you, brother. You'll get through this."

Ed is tired of being assured he'll be all right.

Chapter 22

Pete and Bonnie on day seven. Preliminary meeting with lawyers on day fourteen. Parenting plan established on day sixteen, an even split of time. On day twenty-one, exactly three weeks after Laura got takeout and told him she was leaving, Ed bangs on the door of her new house at midnight, drunk, crying, begging, and a man arrives in his boxers. Ed tries to hit him and misses, bringing his hand against the doorframe. Laura appears, an apparition in an oversize men's T-shirt, those long legs bare, and Ed lunges toward her, needing to hold her, needing to be held, but the man stops him. An arm catches Ed's chest and sends him to the floor. He can hear Laura talking, those same words, "Ed, you need to go. Ed, this isn't okay," and new ones, "Ed, if you don't get off my porch, I'm going to call the police," words that make him crawl back down the steps and push himself to standing in the middle of her new yard. "At least give me my goddamned dog!" he shouts, and he's surprised to hear the clatter of Beau's toenails on the porch, then the warmth of his breath. When he looks up, the man is standing there, this stranger giving up the dog Ed and Laura have shared. Ed loads Beau into his car and somehow manages to drive home.

— —

Every night, the house is dark when Ed arrives. Every night, he thinks the same thing: *Why is the house dark?*

And every night, he remembers.

The night after he showed up at Laura's and swung at that man—*Who the fuck was that man?*—he went to Dorothy's and took Lynn to a hotel after her shift. He was too drunk to remember whether it was any good.

— —

On day fifty-three or fifty-four (he's lost one somewhere), Laura brings divorce papers to the house for Ed to sign. It's eight in the evening, and he's drunk already, starting into a bottle of whiskey the moment he walked in the door.

"Where's Ben?" he slurs.

"At home."

"With that guy? Who the fuck's that guy, Laura? I don't want him around my son."

"Jesus, Ed." She goes to the sink and fills a glass of water, brings it to him. "Drink this. Want me to come back later so you can look these over when you're sober?"

"Laura." He reaches for her, again and again, and she steps away, again and again.

She is scratching Beau's ears. "I'll leave them on the table here, and you can look at them in the morning, all right?"

He slumps into a chair and rests his head in his arms on the table, a sad, broken child. His eyes are closed, but he can feel her hesitating, hovering. Soon he's crying again, his shoulders shaking, everything rattling loose in him, and then he feels her hand rubbing his back, small circles. He makes himself stay seated, makes himself keep his head on his arms so they won't grab for her because he knows his touch will drive her away, like a scared animal that's carefully initiating contact. He has to prove he's tame and good and kind. He can sit here and be petted, see? A gentle, good beast.

"You're going to be all right, Ed." He loves her voice. There are so many other things he wants it to say. "Lay off the booze a little."

And then her hand is gone.

— —

On day sixty-seven (or eight), he reluctantly signs the papers that will end his marriage and resign him to being a half-time parent.

"We're still married in the eyes of the Church," he tells Laura.

"You don't believe in God, Ed. We got married in the Church for your mother." She takes the papers from his hands. "Thank you."

He brings Lynn home that night, a woman named Kathy the night after, then Lynn again, and then a twenty-one-year-old college girl, so young and innocent that he drinks himself into oblivion for days trying to forget.

— —

Sometime later—he's lost count of the days entirely—his mother arrives. She slaps him across the face and then holds his head in her lap for exactly ten minutes. Then she takes him by the shoulders and says, "We learn from our failures." She firmly pats his cheek. "Go take a shower. I will make you a meal."

She stays for three days, cleaning the mess that has accumulated in the house and cooking large meals Ed stuffs himself with.

"You are all right," she says the day she leaves. "Stop feeling sorry for yourself. Walk your dog. Or you will both be fat."

— —

The following Monday, he wakes early, makes a pot of coffee, fries an egg and puts it on toast. He takes Beau for a hike, then showers and gets dressed and goes to Boulder, where Martha says, "It's nice to see you again, Ed."

"It was only a weekend."

She hands him a stack of mail and notes. "It was longer than that, but we made do. Welcome back."

His office waits for him, his patients, his doctors and shoddy staff. He is good at this, and he will give it everything he has on the days when he doesn't have Benjamin, and give it enough on the days when he does. He thinks briefly of Penelope, out there in town somewhere. Not a patient. Just a healthy young woman living her life. He doesn't know if he's responsible for any of her success, but he knows she's responsible for much of his failure. He remembers that moment by the river. Her hands.

Still, he has to believe he's a good doctor.

Should

—

MAY 1976–FEBRUARY 1977

Chapter 23

— *Laura* —

Ed and I have been divorced nearly a year, and I am in Thriftway buying groceries and a pregnancy test. George is my bagger, and he chants my name as he nestles my items into paper bags. "La. Raw. La Raw."

"It's good to see you, George."

I don't look at the checker or George as they handle the small box.

A woman pushes her cart up behind me in line and starts unloading her groceries. A teenage boy clings to the cart's handle, his eyes a bit too wide-set, his lower lip too forward, fat and pink. When he turns his head, I see a scar at the base of his skull, running down his neck, disappearing into his shirt. He would be at home out in Boulder. I would've invited him into my art class.

"So this girl likes you?" the mother says absentmindedly, her eyes on the food she's unloading.

The boy huffs, frustrated. "She doesn't just like me. She's *in love* with me, Mom."

"Ooh-la-la." The woman dances her hands, mocking him, and I want to tell her about Frank and Gillie out in Boulder, their mismatched heights and their deep, devoted love of each other, a romance as sweet as any I've seen. They drew pictures for each other, picked grasses and flowers to form bouquets, walked hand in hand through the yard. They fought, too, like any couple. Theirs was a true relationship, as real as any out here, and I want to defend them to this woman and, in so doing, defend her son and his wistful heart.

These are the people Ed is saving, and the anger gives way to sadness.

I am pregnant with another man's child.

I decline George's offer to help me out to my car, and I load my bags into my trunk and rush the cart back as quickly as I can, so I can leave this place with its reminders of Ed.

Bonnie warns me regularly about Tim. "It's all bright and shiny with this new guy now, Laura, but it's going to get hard and ugly pretty damn quick. The same problems haunt every marriage."

"I'm not looking for marriage, Bonnie."

But that comes with a baby.

Bonnie is still rooting for Ed, slipping in stories that cast him in a favorable light, and I keep slapping her away, firm in my decision, but I am struck by the enormity of all that I've slapped away. I was not wrong to leave Ed, but I am missing him right now, and I would deliver him to the seat next to me if I could, lean my head against his thick shoulder, and ask him what I should do. He was always so good at helping other people direct their lives. *So there's this hypothetical woman,* I would tell him, *and she's pregnant with a hypothetical baby, and the father of the baby isn't her husband, and her husband isn't her husband, either, though she catches herself thinking of him that way still, in fleeting moments, and mostly, she feels relief and freedom, but there are times—like right now—when she is doubled over with the pain of what she no longer has. Tell me, Doctor, what should she do?*

He would tell me to marry Tim, have the baby. He would tell me I've already made a new life away from him, what are a few more steps?

Ed is all smiles when I see him at the Benjy exchanges. He's polished and strong and healthy, though the stories I hear say otherwise.

Ben comes home with his own tales of their adventures, a three-year-old now, with so many words.

"We built a cabin from logs."

"We collected ants."

"We hiked up the mountain."

"We built a fire in the pit in the yard."

I admit it's painful how good a father Ed has become in my absence.

— —

Benjy is with Ed, and I am alone in my little green house, and I sit at my kitchen counter and pour myself a short glass of wine. Tim will be over soon to take me to dinner, and afterward we will come back here and have quiet, pleasant sex that makes up in comfort what it lacks in excitement.

Tim walks in the back door and immediately folds me into his arms. "What sounds good for dinner?" he asks.

I don't know what sounds good—I'm a little nauseated—so I say, "I'm pregnant."

He pushes me to arm distance. I have been so focused on my own feelings that I haven't given a thought to what Tim might think or want. He is good with Benjy, but I have no idea if he wants children of his own, and I am suddenly frightened that he will ask me if I want to keep it, which will mean that he doesn't, and then—I can't see that road, what it looks like, where it might go, and whether I might prefer it, too.

His hands are on my upper arms, and I can't bring myself to meet his eyes, too fearful. "Laura," he says, "look at me. Is this good news?"

I don't know. "Do you want to be a father?"

He takes a deep breath. "Hypothetically, I do. I mean, I've always thought I would be. It wasn't in my immediate plans, though. Aren't you on the pill?"

"We don't have to keep it," I blurt out, not sure whether it's a real offer.

"Laura." He pulls me against him, and I'm relieved to hear him say, "I'd never want that." He pets my hair and answers his first question: "It's good news," though I'm still not sure.

— —

I arrive early for my lunch with Ed. I tried to get him to meet me at the Grille, or the tea shop—someplace that isn't dripping wet with our history—but he refused. "Dorothy's," he said. "I eat nowhere else."

Benjy has been asking if Beau can go between the two houses with him, and that's the main subject for our lunch, a change in the dog plan. I will tell Ed about the baby, too. My upcoming marriage. Small asides at the end.

Gail is hostessing, as she always is, and she sits me in our old spot, a two-top against the north wall, rough wainscoting about four feet up, giving way to old stone. A black-and-white photo of the Marlow Theatre hangs over us. It was torn down the second year we were here—urban renewal claiming so many of Helena's old buildings. Every table at Dorothy's has its own tribute. When they took down the Marlow, the streets smelled like popcorn for a week.

"Get you anything to drink while you're waiting, hon?" It's Lynn, one of the newer waitresses, though she's been here for years.

I order a beer and a shot of Jameson. I will meet Ed on his own ground.

I take a cigarette from the pack I bought on my way over. Tim has gotten me to stop smoking, but it's a constant longing, and the smoke that fills my lungs feels like a past home, someplace I once knew well.

Ed is ten minutes late. My shot is gone, and half my beer. I stand to greet him, somehow expecting to shake his hand in some new formality, but he folds me against his chest as though we are still the most intimate of lovers. I have always liked the shape and warmth of his body, how it can envelop me, swallow me whole. I make myself pull away after staying longer than I should, and when my face is free, he grabs my neck and kisses me on the mouth. Again, I linger too long before putting a hand to his chest. "Ed."

"A friendly kiss, that's all." He holds his hands up, innocent. "You taste like whiskey."

"I had a shot."

"I better catch up, then." He waves his hand in the air like he is the conductor of his life, all the world swirling around him, ready to follow his orders. Lynn bristles a little as he requests two rounds for himself and another for me, which I shouldn't have.

Our new drinks arrive. "Would you like to hear the specials?" Lynn directs her attention to me.

"I don't need to," I say. "Ed?"

"Oh, I know what Ed will have. He always orders the same thing." The woman looks too long at him now. "Or are you shaking things up today?" He must have gone to bed with this woman, one of many, I'm sure.

He doesn't look at her as he says, "No, I'll have the regular." Teriyaki burger with Jack cheese cooked rare, fries, a vat of ranch on the side. I order a turkey club and fries, though I doubt I'll be able to keep much down. The confirmation of the pregnancy seems to have set all the symptoms into action. My breasts hurt. I'm exhausted. I'm throwing up everything I eat.

When Lynn's gone, Ed says, "Damn, it's good to see you."

"It's good to see you, too." It's an automatic response I recognize as true once it's out. It is good to see him, to be in this place. We were happy here, for the most part.

"You look amazing." He does, too, his beard shorter, neater, everything even tidier yet still strong. But there's a redness to his eyes that speaks of late nights and too much booze.

I thank him for the compliment, and he begins talking. "Man, life is crazy right now. I'm sure you're following all of it in the papers, but we're so close, Laura—Boulder is way out in front of the deinstitutionalization movement, and I'm making incredible headway with the governor's office. We're going to see everything change—everything. Institutions, as we know them, will be gone—" And I am back in that life, just one more audience member in a sea of listeners.

"—Ed." The interruption shocks him silent. "I need to talk to you about something." I said the same thing when I told him I was leaving, though he clearly doesn't remember.

He returns to his initial warmth, the staggering charisma that has always disarmed me. I am the center of his attention. All he sees is me. It was all I wanted for so long.

"I knew this would happen, Laura." He reaches under the table, his fingers brushing my thigh in their search for my hand. His blindness makes him ugly, and I draw my hand away to reach for my beer.

"If you knew that the man I've been seeing would accidentally knock me up, then you're exactly right, Ed. I'm amazed at your powers of intuition." The moment it leaves my mouth, I know it's too mean. But it's the only defense I have.

"What the hell are you talking about?" Everything about him changes. His shoulders shoot back, ready to fight, all his natural ease gone. "What?"

"I'm pregnant, Ed. And I'm going to marry Tim. Just a small wedding. We're doing it at the courthouse next week."

I told Tim I had to tell Ed in person. "I can't have him read about it in the paper. I just can't. He's Benjy's dad."

"You're not going to lunch with him for Ben." And that is true. I have told myself I'm doing this to prove I can leave Ed—permanently. But the meanness? I don't know what it's proving.

He gulps his beer, shoots his whiskey, wipes his mouth. His eyes bounce—to the photo of the Marlow Theatre, to the bar, to the wait station, to me, away again. They are watery in the dull light. Edmund Malinowski is not a man who can be hurt, and seeing that pain in him was the hardest part of leaving. Ed is not made for sadness.

He blinks and pastes on a smile I can barely stand to look at.

"Well, my love, I confess I was not expecting that." He raises his second shot, nodding to me to do the same. "To you," he says, "and your bright future."

It is the worst thing he's ever said to me, and the kindest. I excuse myself to the bathroom, where I heave into the toilet. It's only liquid, hopefully enough of the booze to sober me a little. Afterward, I sit on the wide ledge of the window that reaches nearly to the ground and nearly to the ceiling, its glass painted over with a panel of Renoir's *Dance at Le Moulin de la Galette,* a painting I was surprised to see here, in this saloon bathroom in the middle of Montana.

There is a tentative knock on the door.

"One minute," I shout, relieved by the distraction. I am monopolizing the women's bathroom—there is only one. I rinse out my mouth with cold water, pat my face with a towel.

"Laura?" Ed's voice is soft, hesitant.

Without thinking, I let him in, and he is closing and locking the door behind him, and our bodies are so close, and his hands are on my face, and *I should go,* but all I can glean of my own desire is the want of his strength and comfort and attention, which I have—his full attention—and when he kisses me, it's with all the history and regret of our life together, all the warmth and tenderness, the humor and bravado, the songs, the food, the drinks, the sex. My hands are on the buttons of his shirt and then his belt and his pants. These are my hands doing these things, though his are mirroring them now, and he lifts me easily, my legs around his waist, my back against the wall, his body against mine, our mouths together. I want to stay in this bathroom with him forever, Renoir's dancers smiling out over us. We will drink from the tap and turn our backs when the other one needs the toilet.

He is done, and still, he holds me. Maybe I want this instead—to ride around on his chest like a baby, legs and arms locked around his torso, all the strength of Ed right there to protect me.

He whispers, "I'm so sorry, Laura."

He said the same thing the last time he left the Third Street house when it was still ours.

I said the same thing, too.

He lowers me slowly to my feet and we clothe ourselves, stand side by side in the mirror, wipe our faces. I look at him, that thick politician's hair, those blue eyes he gave our son.

"I can't stop loving you," he says, and I nod. He smiles sadly. "Ben will be happy to have a brother."

"You're predicting the sex of this one, too?"

"You grow boys." He says it with absolute authority.

There is a knock on the door that makes us both jump and then laugh.

"One minute!" Ed hollers, and then in a whisper to me, "I'll go first and tell her there's a plumbing issue. Count to sixty, then meet me at the table."

The hall is clear when I emerge, and Ed is at our table, calm and settled. Our food has arrived, and I'm able to eat half my sandwich, and somehow we switch back to regular conversation—Ed's work, the new series of paintings I'm working on, Benjy, shared dog custody, which Ed refuses. "Dogs don't understand that level of nuance, Laura. Beau's staying with me." I let it go. If Ed needs the dog, I can let him have the dog. Lynn is even pricklier when she brings our bill, suspicious of our extended absence, but Ed leaves an extraordinary tip, and we walk outside together. I have to fight myself not to take his hand. He looks at the sky, big and brilliant and blue, takes a deep breath.

"This is a beautiful place, isn't it?"

"Yes."

He's looking at me now. "I can't regret moving us here."

I shake my head. "No, Ed. You can't regret that."

He pulls me into a final embrace and says into my hair, "I want only good things for you, Laura," and then he is walking away.

Chapter 24

Ed stayed away from Penelope while she was recovering in Great Falls, but he hasn't been able to stop himself from keeping tabs on her. He tells himself it's for data collection as he watches her from a distance through reports from one of her therapists, an old buddy of his, Russel Dougherty.

"Still doing great," Russel says. "Working at the library now."

Ed made himself stay away during his separation from Laura. He'd known, even through the fog of that time, that if he'd been given a scene like the one by the river, he would have returned Penelope's advances tenfold.

But Laura is pregnant with her new husband's baby.

And Penelope is an adult now.

Still, it takes him an hour of drinking at Dorothy's to work up the nerve to go in the first time. Everything he needs is at the state library, so he never comes to this one. In his imaginings, he walks in and she is right there at the front desk, perfectly whole.

Instead, an ugly, yellow-toothed man says, "Help you?"

"Is Penelope Gatson working, by chance?" Ed's voice is too high.

"Out in the stacks somewhere. Your guess is as good as mine."

Ed goes to the fiction first. He walks up and down the aisles, A–Z, running his fingers along the books' spines. No Pen.

He goes through the nonfiction chronologically, pausing in the psychology section to flip through part two of Skinner's recent autobiography. Ed has skimmed part one but found it ultimately no more insightful than any other case study.

He is stalling.

He looks at a few pages in an oversize book about elephants in the 500s, a book on classical guitars in the 700s, then he turns down an aisle of 800s, and there she is, in the poetry section. Ed watches her for a few seconds before she lifts her eyes from the book in her hands. Her hair is longer, and if he didn't know where to look, her scars would go unnoticed. There are the faintest starts of lines at the corners of her eyes. Penelope shouldn't be capable of aging. He often wanted her to be older, but he never thought she'd show it.

"Dr. Ed?"

"Hi, Pen."

He is older, too, and he sees her see it. The gray threads above his ears, the salt through his beard, the deeper lines along his nose.

"Where have you been?" she asks.

"Your parents wouldn't let me visit. They banned me from your care."

"I've been away from my parents for years."

Ed looks at the books level with him, all these collections of poetry. Penelope's world. She's clearly landed well.

"I had to focus on the institution. And my marriage. My son."

"You have a son?"

"He was born when you were in the hospital in Great Falls."

"So that's why you didn't come?"

He steps toward her, just the book between them. "I was there, Pen. The second I heard. And then Ben was born, and I had to go."

"Ben."

"Benjamin Edmund Malinowski."

She touches her head where Ed knows a puckered scar runs. "So, he's three and a half now?" She will always know Benjamin's age, Ed realizes. "And Laura?" she asks. "How's Laura?"

"Pregnant with her new husband's baby."

"Oh," she says, surprised. "Are you all right?"

"All right enough." Ed nods to the book in her hand. "What are you reading these days?"

"Thomas. I took a class on Eliot, Auden, and Thomas at Carroll, and I've fallen in love with all of them. Thomas is my favorite, though, and this is my favorite of his right now. 'Before I Knocked.' It would've been too complex for my group in Boulder, but I could've used parts of it. Like these lines." She reads: " 'I, born of flesh and ghost, was neither / A ghost nor a man, but mortal ghost.' "

"What do they mean?"

"You have to figure it out yourself."

"But you're the poetry teacher."

Ed can feel the same energy that pulled them together in Boulder, he's sure of it. He will invite her to have a drink with him, and if more comes of it, that will be all right. There are worse starts out there, worse improprieties.

"Pen," he is starting to say, "come out with me tonight—"

Another voice bellows from the end of the aisle. "There she is!"

And then Ed feels her transfer the book to his hands and move away.

"Billy!" She turns and accepts an embrace from the tall young man who's suddenly arrived. They kiss quickly, and then Penelope smiles back at Ed, her face radiant. "Dr. Ed, this is my boyfriend, Billy. Billy, you remember me telling you about my amazing doctor out in Boulder? This is him. The one and only Edmund Malinowski."

Ed doesn't know whether her words are genuine or feigned, doesn't know what she's chosen to tell Billy of their past, but Billy is shaking his hand and rambling. "Oh, sir, what an honor. Man, I can't thank you enough for all you did for my girl. From what she tells me, she wouldn't be here if not for you, so I'm indebted. Really."

All Ed hears is *my girl*. Again he is too late.

"Great to meet you, Billy." He holds up the book to Penelope. "May I check this out?"

She smiles at him. "Of course, Dr. Ed. You can study that poem and let me know what you come up with next time you're in. Bring your son. I'd love to meet him."

He is her former doctor with a young son she'd love to meet. A man who helped her once. A relic.

He walks to the circulation desk and fills out the paperwork to get a library card so he can take this collection of poems home. This book Penelope held and shared with him. He knows he should be happy for her. This is the life he imagined when he discharged her from the institution. The life he told himself she should have. She is his poster child, after all—his life's work incarnate. And that is more important than taking her to bed. More important than sharing his own life with her.

But he hates the cruelty of their timing. He hates Laura for leaving him when she did. He hates himself for not allowing one full indiscretion with Penelope. He hates Penelope for falling in love with Billy. He hates Billy for existing.

He misses—for just a moment—the complicated days when he had both Laura and Penelope. Wife at home. Patient at work. Yes, it was that very situation that led him to this place, but there had been a surplus of affection then, at least. Two women to love and adore (if he loved Penelope in some way, so be it; what did it matter?). But now they are both gone, their arms linked with Tim and Billy, while Ed walks back to Dorothy's with only a collection of poems in his hand.

Chapter 25

The Boulder River School and Hospital is receiving attention for its system of deinstitutionalization—which Ed designed—and the legislature will soon implement the system statewide.

Ed is often quoted in the paper, eloquent lines from his many speeches and letters: "The goal of deinstitutionalization is simple—remove citizens from institutions if they don't belong there."

He thinks of Penelope, there at the library, there with Billy.

In another article: "The principles of our plan assume a *developmental* approach to individuals, as opposed to the common *medical* approach used by most institutions. The medical model overemphasizes pathology, which makes people view mental retardation and developmental disability as static and hopeless conditions. In contrast, the developmental model places emphasis on potential rather than limitations; *individuals are recognized for their capacity to grow and learn.*"

In the midst of it all, Dean pulls him away from the institution for a meeting at the capitol complex. Dean's office is all windows on one wall, the valley spilling out wide and open. Like all of them, the man is starting to show his age. Ed still considers him an asshole, but they've long since found their rhythm, and Ed wouldn't have accomplished half the things he has without Dean's help.

"I'll cut to the chase. The state hospitals are being moved from the Department of Institutions to a new department, Health and Human Services. Folks seem to think it's a more fitting place, get them away from the prisons. Suppose I agree. I've put your name forward as director of the new department."

"What about Boulder?"

"Jesus, Malinowski, that's your first thought? I know you love your patients, but you'll be doing them more good on the policy end than you'll ever do out in the field. Real change has to come from within these buildings. It's got to be written into law. This is the job where you have the power to do all the damn things you want to do instead of wasting your time kissing the asses of government pricks like myself. You've done great things out in Boulder, and we'll get someone in there to keep up the momentum. But it's time to move up. You'll be the youngest director this state has ever seen." Dean turns his attention to the papers on his desk. "I want your answer tomorrow."

Ed stands and leaves, slightly dazed. He waits for the sense of accomplishment to flood him, the warmth of hard work recognized. He should be rushing out to a bar to celebrate with his pals.

I am deeply suspicious of the word should.

For the first time, he truly understands his mother's words. *Should* hides *is. Should* indicates fantasy, something wanted and not attained, a plan never embodied. It implies what is not. For Ed to acknowledge what he should be thinking and feeling, he must also acknowledge the absence of those things. He should be, and he isn't. He wants to talk to his mother. She will slap him awake with her prudence and discipline, just like she did after the separation.

He calls her when he gets home.

"Congratulations, Eddy," she says, then hollers back to his father, "It's Eddy. He got the better job! See, Eddy? This shows you're learning. You will do things better now." As though this job is another marriage.

He says his goodbyes and looks around his messy kitchen—dishes in the sink, a dirty pan on the stove, crumbs on the counter, a cold half-pot of coffee. He's taken over the dining room table as his home office, and it's piled with files and papers from Boulder. The living room is disheveled, sofa cushions skewed under the pillow and blanket that have taken up residence there. He sleeps on the sofa most nights, letting the television lull him to sleep, the narrow shelf of the couch more comforting than the wide expanse of his empty mattress.

He should clean the house.

He should celebrate his new job.

He should decide between the two women he's dating.

"Only two?" Pete chided the last time they were out. "Down from what—eight?" The other guys at the bar laughed, and Ed laughed along with them, letting them exaggerate his conquests, just as they let him romanticize their marriages and kids and family vacations. He is the only divorced man among them, the errant gander who discarded monogamy for dabbling. He doesn't tell them how dirty his house is, or how much he misses Laura's hair in his brush, the two degrees warmer she kept the house, a painted nail clipping on the bathroom floor. Nor does he tell them that ever since he saw Penelope at the library, he finds himself missing her, too. How he would take the conflict of those years over the emptiness of these.

He tells his married friends that he's about to make a decision about a woman, but he knows he'll never remarry. He had one wife, and she is gone. He prefers to think of Laura that way—gone—rather than see her with Tim, her belly big with his goddamned child.

She's moved across town, into Tim's big house on Jerome Place, a stupidly named street. It hurts to drop Benjamin there after his days with him, hurts to see his small son walk into another man's big ugly house, hurts to know his wife is in there cooking another man's meals.

He knows he shouldn't call her, but he does, present actions overwhelming that well-intentioned future. He hears the line connect, then a fumbling, a small crash. "Benjy, stop," Laura's firm voice says, and "Sorry, one minute," and then, "You will go to your room, young man, and not come out again until I tell you."

He wants to be there, wants to be part of the scene, whatever trouble Benjamin is getting into, whatever mess he's made. Ed would go for the broom and dustpan, sweep up the broken plate as Laura counted to sixty and then went to Benjamin's room, where she'd soothe his tears, because Benjamin would be crying. He always cries after he does something wrong.

"Sorry about that—hello?"

"Hi."

"Ed?" Every time she says his name, he tells himself to treasure it. Every time, he also fears he'll never hear it again. He has a running list of last things: the last time he saw her fully naked, the last time they shared a bed, and the lesser things that nearly hurt more—the last time she slept in one of his shirts, the last time she cooked him an egg, the last time he drank coffee she brewed, the last time she sat across from him at the kitchen table, reading the paper. He is always anticipating more lasts, looking for them everywhere.

"Everything okay over there? Sounded like a minor catastrophe was under way when you picked up."

"Nothing too catastrophic, just a mug your son broke on purpose. He doesn't have the right-shaped pieces for the LEGO structure he's building, and he chose to bust apart a mug to try to accommodate his needs. You wouldn't know where he gets these ideas, would you?" Her voice is light, not accusatory. Ed knows Ben shares all their adventures with her, all the things they build and take apart. Nothing is sacred at Ed's house, everything an experiment.

"I admire the ingenuity, though not the reasoning. Ceramic shards do not mix well with plastics."

She laughs. He loves to make her laugh.

"What's up, Ed?"

He does not get to casually call anymore. That is not part of his new role.

"Dean offered me a director position today, head of a whole new department—Health and Human Services."

"Ah, the great Edmund Malinowski finally gets his government position. What are the hours with that? Eighty to ninety a week?"

He isn't prepared for the bitterness.

To his silence, she says, "Sorry. It's good news, Ed. Really. The state is lucky to have you."

The state is lucky to have you, and she is not.

"You should go celebrate," she says. "Let me know if we need to rearrange Benjy's schedule."

She thinks he's calling about the schedule.

"I wish I could celebrate with you."

"No, you don't. I'm a fat pregnant woman who can't drink like she used to. Go have fun."

He hears the connection click closed, the dial tone in his ear.

— —

The next afternoon, he takes a few shots at Dorothy's and then walks to the library. He finds Penelope in the reference section, helping an elderly lady look up the definition of the word *sonorous*.

"So we're in the S's, and now we're looking for S-O. See right up here—these words at the top tell you where you are." How can this woman just now be learning how to use a dictionary? "Okay, here it is—'sonorous: able to produce an imposingly deep or full sound.' Does that help, ma'am?"

The woman pats Penelope's arm, calls her *dear*. She's tiny, her head barely reaching the top of these low shelves.

"Pen?"

"Dr. Ed," she says, slipping the dictionary back onto its shelf. "Did you figure out 'Before I Knocked'?"

"I was hoping you'd come discuss it with me down the street. Let me buy you a drink."

She laughs. "I'm working."

"Call in sick. Come on. Where's that wild girl I used to know?"

She looks at him quizzically. "You all right?"

The promotion won't mean much to her, and it doesn't make sense that he's seeking her out to celebrate with him, so he chooses a blunter reason instead. "Listen, Pen. I miss you. Even if it's just this one time, I want to have the chance to sit with you in a bar and have a conversation as two adults out here in the world."

"I'm dating Billy."

"Nothing like that, Pen. Just a drink between old friends." Now he's lying, an effective strategy. People are most compelling when they deliver a mixture of truth and dishonesty. Lovers can never be old friends, and Penelope is more lover than any of the women Ed has taken home since Laura left. He understands that now.

"Okay," she says, her sudden softening a surprise. "Okay. Meet me out front in five minutes."

"Thatta girl."

Because he's already a few drinks in, he lets himself grab hold of her when she emerges from the front doors moments later. She returns the embrace, their history unfurling in Ed's mind. There she is in the corridors of Boulder the day he came for his interview. *You hear that? It sounds like music if you listen right.* There she is in his office with her lines of pistachios. She is walking his rounds with him. Steering Margaret and Barbara back from the river. She is pressing her lips against his, her hands on his belt. He has always wanted her. And the weight of that desire presses him closer to her now, makes his hands grip harder.

He feels her breath near his ear. She whispers, "You still want me, don't you, Dr. Ed?"

"So much."

She pulls away enough to look at him. "You have something to drink at your house, I assume?" She walks toward the parking lot. "I don't have a car here, so you'll have to drive."

He hasn't moved.

"Coming?" she asks.

He can't move.

"What's the problem, Dr. Ed?" Her voice is different, sharp and angry and loud. "Nerves?" she shouts. "Conscience? Can't fuck your former patient after all?"

"Stop yelling, Pen."

"Why? You invited me out here in the open. Embraced me in front of my place of work. It's perfectly legal. I'm of age. You're not married. Aboveboard all the way."

"Pen—"

She's storming back to him now, her face angrier than it ever was in Boulder. He has time to think, *This is what hatred looks like,* before she's shoving him in the chest. "You think you can show up here after everything that happened and whisk me off my feet? You're a *psychiatrist,* for Christ's sake. What the hell do you think's been going through my head these past four years? You think I've just been sitting around pining after you? Waiting for you to arrive? You don't think I've replayed over and over everything that happened in Boulder and afterward? Maybe—maybe—if you'd stayed away, I could've cast you in some sort of heroic light. Even if you were a selfish bastard, I could've at least credited you with the start of my recovery. I never would've gotten to Dr. Wong if you hadn't discharged me first, so for that I could've remained grateful. I could've forgotten all the attention and flirtation and let you just be the amazing doctor I've bragged to everyone about. But no. You are everything I was afraid you were." She pulls the hair from her face, absently touches the scar on her head. "I was so jealous of Laura. But I pity her now. Pity her those years of your marriage. She's lucky to have left. I'm right about that, aren't I? She was the one to leave?"

Penelope steps back, and Ed remembers the moments he had to force himself to do the same. *Remove your hand. Step back. Another step.*

"Here's my offer," she says. "I'll keep my side of the story going—the great Dr. Malinowski and all he did for me—and you'll stay away from here."

"Pen—"

"Deal?"

"It's a public library, Pen. You can't ban me. My son needs books—"

"Laura can bring your son. Do we have a deal?"

He stares at her.

"I can make the story worse, Ed. You know I can. You convinced me no one would listen before, but I know I could get some attention now. You may not have a wife to lose anymore, but I bet you're not willing to lose your job."

His promotion. There had been a moment when he thought he was going to get both the promotion and Penelope. More than he could ever have dreamed.

"Deal," he says, his voice small.

"Goodbye, Ed."

He'd so wanted to hear those words when she left Boulder.

Chapter 26

Ed takes a week off before starting his new position with the state. He gets Pete to come camping with Beau and all their boys.

Benjamin and Justin dump the tent out of its sack and help assemble poles. Ed sits in a camp chair, Beau at his side with his heavy head in Ed's lap. Beau is always at his side, and Ed absently tugs on the dog's ears. He's on his fifth beer.

Hank takes a pole to the creek, and the younger two grab their own and follow.

"Hey now, Ben. You have a fire to help build."

"I want to fish."

"Not before you build the fire. Everyone's got a job."

"Oh yeah? What's yours?"

"My job's to drink this beer!"

"That's not a job."

"Go fish," Pete says. "I'll build the fire. Don't argue, Ed."

Pete splits wood, tepees kindling. Ed holds out his lighter. He hears hollering from the creek, a fish on someone's line.

"Nothing better, is there, brother?" Ed raises his bottle, and Pete tips his in return.

— —

Ed awakens in the dirt by the dwindling fire, stars overhead. He walks to the tree line and takes a piss, fishes a bottle of whiskey out of his backpack, rights the tipped chair, sits down.

The boys are snoring in their tent, Pete, too.

Ed came to Montana for these moments, damn it. Fire and whiskey and fishing. He's right where he's supposed to be. Director of Health and Human Services! Youngest director in the state! More women than he knows what to do with. Easy women who don't demand anything. He'll string them all along with him. No promises to any particular one. No wives yelling at him to get home early. Just this—a fire and a bottle of whiskey.

He lights a cigarette, drops it, tries again.

Fire and whiskey and cigarettes. A whole goddamned sky full of stars.

— —

He wakes again briefly to someone shaking his arm and Benjamin's voice shouting. "Dad! Dad, wake up! Uncle Pete, he won't wake up!"

"He's all right, son. Just had a little too much to drink last night. Let him sleep a bit longer."

— —

The sun is high the next time Ed wakes, and he's sweating in his night's coat.

"Good afternoon, sunshine."

Ed opens his eyes to see Pete standing over him.

"You slept on the ground, brother, cuddled up to your bottle. You know I don't like to put on airs, but you've got to clean it up around the boys. If you needed this kind of camping trip, you should've come out alone."

The sun is too bright. Ed's head throbs behind his eyes. "Drugs, good doctor. Bring me some drugs."

Pete laughs.

— —

He joins the boys at the creek in the evening, and they make a good haul of brook trout. They fry them whole to eat with potatoes cooked in the coals, a couple cans of beans heated in their tins. Ed sits back, sips a beer—he'll stick to beer tonight. The air chills with the darkening sky. Stars appear. Hank and Justin tell stories. Benjamin stares into the fire and rubs at his neck.

"Your neck sore, son?"

"It's okay. I slept on it funny."

"Tent sleeping will get you every time." Ed scoots his chair back from the fire and stomps the dirt in front of him. "Have a seat. I may not look it, but I give a great massage."

All the boys laugh, and the anger Benjamin has been sending toward Ed dries.

Ed digs his fingers into the skin and muscle of the boy's small neck and shoulders, promising himself he'll do better.

— —

After the camping trip, Ed drops Benjamin at his mother and Tim's house and goes directly to Dorothy's, where he gets exquisitely drunk. He will do better when Ben is around, but that is a part-time responsibility. The woman he goes home with asks if he has kids.

"Occasionally, I have a son."

— —

The day before he's due to start his new position, he lays off the booze and the ladies. He takes Beau for a long hike on Mount Helena. He goes to the barber. He polishes his shoes.

He will always be a good doctor.

Chapter 27

— *Laura* —

Benjy is thrilled to have a baby brother. "I'm going to teach him everything."

"That's right, love. You are."

We've named him Charlie, after Tim's father. Charlie Benjamin Cooke, so he can share a name with his brother, whose last name could not be more different. Neither could his father.

"I'm going to teach him how to build fires and carve sticks and roast marshmallows and shoot BB guns. And Dad and I will take him out duck hunting with Beau as soon as he's a little bigger and the noise won't scare him so much. I think it'd scare him now, the shotgun, but he'll get used to it, and then Dad can teach him to shoot, too."

Benjy doesn't understand that his father is not Charlie's father.

"It's okay," Tim said when I told him my concern. "He'll figure it out."

Tim was here through the whole labor, talking me through the pain, the coach Bonnie was when Benjy came. He is down in the cafeteria now, trying to find me some real food.

The baby is asleep, wrapped tight in his blankets, only his tiny red face showing. His brow is furrowed, and I wonder what this new mix of genes will produce. I know somehow that he will be nothing like my first son.

"We have to tell Dad!" Benjy shouts. "Dad doesn't know the baby's here. We have to tell him!" He jumps out of bed and rushes to the phone on the wall.

I let Benjy call his dad whenever he wants. "Dial nine first."

Benjy twists the cord around his finger like I do while he waits for his father to answer. It's eight-thirty in the evening, past Benjy's bedtime, and as the silence continues, I realize there's no way Ed will be home at this hour.

I'm just starting to tell Benjy to hang up when his eyes light and he shouts, "Dad! It's me! The baby's here!" And then a stream of words, the same focus and density as his father's speeches. Benjy is telling Ed all about Charlie's face, and his light hair, and his gray eyes. "Mom says they won't stay that color, but I hope they do." He's talking about how small the baby's fingers are and his feet, and how he's sleeping right now, but he was awake earlier, and crying, and it was sad to hear.

"Sure, hang on. Yep. Love you, too, Dad." He holds the phone out to me. "He wants to talk to you."

I don't want to talk to him, but I say hello, aware of my scratchy voice, ragged from screaming. Birthing children is such a glorious, devastating war with oneself. I am torn and bloody and tired, and I hate the comfort that comes with Ed's words. "Good work, lady. I told you it'd be a boy."

It hurts to laugh, all my guts loose and aching.

"What are you doing?" I ask, as though he's a girlfriend I've called for a little chat, nothing in particular.

"I'd prefer not to say."

"Are you with a lady friend?"

"I'd prefer not to say." I laugh again, and wince again, and marvel at this banter with my ex-husband. It isn't devastating, but it isn't benign, either. Ed is a bit of a whore, and I suppose I'm glad for him—the bachelor life is what he was made for.

"I'll let you get back," I say.

"Congratulations, Laura."

"Goodbye, Ed."

I pass the phone to Benjy to hang up.

"When is he coming?"

"Your dad's not coming to the hospital, love."

"Why isn't Dad coming?"

There is a right way to answer this question, I'm sure, and I would like to know it. I would like to wave down a nurse and say, "Could you please get me the pamphlet called 'How to Talk to Your Son About His Half Brother'?" The pamphlet would contain ten easy steps, and it would lead us all to great understanding and acceptance.

I think of our conversation about Tim's and my small wedding. "Do you want to call Tim something other than Tim?" I asked him.

"Why? His name's Tim."

"But he's your stepdad now."

"Do you want me to call him Stepdad? That doesn't sound good."

I conceded. "You're right, honey. It doesn't."

I am still not sure what Benjy thinks of Tim, this semi-father.

I pat the bed next to me. "Your dad's not coming because Charlie isn't his son. Charlie is Tim's son."

Benjy's face scrunches in confusion. "But we're brothers."

"Sometimes brothers have one parent who's different. You and Charlie have the same mom but different dads." I feel like we're scripting out a PBS special on broken homes. It'll be delivered through puppets to make it easier to absorb. We'll be a family of woolly mammoths, long extinct to allow for some distance, and we'll talk in deep mammoth voices, our trunks swaying.

Benjy still looks confused. He likes clean lines, tidy explanations, proof, evidence. He is empathetic but protective of his own feelings, a champion of underdogs, incapable of admitting when he's the one who needs championing. Already, he is so much like Ed.

"Do you understand?" I take on the mammoth voice.

"Why are you talking like that?"

"Because I'm uncomfortable with this conversation."

"Why?"

Benjy is also inquisitive.

The baby is starting to whimper, tiny puppy sounds, and I will need to feed him and direct all my maternal energy back in his direction, but first, I have to make this right for Benjy. It suddenly feels like the most important thing I'll ever do as his mother—make him understand that he can have a brother who doesn't share the same father and still love him ferociously and still teach him to build fires and shoot guns (please, no) and take things apart and put them together. And he can have one mom who loves him with all her heart and one biological dad and one stepdad, and instead of loss, he should feel a surplus of riches because there are extra people to love him.

I am saying these things aloud in an Ed-inspired rant, and Benjy is nodding and staring and absorbing, and I feel his little hand lay itself on my wrist, and I hear his little voice say, "It's okay, Mom," because instead of reassuring him that he is fine, I have shown him that I am not.

I hold him against me with my free arm, and the baby starts crying, and Tim arrives with a burger and fries, Pete and Bonnie and their boys behind him—"Look who I found wandering around downstairs!"—and am I not all right because Ed isn't here?

The thought is quick, and I dismiss it quicker still.

I quiet Charlie with nursing and let Tim feed me fries, then the burger. We laugh at the mess I make of my face, the mustard we drop on the baby. I accept a shot glass from Pete, and I raise it with my free hand, like I did when Benjy was born, and then Justin, and now Charlie.

"We welcome you!" Pete shouts, and we drink and refill. It is warm and comforting, and it is incomplete. Maybe this is what the mammoth tells her inquisitive child. *Listen, little one, you have more people to love you, and that is a wonderful thing, but nothing in your life will ever be whole. Understand me: You will live a life of pieces.*

Chapter 28

It's a mess. The entire state. Patients being discharged who have no business leaving their institutions, others rightly discharged but abandoned to families ill-equipped to deal with their illnesses and disabilities. The group homes Ed promised haven't materialized in great enough numbers. Former patients are walking the streets, committing crimes, facing criminal charges.

His secretary is wary when she brings in the morning's paper. Her name is Eleanor, and she is young and attractive, and efficient and smart, but nothing compared to Martha.

"There's an angry editorial on page two. You'd better just get it over with."

Ed reads: "Close your eyes and imagine a prisoner of war coming out of isolation after being locked up for months on end. Now imagine a person in the final stages of Alzheimer's—confused, mumbling, hands shaking. Now put those two images together into one person. That person is my son, my son who suffers a severely disabling mental illness, coming out of months of isolation at the Montana State Prison. Mentally ill people often leave prison sicker than when they entered, as my son did. Zookeepers are not allowed to keep animals like this. Why do we allow our prisons to keep inmates in such conditions? My son is not a criminal. He is sick. He should be in an institution that can serve him."

At least there isn't another news article today. There have been too many headlines already: "Deinstitutionalization: Good Intentions, Unintended Consequences"; "Prison, the State's New Mental Institution"; "State Criminalizes the Mentally Ill"; "Mentally Ill and

Disabled Populations Outpace Available Services"; "Local Services Assume State's Responsibilities." It goes on. Ed's office floods with letters and phone calls from parents, providers, patients themselves. A few days ago, the paper printed an op-ed by a local psychiatrist: "There is a limit to society's tolerance of mentally disordered behavior. If we impede the entry of persons exhibiting that behavior into the mental health system, community pressure will force those people into the criminal justice system instead. This is a by-product of social control. We are trading one institution for another, in this case a qualified institution for an unqualified one."

Ed looks out his window across the capitol grounds. Everything is gray. Gray trees against gray buildings against the gray sky. Montana clings to its monotones in the winter months, varying degrees of a black-and-white scale, and spring usually holds to its word—a surprise no one sees coming. His head hurts, and he takes two more Tylenols even though it's been only an hour since his last dose. The headaches are chronic these days. He keeps meaning to get to the doctor, but there isn't time. Every moment not spent with Benjamin is spent in this office. He has his staff working all hours.

Eleanor buzzes in. "Call for you. It's Laura." Laura is his most frequent caller, their conversations mostly short and businesslike, working through plans around Benjamin, schedules, extra time with one of them to cover for a conference or a trip. Occasionally, one of them will slip. "Where are you going?" Ed might say when Laura asks him to switch a weekend. "Paradise Valley, huh?" And he will remember all the times he meant to take her there. He made reservations once, but something came up, and they never went, and now she goes with Tim.

Sometimes she slips, too. "Still dating Kathy?" or "Bonnie saw you with someone she could only classify as a child. You dating teenagers now?" He hears what he hopes is jealousy behind the playful judgment.

Mostly, they keep to business, though, and Ed welcomes it now, a distraction from the shit on his desk. Also: He makes a point to answer Laura's calls every time he's in his office, even if he's in the middle of something important. Eleanor has clear orders. It is an apology, a penance. Too late, he knows, but something nonetheless.

"Patch her through," and then the silence of an open line. "Laura?"

"Hi, Ed." His name in her mouth again, still not on the last things list. "Sorry to bother you. I know you're swamped."

"Nonsense." He also makes a point of *acting* available every time they talk, as though he's been sitting at his desk waiting for her call. This isn't an act, actually. He is constantly doing other things, but he is also always waiting for Laura.

"It's ridiculous, but— I left my keys in the ignition and locked myself out of my car. I don't think I ever got the spare from your place. Do you mind if I run over there and check? Or do you want to check for me? I'm downtown by the library."

The library. He has made it not exist. The gulch goes no farther south than Dorothy's.

Ed tries to remember the state of his house—definitely dirty, but how dirty? He tries to gauge what effect it'll have on Laura, how much it would put her off, because he wants to meet her there, and he has to assume she wants to meet him there, too, to see him in person somewhere private. Why else come to him with this request that's so obviously an excuse? How could she not have made a copy of the key sometime in the past couple years? The thought of her creating a reason to see him makes him giddy. He hasn't seen Laura alone since their last lunch at Dorothy's.

"Want to just meet me there and we can both look? Or I can come get you?" Maybe Penelope will be outside to witness him picking up his ex-wife. *See, Pen? Not all bad.*

Laura agrees to the meeting, declines the ride. "It'll be a nice walk."

He rushes home to tidy up what he can. He's sweeping crumbs into his palm when she knocks on the back door. She has never knocked before. He adds: *Last time she walked into the house without knocking*. He hollers her in.

She is remarkably older, he realizes. As in him, her age is beginning to write itself across her face in lines, through her hair in white.

He was supposed to be next to her as it happened, the changes so subtle he wouldn't have noticed them from day to day. But he has missed whole years, and he finds himself wanting this new version of her even more than the one he married. He lets himself hope that the last lunch at Dorothy's wasn't the *last time we made love*. Let there be just one more.

"You look amazing."

She laughs and looks down at her clothes—jeans, a sweater under the winter coat she's been wearing since Michigan, old snow boots. "You've always been loose with flattery." Her expression changes, grows contemplative. "You look good, too." Her eyes flick toward the bedroom as though she's heard his thoughts. "Do you have a cigarette?"

He pulls his pack from his pocket, grateful for a reason to cross the room and stand in front of her, close, and light the cigarette she places between her lips. "I thought you quit."

She sighs through the smoke she exhales, and he imagines the exquisite taste of tobacco after a dry spell. He's halfheartedly attempted to quit a few times. It never sticks.

He loves to watch Laura smoke.

"I'm tired of the quitting," she says, inhaling again.

He lights his own cigarette, suddenly nervous, unsure what to do with his hands or the rest of his body, whether he should step away or move closer.

She is sexier than she ever was when they were married. There is a rawness to her now, something frayed, something rough. And strength—she is so much stronger.

He's trying not to look at her when she says, "I didn't lock my keys in the car."

He goes to the fridge and gets a couple beers. She sits down across from him at the kitchen table.

"Why are you here, then?"

She takes a sip of beer, a drag off her cigarette. "The problem is—" She interrupts herself with a long, hovering silence. Then she laughs bitterly and says, "I can't stop thinking about you."

He hears the heater kick on, warm air in the vents, blowing against their legs. Laura stares at him, and his eyes go to her new wedding ring with its big diamond, gaudy in comparison to the simple bands they exchanged. Ed's wedding ring is in a box in his top dresser drawer.

She can't stop thinking about him? She's concocted a bullshit excuse to get him to meet her here at the house they once shared because *she can't stop thinking about him?*

Anger supplants his desire. "And you want me to help you with that? *Me*. Your ex-husband. The one you left."

"You didn't give me a choice, Ed."

"Oh, I know, Laura. You've made it painfully clear that I was the one who failed us."

"I loved you so much." Past tense.

"And now you don't. Now you love your attentive little builder and your clean new house." Ed is tired, he realizes—tired of interrogating himself, tired of regret, tired of loss. "You should go, Laura."

"Ed—"

He shakes his head.

Snow is starting outside, giant flakes, and evening is coming, the days so short in winter. The anger dissipates as quickly as it came, and he feels the headache return, throbbing in his right temple. He holds his head in his hands, eyes closed. He hears Laura stand and walk to the door. He hears her leave, and it feels more permanent this time than any other. He will move on, too, completely this time, embrace his bachelorhood, fully embody this new version of his life. He has had these thoughts before, but he begs them to stick this time. Let it really be over.

He goes to the bathroom for more Tylenol, then drives back to the office. He stays late, writing more letters, demanding more money. The situation is a mess, but it's been a mess before. This mess is at least moving toward something better. Progress is messy, like all great things—the blood of childbirth, the mud of spring. Marriage and divorce.

Third and Chaucer

—

MARCH 15, 1977

Chapter 29

Ed is alone with his dog when the headache in his right temple switches from throbbing to gnawing, a chisel in his brain. It will stay with him, this chipping and churning. Later, he will talk to a woman who will tell him, "Our lives are like giant wood lathes, our bodies the spun spindle, the bowl, the table leg, things carved and whittled down."

When the chisel starts, he stands from his chair. He touches the side of his face as if checking for blood and then reaches for his cigarette, its ash growing long. His hand moves fitfully, a box attached to a crane. His fingers knock ashes and butts to the floor, but the lit cigarette holds tight to the cover of his book. He knows to flick it away, his right arm replacing the clumsy club that has become his left. He stomps the smoke into the carpet. He can't handle a fire with this whirling in his head.

"Outside," he says to Beau. "Gotta get outside, get some fresh air." He says these words, but they don't come from his mouth. Other noises do, feral and stray, something from the mountains where he camps with his son, a winter-den noise, he thinks, a brooding clutch. He doesn't know what a clutch is. Or brooding. What are these words in his mind that don't match their sounds?

Walking is difficult, slow. His left leg is like his left arm, clubbed, unformed. The lathe that whittles away his brain works in reverse on his limbs, turning them back to clay and stone, lumps to be molded by a creator's hands. *God?* he asks, but as usual, God doesn't respond.

Beau whines, his tongue on his master's right palm, a lick, a nudge. These gestures ask, *Okay?*

Ed puts his hand on the dog's head, sloppy, a bit too rough.

Together, they make it through the dining room and kitchen, into the mudroom, to the back door, its knob a mystery he knows he could solve if concentration would come, if the damn knocking would stop. Somehow he makes his right hand turn the doorknob, and then they are outside in the sun. The trees are still bare from winter, the air chilled, though it is technically spring. Frost clings to the rock garden beds in the shade, patches of snow around the corners of the deck and yard. Paths of ice run to the garage and driveway, formed from the days he was too lazy to shovel. He is talking to his dog, telling him to close the door and get the mail, to call Laura, see what Ben's doing. It's nearly time for their first spring camping trip, and there are fish to catch. He has a date tonight—don't let him forget.

Ed's nonword noises make Beau bark, concerned, and then Ed falls, his head to a mound of old snow, no softer than the wood of the deck, but somewhat softer than the ice where his shoulder and hip hit. A small cut begins to bleed on his forehead, a slightly bigger one on his right arm. Beau licks them both. He pokes his snout into his master's face, into his armpits, his stomach, his groin, but Ed doesn't move. Beau whines and nudges, then turns circles before curling against Ed's ribs, a small ball of warmth.

Patient

—

MAY 1977–MAY 1978

Chapter 30

Ed will remember waking up for the first time nearly a month after the aneurysm felled him. Doctors will tell him he's been lucid several times before, but Ed will remember only the one time. Pete is in the room, his old pal Pete.

"Gave us a scare, you son of a bitch."

Ed laughs, the left side of his face heavy and numb. "Would you believe me if I told you I have no idea why I'm here?"

Pete grimaces. There is no other word for it. "Didn't catch that, Ed. Maybe try talking a little slower?"

Ed hasn't yet recovered words. His mouth and tongue are waiting to be taught their functions, impatient children. He knows the words. He says them in his head. He just can't transfer them to his body.

He tries to sit up taller in his hospital bed and finds his whole left side as heavy and numb as his face. He looks at Pete, and Pete looks away.

"What's wrong, pal?"

"Maybe you should rest," Pete replies.

Ed's head hurts, and he doesn't know why Pete won't answer him. He doesn't know why Pete looks so damn *sad,* and as he thinks it, the word *sad* balloons in his mind into a great white swatch of fabric, a gauzy blanket coating the room. It quiets the beeping monitor and the heaviness in his legs, the pain in his head, the face of his friend. Quiet, rippling white.

His next memory will come nearly a month later.

— —

"When is your family visiting next, Edmund?"

"Tue. Sss. Day. Come."

He hears the therapists tell him about his progress. He hears *language rehabilitation*. He sees words in his brain, though they don't look like the words on the pages of books. His therapists tell him these are words—these jumbled nonsensical characters—but he knows the therapists are lying. *Words* are objects, like the objects in the bag he carries: pencil, paper, toilet paper, spoon (for hunger), cup (for thirst), a photo of Benjamin, a photo of Laura. Words are textured and colored, bright and vivid. They walk across his thoughts. Sometimes they speak. The *word* Laura pausing in her stroll to say, *Hello there, handsome. Where have you been?* The *word* Edmund (self) saying, *Right here, my love*. He remembers his wife and son. He remembers his friends Pete and Bonnie. The word-object *Penelope* comes often, and he tries to move it to his mouth, out into the room where he can make it real, but his therapists just hand him pens of varying colors, more and more pens.

The left side of his body is heavy, always, and he can't walk, though he forgets every morning, swinging himself out of his bed onto legs that don't stand. He sees and feels *anger* at his physical therapists. He needs no object for the word *no*.

Benjamin comes sometimes, and Laura, and a new word, *Tim*, who doesn't stay.

"Tim is my husband," Laura says. "You and I aren't married anymore, Edmund. I am married to Tim."

"No."

With his good hand, he reaches for her, and when he feels her soft fingers in his, the word *Tim* disappears again.

Chapter 31

— Laura —

We've been going to Great Falls every weekend, me and Ben and Charlie and Tim. This is the first time I've gotten Tim to agree to stay home with Charlie. "Please, Tim. It's so confusing for him, and Charlie really doesn't need to be a part of this."

When Tim conceded, he made me promise not to let Ed believe he's my husband again. "I know the man's in a rough place, Laura, but letting him believe something that's not true isn't going to help him get back to where he was."

I was angry at the insinuation, but mostly because he'd foreseen a realistic possibility. Ed just needs something to grasp, something to ground himself. More of his memory returns every time we visit, and the doctors assure us this is a great sign, an indicator that he could get nearly all of it back at some point, but he is years behind: Benjamin is small and I am his wife. He is working out in Boulder. He's trying out a new behavioral model for Penelope. He is speaking in clear if broken words, and concise, vivid sentences that have no articles or conjunctions, just the meat. His doctors say he's starting to read again, slowly, like a child. *The cat sat. The dog ran.*

I hear myself say, "I can't stop thinking about you," the last time I was in our old house. I feel his anger, the finality of it. We were done then, in a way we hadn't been before.

In the car, I tell Benjy, "I'm going to pretend your dad and I are still married today. He seems to think we are, and I think it might help him find more memories if I play along. Is that all right?"

Benjy is looking out his window across the grasslands. We've left the curves of the canyon, the wetness of the river, and now we're out on the plains, everything gone gold in the late-summer heat.

"Antelope," he says, pointing.

It's a big herd, closer to the road than I've seen, and I can feel the longing in my son to go stalk them, belly-crawl through the furrows of stubbled wheat next to his father. Ed has told me our son is a good shot. My freezer is full of their bounty.

"Did you hear what I said, Benjy?"

"You're going to pretend you're married to Dad again." He looks at me, and he is suddenly old, this boy of mine, resignation tugging at the corners of his mouth. "I don't care," he says. "He isn't Dad anymore."

"He's still your dad down in there. He's just sick." Again I find myself reciting facts to Benjy, though he's heard them too many times now. The story is our lullaby, my go-to song to calm these fears. *Hush-a-bye. Don't you cry. Go to sleep, my little baby*. I talk about the damage done to Ed's brain during the surgery to stop the bleeding. I talk about the inadvertent deprivation of oxygen that caused the *temporary* paralysis. Benjy and I have checked out books from the library. I've sat with him, pointing to the different parts of the brain. "The frontal lobe does reasoning, movement, emotions, problem solving, and planning," I repeat now. "Most of the damage was there, but there was also some damage to the temporal lobe, which does sound, memory, and speech. The doctors say the damage isn't bad, and your father is a very strong man. He's going to recover from this, Benjy." I know he doesn't understand, but it's a story with a happy ending that I have to tell.

He's going to recover. Hush. Go to sleep. In the morning, your father will be mended.

I am a liar.

Benjy shrugs and returns to his staring.

— —

"He'll be done with occupational therapy in about ten minutes." Ed's primary psychologist directs us to a small room off Ed's. "Why don't you two watch this last bit. I've found that it helps family members with their own communication techniques."

We watch Ed through a two-way mirror. The voices are piped in through a microphone, and it feels like spying—furtive and wrong.

"This is weird," Benjy says.

"It is."

Ed is hunched over a notebook with a pencil gripped in his hand. He holds it like Chip would hold his pencils, his fist a clumsy paw wrapped around the instrument, the lead ripping paper. He is close enough for us to see his work.

"Write *no,*" his therapist says.

Ed scratches at the paper a few times, then lifts the notebook and throws it across the room, the pages fluttering, momentary wings in flight. *"Fuhhh . . . ck. You."*

Benjy snorts at my side. "Dad cursed."

"That's not so different from the dad you know."

The therapist working with Ed is a man named Martin whom we've met several times. All of us have taken a liking to him. He is patient and has a great sense of humor.

Now he says, "Great pronunciation, Ed."

We can see Ed smiling. "He gets it," I whisper to Benjy. "See?"

Benjy nods.

Martin retrieves the notebook, talking all the way. "Your speech is brilliant, Ed. I know the writing is frustrating, but I want you to try again."

Ed shakes his head.

"One word, Ed. Just one, and we can be done with writing for the day."

"Puh . . . Puh . . . Pen."

"Oh," I say. *Pen.* He is remembering Penelope.

"One word, Ed. Pen's a great one. P. E. N. Let's start even smaller, though. Try *no*."

The pencil touches the paper. Ed squints in concentration, and I can see his broken brain trying to find the letters, the meaning, the instructions to send to the hand to move the pencil to prove the point. *Straight up-and-down line, then a diagonal line from it to the horizon where it landed, then another straight up-and-down line from the bottom of that diagonal to the horizon where the top started. Lift pencil, move over slightly. Draw a circle, a round sun, a ball, a penny.*

He makes marks on the paper, lines and dots. No letters, no words.

"Good," Martin says. "Good try, Edmund. We'll come back to it tomorrow."

— —

We're in a big common room now, cleaner and brighter than Boulder's but similar. This is our usual meeting place. We regularly play board games, an activity suggested by Ed's therapists. The distraction helps our conversation; it's also hand-eye practice for him, sequencing, process.

Martin has brought Ed to us in his wheelchair. He has begun walking, but it is difficult and exhausting.

"What'll it be today?" Martin asks. "Chutes and Ladders, checkers, Yahtzee? Go Fish?"

"Yahtzee." Benjy loves Yahtzee.

Ed grunts an affirmation. I nod my agreement. "Good choice."

Ed reaches for my leg as soon as Martin turns his back, his touch feral and needy. "Good. See. Laura." He moves his eyes in the direction of his room. "Come. Bed." His smile is leering, his excitement obvious.

Oh, God. I check to see if Benjy has understood, but he looks confused, not disgusted.

"We're here to play a game with our son, Ed. Family time."

He keeps his hand on my leg but smiles over to Benjy. The left side of Ed's face has regained nearly all its muscle and movement, and it's a relief to see symmetry in his expressions again.

Martin brings our game, and it is just the three of us at a small table in this common room for brain-injured patients. There's one other man in the far corner, sitting in a wheelchair with a blanket over his lap, staring vacantly out the window. There are no bars on these windows, no grates or screens, unlike the ones in Boulder. There are plants instead, books and magazines and games, all clean and ordered. It is nice but sterile, and I find myself wishing for the messy din of Boulder, the smiles on the faces of my students, sloppy artwork on the walls.

Benjy sets up the game, and over the noise of our dice, the shaking and scattering, I listen to him ask the simple questions we've prepared. Benjy wanted to ask about going camping; instead, I've encouraged him to ask where his father's favorite camping spot is.

"I already *know* that, Mom. It's up on Trout Creek."

"Your dad might not know it, though, Benjy. We're trying to help him remember."

And so Benjy asks this new, strange father where he most likes to camp, looking away as the man tries to form words with his clumsy mouth.

"Trou . . . Ta," Ed says.

"Trout Creek?"

Ed nods, and Benjy smiles, and my whole body tingles with the warmth of this word from Ed. This is how I felt the first time Benjy spoke, excited not for the word itself but for what it symbolized—this great start, this wide door opening into the world of language.

Ed's fingers are exploring my leg again.

Benjy seems buoyed by the mention of Trout Creek, and he launches into one of his stories. "Do you know why Helena's nicknamed the Queen City?"

Ed shakes his head.

"I just learned it from Hank. He learned it in school, so I'll be ahead when I get there. There was gold here, and gold is worth more money than the copper they mine in other towns, and they were fighting over where to put the capital, so there was this great—*rivalry*." A word he recently learned, also from Hank. Benjy loves new words. "The Helena folks were very fancy, so the copper kings called them *Queen City*."

Ed snorts a laugh. "Why. Hel. Eh. Na. Be. Cap. It. Al?"

"Why did Helena become the capital?" Benjy scowls at the ceiling, an expression he's taken from me.

Ed nods. *Go on.*

"I guess people like to feel fancy."

"Hah!" A bark of laughter, more emotion than we've seen in Ed since he woke up. He struggles to lean forward, to drop his left hand onto his son's knee, to pat it a bit too roughly. I'm proud of Benjy for not pulling away, though Ed's face is terrifyingly close, his open mouth, his bad breath.

"Your turn, Dad."

Ed pulls back, stealing his hands from our legs. His left arm is still clumsy, and the dice spill out haphazard on the table, one of them plinking to the floor. Benjy rushes over, calling out its number. He is adamant about not rerolling when a die goes astray. One night he argued with Tim about it over a game of *Sorry!* "Why should you get a redo when it's your fault for throwing your dice too hard?" Tim conceded quickly. He doesn't argue.

Ed picks up five sixes, and Benjy marks it for him, our scorekeeper.

"You're going to beat me again, Dad."

"This is still anyone's game," I say, taking the cup from Ed's hand.

— —

Ed tires easily, and after one round of Yahtzee, he's ready for a nap. Benjy says his goodbyes and heads to the television to wait while I return Ed to his room. I blather as I push his chair, a long string of words that describe things Ed should know. "The more you can talk about his life," his doctors tell us, "the quicker these memories are going to come back." I talk about Beau, whom Tim and I have taken back full-time, like Benjy. Sole custody now and likely forever. "We're taking Beau to the lake for dummy throws," I say. "He's already anxious for duck season."

Ed makes his hands into a shotgun, fires it toward the ceiling. "Duh. Ck."

"Yes, Ed. That's right."

I talk about the perennials coming up in the beds at Third Street, the bleeding hearts, the wide leaves of hollyhocks. "The Lewises are back," I say. "Eating all our peanuts."

Ed slaps his leg. "Nuh. Ttt. Crack. Ers."

He recognizes the Lewises, and it's this that wets my eyes. Our birds.

I can't cry in front of him, though, so I swallow and blink as I turn in to his room with its flood of flowers and balloons and gifts, every surface covered. His fans have sent their condolences—colleagues in Boulder, colleagues at the state, some of the legislators he wooed, the governor. There are also notes and gifts from bartenders and waitresses and lovers I've never heard of. Pete and Bonnie make regular visits, and Ed's parents have rented a furnished apartment in Great Falls to be here during his recovery. All of us leave the room with bottles of whiskey to store away for him until he's well and home. "No drinking," the doctors say. I took two bottles home last week, and there's another new one today, a regenerating whiskey plant.

"You want to lie down?" I park Ed's chair next to the bed and come around in front of him, where he grabs for me, his good hand on my hip.

"You. Too."

I kneel and take his hand into mine. "Not yet, handsome. You have to get well first."

He rearranges his grip so he can bring my hand to his lap, smiling at me, his eyes bright. *Feel that? I'm well enough.*

I can hear one of those doctors saying, "This is a tough road. Trauma to the brain often exacerbates existing tendencies and character traits, usually in the—" He struggled to find a diplomatic way to put it. "Usually on the negative side rather than the positive. Let's say someone's a little messy; we often see that become worse after a brain injury, to the extent that a housekeeper might be needed." What were Ed's negative traits? Messy. Stubborn. A voracious appetite for food and drink and women. Of course Ed is ready for sex.

I take my hand back and stand, repeating, "Not yet, love. Not yet."

Not ever, love. Not ever.

I am devastated by the idea of Ed's celibacy. The Ed I know would forfeit life entirely before accepting it under these terms.

His face reads fear suddenly, his eyes bouncing in discomfort like those of a disoriented beast. Panicky, ready to flee. I don't know what has scared him, whether he's heard my thoughts or whether it's just one more wave of confusion that's caught him and knocked him back under.

"Let's get you into bed." The physical therapists and nurses have taught us how to help Ed from chair to standing, standing to sitting on the bed, sitting to lying down. We brace ourselves as he heaves his weight forward. We lift his left leg onto the mattress after his right, the limb stiff and foreign, a dead thing tied to his body. The therapists have shown us how to massage the muscles, to loosen them back into the memory of motion. They tell us, "It's just going to take time." They tell us this over and over, but it has been nearly six months, and I don't know how many months or years it will take to finally amount to Time.

I prop pillows behind Ed's head and shoulders as his eyelids flutter. He snaps his eyes open and then closes them softly, just like my boys when they're fighting exhaustion. I sit on the edge of his bed and watch as his breathing grows smooth and even. I push a thick swatch of hair back from his forehead, the dark flecked with gray I haven't noticed before. This new Ed is aging quicker than his predecessor, and I worry that he'll be an old man before he's released from this place, withered and stooped, resting on a cane. We'll all be our same ages, and we'll gather around him, children at his feet, waiting to hear his stories, all the life he lived before this moment.

Chapter 32

— *Laura* —

Tim has dragged me to this appointment. It isn't his, but he insisted on coming with me, and now he sits stiffly at my side, uncomfortable. He's never visited a therapist before, either.

The office is done up in Easter pastels. Light yellow walls, lavender curtains, a rose and baby blue plaid sofa. I am sitting next to a stuffed bear. Tim rests his arm on the head of a duck. A bowl of potpourri sits on the low table before us, a blend of cedar and cinnamon and sage, too strong. I feel a headache starting at the back of my skull.

The therapist stares at us. I can't remember if she's asked something. I don't know whose turn it is to talk, or if anyone has spoken at all.

Her name is Helen, and her eyes are enormous, amber-brown, the most beautiful I've ever seen, overshadowing the brightest blue or green, and I find myself envying them, though the rest of her is bland and thick. She is tall and wide-shouldered, and she towers over me when we shake hands.

"I'm sorry to hear about Edmund," she says, and I try to remember if it's the first thing she's said. "We worked together a few times throughout the years. He was a great asset to the state."

"He still is." My voice is too defensive. I hear it.

Tim takes my hand, and I have to make myself not draw away. He feels less of a husband now that Ed is less of a man.

A week ago, Bonnie and Pete and Tim cornered me in the kitchen of our house. They'd occupied the children with a movie downstairs.

Pete poured us each a whiskey, and Bonnie said, "You need to let Ed go." Pete was nodding at her side, Tim, too. They were staging an intervention. I thought again about that last day with Ed in his kitchen, all that broiling anger. I thought I'd let him go. I thought I was done.

But he is sick now, and everything is different.

Tim said, "Baby, this is too much right now. It's hard on all of us, but you're taking the brunt of it. I've made us an appointment with a therapist."

"She's wonderful," Pete added. "Bonnie and I have seen her, and she really helped us work through some of our shit. She'll be able to help you sort this out. There's no guidebook here, Laura. You've got to talk to someone."

I took my whiskey to my room and stayed there through dinner. But they were persistent, and here we are.

Helen says, "Tell me what's going on."

Tim speaks first. "Laura is driving to Great Falls twice a week to visit Ed. His parents were here for a while, but they had to get back to Michigan, and Laura has taken on the bulk of Ed's care. He still thinks they're married, and I think—Pete and Bonnie and our other friends, too—that it isn't good for either of them. Ed needs to understand what his life really looks like, and Laura needs to focus on her own."

"You mean I need to focus on you."

"That's not what Tim said, Laura." Helen's voice is calm and even. She has a notepad on her lap, a pen in her hand. She blinks at me.

"It's what he meant, and of course he deserves my attention. But I'd appreciate a little understanding while I help Ed get back on his feet."

"Why is it your responsibility to help Ed get back on his feet?"

Her voice is like a metronome, a steady unbroken rhythm. I don't want it to soothe me as much as it does.

I say, "He's my son's father."

Tim says, "I'm your other son's father, *and* I'm your husband."

Helen says, "Can you understand how this might be hard for Tim, Laura?"

I look away from her, my gaze catching on the prints and posters she's chosen to display on her walls—waterfalls and meadows and mountains, their natural colors at odds with the room's muted tones. Near the window, she's hung a framed copy of the Serenity Prayer, the words in swooped calligraphy, vines and flowers decorating the border. How can anyone have the wisdom to know what they can and can't change? We learn only after trying.

I remember Ed telling me the Catholic Church doesn't recognize divorce. Ed and I are still married in its eyes, and I am committing adultery with Tim. I am a polygamist, a whore, and I fight the urge to tell Helen that sometimes I feel the same way. *I am still married to Ed,* I want to tell her. *Make my new husband understand.*

Tim isn't even new anymore.

"Laura?" the woman asks. "What are you gaining through this time with Ed?" Her pen is poised over the notepad, ready to scribble down my response, because this answer feels like *the* answer if I can find it. *What are you gaining?* But I can't see it in terms of *gain.* I am focused only on *not losing anything else.* I have lost Ed over and over—to the institution, to Penelope, to policy, to the state, to his friends. I had so little of him left that I had to finally let go of the last bits, which is maybe a new version of the story I've told myself of our divorce, but one that feels true right now. It was Ed who slipped away from me, and I couldn't hold him, couldn't bring him back. He was a bachelor and I was a wife, but we would raise our son together, and I would live just a little through the power of him, the great force that was Ed out in the world.

I have lost him as husband and lover, but it's the idea of him I risk losing now. We build our lives on ideas.

I still have not answered her question.

"Do you feel responsible for Edmund's accident, Laura?"

"Yes," I say. *Do I?* The doctors have given us no cause, no preexisting condition that led to Ed's aneurysm. It could've been due to his smoking and drinking, which were always heavy but grew heavier after the divorce. Still, plenty of nondrinking, nonsmoking people develop aneurysms. Likely, it was some faulty piece of genetic code, passed along from his parents or grandparents, a dormant weapon crouching in the shadows of his brain, grating away at that one vulnerable spot, thinning and weakening it until it burst.

Starburst. Sunburst. Outburst.

"Laura, no one could've stopped this thing that happened to Edmund, not even Edmund himself. You are feeling guilty that Edmund is having to go through this without a spouse, and you are transferring that guilt onto something you have no control over. Tell me, why did you and Edmund divorce?"

"He didn't see me anymore."

"Ed was never home," Tim tries to clarify, and I *hate* him for speaking now, the word *hate* sharp and defined in my mind. "He was completely devoted to his work and had an inappropriate relationship with—"

"Ed's and my marriage is not yours to discuss," I say.

Tim's voice grows tight. "When it's affecting *our* marriage, then I'd say I can talk about it all I want." He turns his attention to Helen. "I'm going to wait outside."

"Are you sure, Tim? It's good to work through these things together."

"I think Laura has some work of her own to do."

I watch him walk to the door, stiff and indignant. He wears short sleeves and shorts even though it's October, and I watch the muscles of his calves, the thickness of his forearms. He is still tan from summer, long days outside building. He built the boys a multistory playhouse in the backyard, nicer than a lot of real homes. It has a balcony.

"How would you describe your relationship with Tim?" Helen asks once he's gone.

"Good, like it's always been."

"You sound disappointed by that." She is a professional, versed in diplomacy.

"It's boring," I say. "Boring and monotonous and safe. There's nothing to complain about. Tim is everything I said I wanted Ed to be—attentive, available, open. He's home for dinner every night. Half the time, he's the one cooking. He takes our boys for walks and bike rides and trips to the library so I can have time alone to paint. He supports my artwork, asks about it every day."

"How's the sex?"

Bonnie is the only one who's ever asked me this question—abrasive, bold Bonnie who asks anything, no subject off limits—and I've never answered fully. "Fine," I've said. "It's great."

"It's all right," I tell Helen. "Rare, I guess, but good when it happens."

She is staring at me, pen poised. Her face says, *Why don't you tell me the whole story.*

"It's good and boring, like the rest of our lives. We have sex in one position in our bed on Friday nights unless something interferes."

She's writing in her notebook, and I worry that I've said too much, that I've betrayed Tim, that I'm being too fussy.

"Do you think it's boring for Tim, too?"

I have never considered what Tim thinks of our sex life, and it makes me feel even worse about my indictment.

"I don't know," I admit to Helen.

"How was sex with Edmund?"

I am in the bathroom at Dorothy's. I am in the bathroom at the hospital. I am in my classroom in Boulder.

"Sex with Ed was exciting, but he used it to take the place of real connection."

Helen nods and writes. "Do you feel like you have a real connection with Tim?"

"Yes."

Helen puts her pen down as though she's just penciled out an answer to the troublesome equation we've been working for days. *Sex times x equals intimacy plus y, in which x is of greater or equal value to real connection; y is less than excitement but greater than boredom. Solve for x and y.*

"It's human nature to second-guess our decisions, Laura, especially decisions of this magnitude. There's no way to completely eradicate that way of thinking. However, you can behave in ways that lessen it. It sounds like you and Tim have some things to work on between the two of you. By focusing your attention on Edmund, you avoid the issues with Tim. Does that make sense?"

I nod.

"If you want to save your current marriage, you must invest in it, and to truly invest in it, you have to let Edmund go."

I stare at her, those giant amber eyes, rich as honey.

"Can you do that, Laura? Can you let Edmund go?"

"I don't know."

"Say *Edmund is not my husband.*"

"Edmund is not my husband." Have I ever said this before? *Edmund is not my husband.*

"I divorced him four years ago."

"I divorced him four years ago."

"I am divorcing him again right now."

"I am divorcing him again right now."

I don't know that I want to.

"I'm just supposed to abandon him?" I ask.

Helen's voice is patient and gentle. "You can't abandon something that isn't yours."

Chapter 33

"Dr. Ed?"

Ed has been dozing in his chair. Not a wheelchair anymore, but a regular chair at a regular table in this regular room. He is walking with a cane and using his left arm again, the fingers starting to obey his thoughts. *Pick up glass. Bring to mouth. Set down.* There are moments when he forgets where he is—a hospital in Great Falls—and who he is—a patient—and instead finds himself back in Boulder, making his rounds. He hears his patients asking for him.

"Dr. Ed?" A hand on his shoulder accompanies the voice.

Ed opens his eyes. He tries to orient himself, tries to place the face before him into the situation his therapists keep telling him is true. *You are the patient, Edmund. Yes, you are a doctor, but right now, you're a patient.* If that is true, how can this person be here?

"Pen?"

She sits in the chair next to him, scoots it close. "Hi, Ed."

His brain is a building gutted by fire, walls smoke-licked, ceiling blackened, floor crumbling. He trips down the damaged hallways. Every now and then, though, he finds an untouched room, everything just as he left it, and the memories rise up in vivid detail. He searches for the room marked *Penelope*. He's sure he was just there.

"Ah! Pen!" There it is, and he beams at her.

She reaches for him and he leans toward her—*a kiss!*—but instead, she pulls the smudged glasses from his face and polishes them with the hem of her shirt.

He blinks, a baby unaccustomed to the light. "What are you doing here?"

"Visiting you. I'm sorry I didn't come sooner. Dr. Pearson came into the library only last week and told me what happened."

She slides his glasses back on, and he takes in the brightly edged world before him, suddenly clear. He can see the common room where they sit, the board games on the shelf in the corner, the television on low, the bookshelves and coffee tables and sofas. There's a table for coloring, and he wants to collect all those bright crayons, though he doesn't know why. Maybe just to look at now that he can see them so clearly. *I'll have to talk to those orderlies about keeping the patients' glasses clean.* He files this note in the *Staff Improvement* room of his brain. He fills this room often, though he worries a window might be open, the screen damaged or gone, all his notes flying out into the grasses behind Griffin Hall, sticking in the sagebrush, fluttering up into the mountains.

A woman is sitting next to him. *Beautiful woman. Young.*

"Pen!"

She smiles, and he remembers that smile, the warmth and radiance of it. She worked with him, just down the hall. *No, not quite.* He searches, sniffs, opens and closes doors. *Patient,* he hears, and the room blazes before him, a jumble of images and words and moments. *Seizures and standing near the river, near-drowning, hand on him, touching bodies pressed.*

"We're lovers," he says.

She winces and shakes her head. "No, Ed. You were my doctor when I was at Boulder."

"Here!" he shouts, raising his hands to indicate the room. "You're here, too?"

"This isn't Boulder, Ed. You're at a rehabilitation center in Great Falls."

He shakes his head, the words misaligning, falling into rubble. This is Penelope, he knows, and he was her doctor, but the room said *lover*. The room said *touch,* and now a door is flying open across the hall, a door marked *Laura,* and he withdraws, unsure. Laura is his wife. Ben is his son. Penelope is . . .

"I work at the library now," she says, and something flashes, a hot coal of anger. She is yelling at him, and he has done nothing wrong, or everything wrong. Penelope is . . .

"I could bring you books, if you'd like."

"I can't read much." The things his therapists call words sometimes make themselves into meaning when he looks at them on the page. He can see them in the blackened halls of his brain, etched into the glass of doors, typed across papers.

"Your therapist said you're regaining that skill. He said you're making great progress."

Yes, his aides told him as well. It's difficult to do his job without reading. He has to have Martha read everything aloud to him.

"I could read to you," Penelope says.

Penelope. He hears the thrum of her words mixing with the rest of the room, the broken patterns of speech, the slurs and hoots and moans. He hears Chip (*Chip!*), his deep voice. Gillie and Frank. He hears Penelope's voice reading to them, coaxing them through the language, dragging them toward meaning.

And there is Ed in the doorway, spying on her, smiling. He can feel himself there, asking, "Is Caesar the fly?" He can feel her elbow in his ribs, the touch sending darts through his veins, a pulse at the base of his stomach. He hears her say, "You're hopeless." He feels her hand fall over his forearm, intimate. "His mind is the fly, moving upon silence."

"The fly," he says aloud, the words tumbling, rushing out of his mouth. "'Like a long-legged fly upon the stream / His mind moves upon silence.' You're teaching that in your reading group. The patients are doing so well." He can almost see the next part, an outline, a ghost, wispy and threadbare. Ghosts trip down these halls. He can hear them skittering off, can feel them. The words. Where are they? "A woman?" he says.

And Penelope recites, "'She thinks, part woman, three parts a child, / That nobody looks; her feet / Practice a tinker shuffle / Picked up on a street.'"

"Ah!" he shouts. "A tinker shuffle!" And he stands too quickly. His left leg works now, but stiffly—a dead thing he drags. Penelope is propping him up and reaching for his cane to help him balance. "You'll dance with me?" he asks, waving the cane away, sliding his right hand around her back, just above her hip. *Beautiful lover*. His left hand interlaces with hers at shoulder level, and they move in a quiet, slow dance he can almost remember. *One-two-two. One-two-two. One.*

Chapter 34

Excerpts from interview between resident psychologist Jeffrey Holht (JH) and stroke victim Edmund Malinowski (EM), one year post-incident, conducted over the course of two sessions.

JH: Anything to drink?

EM: Coffee, no cream, five sugars.

JH: Sweet tooth.

EM: One or two of them. How do you take yours?

JH: Cream, no sweetener.

Coffee delivered.

JH: Could you tell me how long it's been since the incident?

EM: A little bit.

JH: Do you know how long, exactly?

EM: Not long.

JH: Can you tell me where you are?

EM: The hospital.

JH: Do you know what city we're in?

EM: Helena. No. Great Falls.

JH: How about where you lived before you were here?

EM: The house on Third Street. Laura and I bought it when we first moved to Montana . . . We brought Ben home there . . . His changing table is still in there somewhere, that piece of countertop and cabinet from the kitchen—one of those pieces you come by in older houses that doesn't attach to anything in particular—we put that in his room. There's the photo of Laura folding diapers when she was still pregnant, big old belly sticking out front, folding those diapers. I think it was the day before she went into labor. No. I wasn't there. It had to have been taken earlier. Weeks before. A week?

JH: Does your son live with you?

EM: They had him all wrapped in blankets like an eggroll. No, a burrito, that's what Laura called it—a burrito roll.

JH: Does Ben live with you, Edmund?

EM: I could tell he was smart from the start, quiet and smart. Instead of pushing the car on the floor and making those *vroom-vroom* noises, he'd turn the car over and try to figure out the axles and wheels, figure out what made—

JH: Edmund.

EM: Yes.

JH: Does Benjamin live with you in the house on Third Street?

EM: Benjamin and Laura.

JH: Who is Laura?

EM: My wife.

— —

The following initial questions prompt familiar stories supplied by close friends and relatives, used to establish a sense of safety before questioning the patient about telephoning his ex-wife (occurring nightly for seventeen consecutive days).

JH: Would you mind playing a game, Edmund?

EM: Depends on the game.

JH: It's called If/Then, and it's very simple. I'll make an *if* statement, and you'll have to fill in the *then* part. For example, I could say, "If I drink too much coffee, then . . ."

EM: I won't be able to sleep.

JH: Exactly. Could we do this?

EM: All right.

JH: If I drink too much milk before bed, then . . .

EM: I'll have to use the toilet in the night.

JH: If I go camping with my son, then . . .

EM: I'll burn Ben's leg with bacon grease. Grease burns take a long time to heal because they cook the flesh more. That's what the doctor said, and the grease stays on. It's sticky, and we didn't know what we were doing out there, all of us a couple beers gone, even though it was morning—breakfast time, that's why I was cooking bacon—and Benjy didn't cry, is the thing. He didn't cry.

JH: If I drop my beer in the Smith River, then . . .

EM: I'll get wet, and so will Pete.

JH: If I call my ex-wife, then . . .

EM: Not even one tear, and the boys and I didn't take him to the hospital. We didn't realize it was serious, thought it was just on the surface, and Laura had let me take him on my own, just little Ben and his dad and his uncles, and he was so little, but he didn't cry, and when I brought him home, Laura took one look and rushed him off. I mean, we rushed off, the both of us, or more, the three of us—we rushed off to the emergency room.

JH: Edmund, listen. If I call my ex-wife, then . . .

EM: I didn't call her. I just came home, and we went to the hospital.

JH: Right now, Edmund. If I call my ex-wife right now, then . . .

Several minutes pass before Edmund speaks. He does not make eye contact.

EM: *When* I call my wife tonight, we'll talk about dinner. I'll pick something up for us on my way home.

JH: Ex-wife, Edmund.

Patient ends interview.

— —

Note: The patient's memories have become his current reality, though some are confused. His memories appear to stop after the stroke, though he has some awareness of his surroundings. The patient does not recognize his divorce, contradicting previous diagnosis of stable long-term memory.

Diagnosis: Moderate to severe brain damage producing confusion, memory loss, delusions.

Independence

—

APRIL 1980–OCTOBER 1981

Chapter 35

Ed awakens thinking about Laura pregnant with Benjamin, past midway, five months, maybe six. He needs to talk to her, and she should be here in bed with him, but she isn't, and he's learned that he has to call her now when he needs to talk to her, though it doesn't make sense, but it is a rule, and rules are rules. He reaches for the phone. It's five-thirty in the morning.

"Hello?" Laura's voice is tired.

"Good morning, sunshine."

"Ed?" He can hear her waking up, and he can see it, covers falling away, some small nightgown barely covering her. "Is everything all right?"

"Fine, fine. I just wanted to see if you're free for lunch."

"Ed, you can't call this early. We've talked about this."

"I'm worried about Benjamin." Ed doesn't know where the words come from, and he doesn't fully know that they are a lie, either. He knows they can help him get what he wants—time with Laura—and so they can be used. What are words for if not to be used?

Ed hears a man's voice in the background. "Want me to talk to him?" Ed has learned that voice belongs to a man named Tim, whose role in their lives Ed can't quite place right now, this early in the morning. He had it yesterday, understood it fully. He remembers Penelope explaining it. *Penelope*. He'll call her next.

Laura's voice returns. "What are you worried about?"

Ed doesn't know. Is he worried? "Let's talk about it over lunch."

"Ed."

"My treat. I'll see you at Dorothy's at noon."

He'll see Laura and tell her about his dream. Was it a dream? It must have been. She was so close, so near, and he touched her belly and also her face, the sweet young face he'd fallen in love with back in Michigan, but even as he conjures her face, it changes, the glasses bleed away, the hair shifts, the eyes, the form and shape, until his mind no longer holds Laura, but Penelope, pregnant and beautiful under his hand. Pen? He distinctly remembers Laura, but Laura won't return, and her memory is already tiptoeing away, slinking off to its dungeon. *Goodbye, young Laura.* No, not goodbye. He will have lunch with her, with Laura, not Pen. He says it aloud. "Lunch with Laura, not Pen. I'll see Pen tomorrow." They have a date at the library.

He is still in bed. If he lies there long enough, the instructions will come.

"Walk yourself through every step of your day, Edmund. Simplify the steps as much as possible, and acknowledge each one of them in your mind." Martin said that. Good old Martin, one of the few good aides he has on staff. No, not an aide, a therapist. Martin is a therapist. They work together in Boulder.

That feels almost right.

Ed leaves it.

When he first got home, he'd spend whole days trying to figure out where his instructions should start. Waking up from sleep required no instruction because it was subconscious. His body woke itself regularly at five-thirty a.m. But then what? Open eyes. Should his instructions include a description of the eyes? How to open them? The peeling back of the lid to reveal the orb? He would lie in bed questioning, his eyes still closed, those swatches of color playing against his irises, the oranges over the blacks over the greens. When he squeezed his lids tightly, colors exploded, and should he mention this phenomenon in his instructions? Should he practice this action upon waking every morning? One final squeeze of color-drenched darkness before opening those lids to his dark room?

Open eyes.

Roll onto left side. Ed sleeps on his back.

Open eyes.

Roll onto left side.

Swing legs over edge.

He goes through the steps and rounds a corner to his kitchen. *My kitchen!* Slick with blueberries—there they are, the squish and pulp and stickiness, a mess of them on the floor. Pete got the berries because of some health they imparted, and Ed didn't close the bag entirely before putting it back in the freezer upside down. And then it became morning (*Weeks ago? Days?*), and he gave himself instructions to *Rise* and *Go to kitchen* and *Make coffee* and *Eat something,* but there weren't instructions for upside-down unclosed blueberry bags, and though he didn't move quickly once he grabbed the bag, it seemed like a fast-forwarded moment, a dancer's spin, a lithe pivot, the bag opening, the berries breaking loose. It was a new bag, and big, and all those berries—hundreds, even thousands—flew across the kitchen. They gathered below the edge of the sink cabinets and rolled under the dishwasher; they scattershot the counter with purple-blue, mixing with the crumbs from earlier breakfasts. They built themselves into drifts, settling like dunes in the corners. And they are still there. Ed sees and remembers. They are still there under all the other accumulation.

He picks up the kitchen phone. "Pete!"

"Goddamn it, Ed, it's really early." Pete's voice is sleepier than Laura's, rough with drink, Ed is sure.

"You out boozing last night without me? Out with the boys? The Tavern. Ladies all around and dinner getting cold, isn't that right?" Before Pete can answer, because it feels like one question, all questions piling together in Ed's mind, a great collection swept up against a door that suddenly and unexpectedly opens, "Did I tell you about the blueberries?"

Silence, a long exhale, and then, "Blueberries?"

"I spilled them all over the kitchen."

"Did you clean them up?"

"Yes."

"Then why are you calling me so early?"

"No."

Pete is the only person who comes to Ed's house, and there are moments—this one, right now—when Ed can see it as Pete must see it, the kitchen spread with dishes and food and mail. Empty soup cans take up a whole portion of countertop—Dinty Moore stew and Campbell's bean with bacon, cream of mushroom, classic tomato. His Crock-Pot still holds the remains of the pot roast he cooked for Pete a month ago. Dark ratty towels are piled on the crusted floor, which is creaky in spots from all the water damage. Hair and crumbs under the cupboards, grease spatters staining the plaster above the stove, crusted tomato sauce and ranch dressing and gravy and milk, and now—blueberries, their juice seeping into the already stained and darkened linoleum, purple-blue-black mixing with the mottled brown.

He should know what to do about the spilled blueberries, but the instructions and processes won't come. He doesn't know how to start. He doesn't even remember why he got the blueberries out or why he had such a large bag of them to begin with. They must've come from Pete. That was it. His old drinking buddy who was trying to get him to eat healthier.

"How about that housekeeper we discussed?" Pete asks over the phone.

"I don't need a housekeeper."

"Ed."

He'll start using the dishwasher again, the dishwasher that isn't built in, that rolls around the kitchen on its shoddy wheels. It moves like a refrigerator, a dryer, a tall, thick-walled safe. He'll just have to screw one of the hoses to the faucet head of the sink, then put the other hose into the basin for draining. The last time he used the thing, he failed to get the drain hose where it belonged, and he caused a small flood in the kitchen. That was the first flood. Then there was the second, a small leak at first—a dribble of water out the bottom of the sink cupboard, drips that grew into a small rivulet, and then into a stream, but a small stream, nothing pressing. It flowed at a weak rate, only a centimeter wide, probably less. And it disappeared quietly through the edges of the kitchen, making for small slivers of open space between the floor and the trim. That stage lasted for a good week, but then the pipe let go completely, the last vestige of strength succumbing to the building pressure, and so when Ed walked into the kitchen for his morning coffee, there was a river running from the bottom of his sink cupboard.

He called Pete, and Pete called the plumber who'd come before, who didn't conceal his outrage when he walked in. "Jesus. You're ruining your house, you know that?" The man waded through the deluge, speaking and shouting as he went, the cuffs of his pants darkening with the water. "You know water is the number one assailant to a home? It'll touch everything it can, go everywhere, and it'll rot and mold everything it touches. Goddamn it. The break's above the damn shutoff valve. Didn't you think to shut the water off?" The plumber crouched in front of the open sink cupboard, his hand deep in the dark interior, shoulder swallowed, head cocked at an awkward angle to look back at Ed, and then the water ceased to flow. The last wave spilled out of the cupboard and scuttled across the shallow lake of the kitchen, slipped quietly down those secret passages into the basement, where it dripped in an orchestra of noise, a sloppy plunk into an existing puddle, a tinny clang on the lid of a metal can, a subtle, barely heard swallow on the upholstery of a rotting sofa.

Pete says, "I'll come over after work tonight and help with the kitchen."

"That'd be great, just great. I'll get us a six-pack."

"All right, Ed."

Ed hangs up and continues with his morning: coffee and cigarette and morning news. His recliner is there and his book, the book Pen recommended about eyes, blue eyes, the bluest, that was right. It's devastating and sexy and awful, and he'll be able to talk to her about it soon, tomorrow.

On television, the newsman speaks to a slight rise in the price of gasoline, a riot in Bristol, a lottery scandal in Pennsylvania. Eight U.S. troops are killed in a midair collision during a failed mission to rescue American embassy hostages. A British plane crashes, killing all 146 people on board. The women's winner of the Boston Marathon is exposed as a fraud: "Ruiz did not run the entire course," the anchor reports. "She is believed to have entered the race a half-mile before the finish line."

Ed chuckles and unfolds the current note sheet he keeps tucked in his book. Under the heading "Find Out," he writes, "Rosie Ruiz." He'll see what he can dig up the next time he goes to the library, what bits of Ruiz's history he can learn, trivia a hook he uses again and again. "Listen to this," he'll say, and go on to tell his son, so big now, how Ramses II's mummy was issued a passport when he was shipped to France, with his occupation reading: "King (deceased)."

"Did you know Oscar the Grouch used to be orange?"

"*Jay* used to be slang for a foolish person, so people who ignore street signs became known as *jaywalkers*."

"The only number whose letters are arranged in alphabetical order is forty. F-O-R-T-Y. The only one!"

He'll tell Laura these facts, too, and Penelope, who brings her own to the table. The last time he saw her, she told him something fascinating. He wrote it down. What was it? He flips his paper over, unfolds, and folds. Yes, here it is: "Only female mosquitoes bite you."

"Ha!"

— —

The day creeps slowly toward noon. Ed dozes in front of the television. At eleven, he opens his eyes, smokes a cigarette, and then hoists himself from his chair. "Beau!" he calls. "Time to go out!" There is no scrambling of paws on the wood floor. He calls again, and then he remembers—Beau lives with Laura now. But Laura lives here. He shakes his head. Laura lives somewhere else. They're taking some space—that's it. She got the house down on Beattie Street. She'll be back soon.

He's still in his robe, and it's time to get dressed. Yesterday's pants crouch near his bed, legs gone to puddles, rippling back on each other. They stand highest of all the floor's accumulation, buoyed by soiled paper towels, girlie mags, plates, silverware, books, mail, other, dirtier clothes. He should have left them on the dresser or draped them on a chair. Bending to pick them up is hard. He sits on the edge of the bed to ease his legs in, his left leg stiff and stubborn, the toes stuck in the pocket of the knee, fabric folded in on itself, caught and catching. He kicks and the fabric loosens. His foot passes through, emerging in the open air at the other end. The right leg goes quicker.

He misbuttons his shirt, the tails misaligned at the hem, the left side shorter than the right, but the error is hidden when he tucks it in. He isn't wearing an undershirt. The thick swatch of hair at his chest leaps from his collar. Like his beard and his head, this hair is mostly gray now. He tells himself it's dignified.

He backs into the trash can on his way out, leaving another white scuff in the dull plastic. He's left lines all over town, his car a great swatch of scratches. He tries to remember the source of all of them, but those moments are as blurry as the instructions for spilled blueberries.

Dorothy's isn't far. It was an easy walk once, but it's steep downhill there and steep uphill back. Ed can't handle either anymore. He drives everywhere he needs to go.

Though he easily could qualify for a handicapped sticker on his license plate, he refuses. He will park in no designated place, accept no charity. The handicapped are not his; he is not theirs. This definition is clear in his mind—always. It does not cloud or waver or need writing down. It is *known*. He knows it like he knows his son, Benjamin, and his wife, Laura, and his own name.

Ex-wife.

He gets to the restaurant twenty minutes early and orders a draft beer. "Anything you have that's cold."

The waitress laughs and pats his shoulder. "You got it, Ed." He should know her name—he knew it once—but he doesn't anymore. She's been waiting tables here for years.

He lights a cigarette and shuffles the sugar packets.

His beer arrives. "You meeting Pete today?"

"Nope. Laura. She'll be here around noon."

"I'll check back."

He usually eats with Pete at Dorothy's, and Benjamin, his boy, sometimes those bastard senators he's still trying to squeeze funding from. Before them, it was his alone with Laura. They had their first meal in Helena here, and they ordered steaks, thick and bloody, baked potatoes, beer and more beer, and then they went back to the Third Street house and made love.

He is good at passing time or, rather, letting time pass him. Minutes ebb by, eddying in circles before they flow on and away, minutes and then hours, days, months. Time passes while Ed sips his coffee and beer, smokes his cigarettes, eats his food, pinches and pulls the fabric of his pants. His brain keeps ticking away, counting seconds, marking them off in folds and drumbeats. He was young—forty—barely a gray hair on his head, and then he was old. It happened in the time between sitting down in Dorothy's alone and seeing Laura walk in. It happened that quickly.

He lumbers to standing. "Hello there, beautiful."

"Hi, Ed." Laura seats herself across from him. "I don't have long."

"We'll order quick, then," he says, and chuckles.

She orders a salad, and he orders a burger, fries, ranch dressing.

"Why are we having lunch, Ed?"

"Old friends can't have lunch?"

"You said you were worried about Benjy."

Did he? Ed doesn't remember saying he was worried about Ben. He doesn't remember saying it or feeling it. Ben is fine. Ben is building block towers and climbing trees.

"Ed?"

He searches: *Worry.*

"Was that just an excuse to have lunch?"

Worry.

"Ed, you can't keep doing this."

Worry. Ed worries the inside of his pocket, fabric between his fingers.

"Ed." Her voice is lower, quieter, and calm. "Ed, Lynn would like to know if you need another beer."

The waitress is there. *Lynn*. That's it, her name. And what's more—her body. It was in his bed, he remembers, bare and lovely. "Yes," he says. "Yes, ma'am." He's found a missing piece. He was searching, and something was found. The search is off. He is back here, in his favorite restaurant, with his beautiful wife, her voice that same beautiful voice that sang around campfires and in the living room and in Ben's nursery, lulling the boy to sleep. Beautiful Laura. They spend their lunch talking about the weather and gas prices, and she tells him about the kitchen remodel she's doing with her husband, Tim, and Ed sees the Third Street kitchen shift under her words, growing an island and new countertops, a refrigerator with ice and water in the door, a window box for herbs.

When their meal is done, Ed pays with cash, insisting until Laura acquiesces, and they walk to the parking lot together, slowly, leisurely, to get every minute they can.

"Same time next week?"

"No, Ed." Laura closes his car door and taps her fingers on the window, her goodbye. He should've walked her to her car, he realizes as he pulls away, should've been the gentleman. *Next week*. He'll do it next week.

Chapter 36

— *Laura* —

The phone wakes me too early again, Ed's voice on the other end, singing, "Good morning, beautiful."

I have to be incredulous. This is my role now, everyone agrees.

"We have to retrain him, Laura," says Pete and Bonnie and Tim. "You can't indulge this behavior."

But I disagree. What can I do for this Ed other than answer his early-morning calls?

I say his name with exasperation, though, and I make a point of rolling my eyes at Tim when he sits up and turns on his bedside lamp. "It's five-thirty," I scold. "I've told you too many times not to call this early. Do I need to change my number?"

"If you did, I'd find it out. Meet me for lunch."

Tim mouths, *Hang up*.

"I can't, Ed. I'm working at the gallery all day." I've started showing my work at a small gallery downtown, working its retail hours several days a week.

"I'll bring you lunch, then!"

Tim is shaking his head. I've spoken too soon, telling Ed my plans, sleep muddying my brain. I'm not supposed to tell Ed where I am. "No, Ed."

Tim takes the phone, and I swallow the resentment like I always do. He is firm and gentle, and *right*, he reminds me. *This isn't good for anyone.* "Ed? It's Tim. Listen, you can't call this early. And Laura needs to work today, so you can't stop by the gallery, all right? You want to meet me for lunch? I'd love to catch up."

I lie back on my pillow, childishly delighted by whatever Ed is saying to scrunch Tim's face into such stern disappointment. Ed won't have lunch with Tim. Ed ignores Tim, forgets Tim, and when he happens to place him in his role as my husband, Ed despises Tim.

"Fine, Ed, that's just fine, but you can't go bothering Laura today, either." Tim says goodbye and reaches over me to hang up the phone. "We need to switch sides. Let me start fielding the calls."

"You shouldn't offer to have lunch with him."

"Why not? I know the guy's been through a lot, but I think I have the right to tell him to his face not to call my wife at five in the morning."

"Would you be doing that for me or for you?"

He has asked me the same kind of question any number of times. *Is this for you or for him, Laura?*

We're facing each other in bed, and he puts a hand on my face. It's the same rough hand I was taken with that first time I met him. The hand of my old firefighter. The hand of my present builder. The hand of everything that is not Ed.

Tim says, "I'd be doing it for both of us, Laura, and for our boys."

He has never before referred to Benjy as his own, and I am both warmed by his investment in my son and furious with his usurpation of Benjy's father.

"My being in Ed's life doesn't hurt the boys."

Tim's hand moves to my collarbone, his mouth to my neck. "It doesn't help them, either," he whispers, and I want to be angry, but he is kissing me and his hand has snaked inside my nightgown, those calluses against my skin. My hair is a ratty mess, and we both have terrible breath, but he is rough and handsome and—in this early-morning moment—he is not boring.

It's wrong that I think of morning sex with Ed as Tim moves on top of me. That I hear Ed's voice on the phone. *Good morning, beautiful.* But the yearning for Ed's attention is ingrained, and I channel it here in this moment with Tim. I sleep with them both—Tim who has never stopped seeing me and Ed who sees me only now that there is so little else he can see.

— —

At noon, a rich couple from Santa Fe is perusing the back hall where several of my paintings hang. I've given them a quiet, self-effacing pitch: "Not a professional by any means. Just something I've always loved to do."

"Oh, sweetie," the wife says, "your work is *astounding*."

The praise is too generous, but still, it warms me.

My work is finally reflecting this place, but only its dirty sides. That burned-out third floor at Boulder, yellow scars left by mines, long trains of railroad cars covered in graffiti, rolled bales of rusted barbed wire.

I am giving the couple some space to make their decision when Ed walks in, a Styrofoam box in his hands.

"Got us a Reuben to split from the Gold Bar." He pops open the container to show a hefty sandwich, a heap of greasy fries, a sad pickle spear. The Gold Bar makes a good Reuben, not that I eat Reubens much anymore. They've always been Ed's favorite sandwich.

The food is stinking up the gallery, clouding the sage and lavender candles I burn every time I work—Montana chic. The Santa Fe folks don't want takeout in Styrofoam.

"I don't eat out here on the floor, Ed, and I have customers."

"I'll just take this back to your office." He is already walking that way, shouting—too loudly—over his shoulder, "I'll save you half."

I watch his asymmetrical walk—the lift and throw of his left leg, every step a swing, something like a golf stroke, full of focused attention, direction, aim. He lifts his foot, pulls it to the side, and then throws the whole limb forward. He should be using his cane.

He walks right past the Santa Fe couple.

Please don't speak to them.

Ed stops and leans over, and I cringe at the thought of his breath—smoky and unbrushed and hot. "That lady's brilliant, you know. I'd buy every piece of hers I could."

"We *agree*." The woman leans toward Ed, intrigued. "That smells *delicious*."

"If you're looking for a good lunch, the Gold Bar down the way makes a hell of a meal. Not fancy like this place, but damn fine food."

"Oh, Lester, how *delightful*. The Gold Bar! We'll have to go."

I watch with horror. Then amusement. Then resentment. Then gratitude. This Ed is such a stranger, such a wonderful, disgusting stranger.

He leaves the couple and closes himself in the back office. I know he'll spill all over the bills and invoices piled on the desk, leave everything smeared with ketchup and grease.

The couple returns to me, the woman's face aglow. "What a sweet man. Does he show his work here, too?"

"He's not an artist."

"Well, he has the personality of one!" The woman takes the arm of her husband. "We're going to take three of yours, dear. *Coupling, Twine,* and *Ghosts*. I'm in love with *February,* too, but I don't think we have space in the car. I might have you ship it to me when we get home."

It's my biggest sale, and they must see the surprise on my face.

"Oh, honey. You're going to be a star."

It is so sweet and so far from the truth. My hands shake as I take the check from the man, and I want to hug the woman, but she makes no move toward me. I hold the door for them as they bundle their butcher-papered paintings out to their car.

"Where's this Gold Bar your fellow mentioned?"

"Two blocks down on the left. You can't miss it."

"Brilliant. Thanks again, dear."

My biggest sale, and now my benefactors are off to the Gold Bar, per Ed's recommendation. It's awful how pleased I am.

We have a decent bar of our own in the back, the varied leftovers of receptions, and I pull out a half-full bottle of Jameson, hold it up for Ed to see.

"Well, all right!"

I pour a couple fingers' worth each into two coffee mugs, pull a chair up opposite Ed at the desk. As I knew they would be, the papers are littered with food, and Ed's beard is flecked with dressing, a few strings of kraut. He hasn't touched my half of the sandwich, though, which nearly makes me cry. He's never been one to share food.

I raise my mug and clink it against his. "I sold three paintings, Ed. My biggest sale ever. And you helped."

"Nah. I didn't. It's all you, Laura. Didn't I tell you, you're amazing? That we'd move here, and you'd have the time and space to really devote yourself to your art, and here you are—famous." His smile is deep and rich and flushed with pride.

Chapter 37

— *Laura* —

Pete and Bonnie are over. We just finished dinner, and the murmur of the television rises up from downstairs, a spatter of voices, and then the boys laughing. Bonnie and Pete's backs reflect in the giant window behind them, night here already, the days turning short. My yard is out there, my gardens, my patio. My husband is doing the dishes, and I am chatting with friends, and my children are laughing downstairs. It is all too easy, and I know from Pete and Bonnie's faces they are about to shatter it, all this comfort, so I sip my wine and close my eyes and tell myself to appreciate it. There is nothing wrong with ease.

Still, I'm hungry for whatever it is they have to tell me.

"Pete thinks it's time to get Ed into a facility." Bonnie spits out the words and sets to her wine, drinking it like water.

"But his memory keeps improving," I say. "He's so much clearer than he was when he first came home."

Pete says, "You're further removed from it than I am. The house is out of control. There's the water damage, but even worse is the daily mess. There's rotting food everywhere and dirty clothes and garbage. You're right that his memory is improving, but it's scattered. And the other parts are declining." Pete rubs his eyes, hiding behind his hands. "I just think we were too optimistic."

"You think we were wrong to bring him home at all?"

Neither Bonnie nor Pete replies, but their faces say it: Ed never should have been allowed to live independently.

"He still listens to you, love," Bonnie says.

"You were the ones to tell me to step away!" I say it jokingly, but I want them to feel it, their flip-flopping.

"Well, that never really happened," Bonnie says, shooting a look over my shoulder toward Tim, there in his own world in the kitchen. "You see him at least once a week."

"He shows up at the gallery."

"None of that matters," Pete says. He sounds tired, all the joy of the evening wrung from him. So many of my Ed thoughts center on us, Ed and me, but now I think about Pete, pal-turned-caregiver, and I realize how hard this must be for him, too. Ed was his best friend, his colleague, his drinking buddy, and now he is Pete's ward, one more patient on the roster.

I have been in the house only a few times since Ed came back, most recently when Pete was out of town and Ed thought he'd left a burner on, remembering at a truck stop halfway to Bozeman. He goes for long purposeless drives, this new Ed. The house was shocking, jarring, sad, and I walked through it like an anthropologist through a lost city, noting the evidence of habitation, the accumulation of things. Jack-off rags by the recliner, more around his bed, pornographic videos, their thick mail-order packaging strewn about the living room, the videos piled on top of the VCR. *Julie Gets Jammed,* alongside *The Godfather,* alongside *Puffy Nipples,* stacked atop *Jaws.* Overflowing ashtrays, cigarette butts on the floor, burn scuffs in the wood. The plate on the side table was covered in foil, layers upon layers that served as a fresh surface each time he ate, earlier meals moldering there under the thin metal sheets. I'd needed the restroom, but I couldn't bring myself to go in there, not with the rest of the house as it was.

Tacked to the wall near his desk was a poem by Dylan Thomas.

And books everywhere.

And his guitar there by the woodstove.

These are pieces of the old Ed, and I know there must be a piece in there still that recognizes how awful the rest is. It's this part that allows only Pete inside his house nowadays, Pete who has witnessed worse out in Boulder, Pete who will understand.

But Pete is done understanding, and I know Ed will feel only betrayal when his old friend comes to him with a plan to move him away from his home. Ed will never let himself live in a facility of any kind. I know this clearly. It is as true as any truth I've learned about Edmund Malinowski. He will live independently until he dies.

"You'll never get him to move," I say, rummaging in my purse for the cigarettes I now buy and smoke openly.

Without turning from the sink, Tim says, "Outside, please."

I don't go outside.

"Give me one of those."

I pass a cigarette to Bonnie, then reach across and light it for her. Pete shakes his head when I offer him one. "Got to follow the rules of a man's house," he says.

"Maybe you could talk to Ed?" Bonnie says through her smoke. "If we can get everyone on the same page, maybe it'll be enough to convince him."

I smile at her, at Pete. I can see Tim reflected in the glass, drying his hands on a towel. He is glaring at me, but I know he won't ask me to go outside again, since Bonnie is smoking, too. Tim would never argue in front of guests, even these two, my oldest friends, compliments of my ex-husband.

"I'll talk to Ed, but I promise you—he'll never do it."

— —

Ed asks me to meet him at the library, a first. I know Penelope works here. I see her occasionally when I bring the boys. I've assumed they see each other, too, but this new Ed knows not to talk about her to me, and most often, I'm able to pretend she doesn't exist.

This new Ed is also forgetful, though, and I find the two of them in the back corner of the 900s sitting in deep chairs, books open in their laps. Jealousy rises in me, rich and angry as those days back in Boulder. I'm tempted to make a scene. *You wanted him, Penelope, well, here you go. He's all yours now. The great Edmund Malinowski. Congratulations.*

I swallow it and interrupt them with a quiet "Excuse me?"

Ed is slow to lift his head and slower still to recognize me. When he does, fear blanches his face, and he is immediately talking, a great stream of excuses. "It's not what it looks like, Laura. There's nothing happening between us. That's long in the past, I promise. We're just working together—isn't that right, Pen? She's helping me with something at the institution. I'm helping her with her reading group. We're trying out different pieces to see if they'll work with the bigger group. I should've called and told you I was going to be late—"

"Ed." Penelope has placed her hand on his arm, and his words dry up as quickly as they came.

The library is quiet around us.

Ed is looking at his lap, a caught boy. Guilty.

The only other time the three of us have shared a room was back in Ed's office in Boulder. He looked the same then. And the emotion is real. He is guilty. Then and now. His relationship with Penelope has never been nothing.

I should let them get back to their book club. It's good for Ed.

But the girl who helped ruin our marriage is sitting in front of me, her hand on my ex-husband's arm. And she isn't a girl anymore.

"How long in the past are we talking?" I ask.

Penelope says my name now. If she touches my arm, I'll slap her face.

"Come on now, Pen. I think I deserve to know just how long my husband was fucking around with you. It's fair, don't you think? I mean, it's all water under the bridge—you two are clearly doing great, and I'm remarried, but humor me. Are we talking months? Years? And I'd love to know the start date, just for clarification purposes, of course."

Ed is still looking at his lap, and Penelope is standing and storming away. "Come with me, Laura."

I hesitate, but my curiosity is stronger than my indignation, and I follow her upstairs to the administrative offices. She closes us inside a small room. There is part of me that hopes we fistfight, a great scrappy brawl here in the library. We'll walk out with cuts and fat lips and missing clumps of hair.

But she leans against the desk and sighs. "I was in love with your husband. You're right about that. But nothing really happened. I kissed him once, and he pushed me away. Then he discharged me from the hospital. I quit taking my meds in the hope that I'd get to go back to Boulder and be with him again, but instead, I sent myself into the nonstop seizures that landed me in Great Falls with Dr. Wong, who did actually save me. I was so sure it would be Ed who'd be the one. I know he came to visit me when I was up there. I know he missed your son's birth. I don't remember seeing him then. I remember him in Boulder, and then I remember him here at the library when he came to find me after you two split up."

He went back to her. It hurts more than it should.

"There was a big part of me that still loved him, of course. But a bigger part that hated him. I know you have to see me as a villain, but I was kept in a place for retarded people, people who couldn't feed themselves or dress themselves, people who couldn't talk. I was given shoe-tying lessons. I was put in the rapid-toilet-training program. Against all that, I had the attentions of my handsome doctor. He was all I had. I'm sorry if it was part of what ruined your marriage, but I'm sorrier still for what it did to me. He was all I knew, and it took me so long to be able to let anyone else in."

"You never slept together?"

"We never slept together. But I don't know if it'd be much different if we had."

I suppose that's true. It was an affair, whether there was sex or not. An affair between an older doctor and his teenage patient.

Still, I'm relieved.

"Why are you helping him now?" I ask.

She looks past me to the drab walls of the little office. It's cold and unadorned. Vacant, I assume.

"Because it would be worse if I didn't." She meets my eyes, and it's clear this is all she'll give me. She walks to the door. "Did you need to talk to him? I can give you a few minutes."

There's more I want to say to her. I want to tell her she might not be a villain, but she's no heroine, either. I want to tell her what it felt like to walk into Ed's office and feel the energy between them. Wrong as it might have been, it was real and strong. I want to yell at her and then thank her. I want to accuse her and then forgive her. She is not the only reason Ed and I divorced, but she helped, and I am grateful. It is awful but true: Our marriage wasn't good, but it would be even worse to be his wife now. And it would be even harder to leave.

Ed is dozing where we left him.

"Ed," I say gently. "Ed, wake up."

He lifts his head and blinks, smiles broadly. "Hello there, beautiful. What a treat!" He looks around, smiling through his confusion. "Looks like we're in the wrong place, doesn't it? We should be down at Dorothy's, throwing back a couple shots."

"You're in the middle of something here." I tell myself I'm not mentioning Penelope's name because I don't want to confuse him. "I just need to talk to you about something real quick."

He smiles even bigger. "I knew this would happen, Laura. The house is all ready for you. Just as you left it." We are back in Dorothy's the day I told him about Charlie. He's sure I'm coming back. Most days, he doesn't know I'm gone.

I can't talk to him about assisted living. There's nowhere for him to put the information.

"Okay, Ed," I say, letting him keep the story for the little time it'll last until Penelope arrives. I tap the open book in his lap. "Better get back to it, love. We'll catch up later."

"I'll take you out."

"Okay, Ed."

I kiss him on the cheek, and when I look back at him from the end of the aisle, his head is bent to the pages of his book, stern concentration on his face.

Penelope is sifting through papers at the information desk. "He's all yours," I say as I pass her, though he isn't. He is ours. Together, we are Ed's dysfunctional parents—I am the one who left and started a new, comfortable life, leaving our needy son in the care of the weaker parent, already a few steps behind, weighed down by her own challenges.

We have our own successes and failures.

And neither of us will get him into a facility.

Chapter 38

— *Laura* —

The reception is the fanciest event the gallery has ever thrown, thanks in large part to Bonnie's help with the setup. "We're doing real goddamned glasses, Laura. None of those ugly plastic cups you use for lesser folks. And Pete insists on bringing Ed, but I'll tell you straight out, I don't know why you invited him. *And,* since you did, and that's all said and done, I just want you to know I'm not playing babysitter. This is my best friend's Big Night, and I'm not spending it nursing your ex-husband."

Bonnie rarely talks about Ed anymore, but her speech is bitter and angry when she does. "It's like having a third giant child. Pete's there all the time, taking care of him," she said the last time she was over. We were alone drinking wine and smoking cigarettes. "I'm sorry. You don't need to hear this. Thank God you escaped when you did. Can you imagine still being married to him? In his current state?"

I can. I do.

"Please shower," I told him on the phone this morning. "And dress up. It's going to be on the fancy side."

"Anything for you, my love."

I don't correct his endearments. There is so much of him in this new series of mine. Let him believe he's my husband again, if only for tonight.

I gave George a postcard at the grocery store. "It's like our art class, you remember?"

"Yes! Ms. Law-Raw! Yes!"

George is still doing well. I noticed the smallest patch of gray hair above his left ear the last time I saw him, and it seems unfair. I can't imagine him tightening down into an old man, his skin wrinkling, his back stooping. Youth is the strength he shakes in the face of his adversity.

My benefactors in Santa Fe have assured me they'll be here.

"It's going to be such a success," Bonnie promises. She is already drinking.

Evening ushers in the first arrivals—strangers who saw a poster somewhere.

"Welcome!" Bonnie shouts, playing hostess. "This is the artist"—a hand on my arm—"and she's happy to answer any of your questions." They help themselves to glasses of wine and plates of food, then stroll along the walls. More people arrive before I have a chance to speak to the first ones, a stream through the door until the gallery is crowded and loud.

George appears with his parents, and all three of them hug me close. From behind George's back, he proffers a canvas.

"For me?" I ask, and he nods, wide-toothed and generous.

"You." He points at my neck. "Lah-Raw." Slightly abstract but a portrait all the same, my likeness clear.

"Thank you, George."

"He's been working on it nonstop since he got the invitation," George's mother says.

"There's my girl!" Ed's voice breaks us apart, startling George into a hop-skip backward, his painting still gripped in his hands. Ed lumbers in and gathers me against him, too intimate, too assuming. I make eye contact with Tim across the room. *You need help?* he mouths, and I shake my head, pushing Ed back to arm's distance. I note the combed hair, the cologne, the suit. He looks fancy, just as I asked, and he smells better than he has in years.

"Ed, you remember George and his parents, don't you?"

I watch the question spread across Ed's face, watch him parse it. I imagine his brain, a dusty tunnel, every question a torch he has to relight, illuminating dark corners, uncovering dusty skeletons. The smile on his face shows something awakening, bones growing muscle and tissue, whole figures rising up and setting to work.

"George!" he shouts, shoving his hand at the man. "Of course! How the hell are you?"

I don't know if his recognition is real. George's face registers terror and confusion. I take the painting from his hands so he can shake, that social habit well ingrained.

"Doc-Tor. Ed?"

"That's right, George," his mother says. "Your old doctor from Boulder." She turns her attention to Ed. "You were always so wonderful with George. Besides Laura's classes, time with you was what he missed most when he left. We'll never forget what you did for our boy."

George's father shakes next, and I watch Ed's face, his frozen smile. He doesn't remember them.

"So good to see you both," the mother says, leading her men away.

"Thank you for the painting, George!" I say.

"Yor. Well. Come." George smiles over his shoulder, the confusion over his former doctor dismissed by my praise. Hopefully. I try to see Ed and George together again, sharing in the same unmooring, the two of them floating in a deep sea of unfiled papers, memories and names and knowledge all churning together. Ed was the one to reach out a hand before, to drag George to the edge of the pool and give him a place to hold on and catch his breath. But together now, they would both drown, I am sure, each unconsciously pushing the other under to get his own head up, to gulp in just one more breath of clear air.

Ed can't save anyone anymore.

"Get you a drink, beautiful?"

"That'd be great, Ed."

I watch him limp to the drinks table, smiling along the way, still able to play the socializer. The food clearly beckons him, but he takes two glasses of wine and returns to me quickly. I remember all the times over the course of our marriage that he offered to get me a drink and never returned, engrossed somewhere else, consumed by everything but me.

He sets a glass in my hand and raises his to toast. "To your success!"

"Thank you, Ed."

"Will you walk me through?"

"No monopolizing, Edmund. I need to talk with some other people, too."

He laughs his rich guffaw. "Go work your magic. I bet you sell everything."

He limps away again, and Tim announces himself with his hand on my back. "Everything okay?"

"Everything's great." I slip my arm around his waist, this other husband of mine. "It's wonderful," I say, believing it, feeling something like comfort, a settling.

"Ed's not too much?"

I shake my head. "Look how much he cleaned up."

Tim kisses my cheek and moves back into the crowd. He will sing my praises, like he always does, and I hear that therapist asking me again what Tim thinks. *Does he find it boring?* She was asking about sex in particular, but there's also the question of our whole marriage. *Is it boring, Tim?* And I am starting to go after him—to ask? to prove something?—when the Santa Fe couple pushes their way in, demanding that I walk them through each piece.

They call everything "exquisite," and when they ask about purchasing, I direct them to the gallery owner. She's handling sales tonight because I don't want to deal with logistics. I want to mingle and drink and eat, bask in attention, be the star. It's a new role, and I love it possibly too much. I talk to strangers and friends. I refill my wine and eat very little, pleasantly. I forget that I have a question for my husband.

The Santa Fe couple recognizes Ed, and they make a great fuss about the Gold Bar and its incredible sandwiches. Ed plays his part perfectly, showering them with his smile and his laugh. Tim is talking to Bonnie in front of the loosest painting of the show—rows and rows of bones lined up like writing, growing larger and fuller as they write themselves down the canvas, expanding into whole limbs and parts by the end. Pete is pouring himself another glass of wine, right up to the rim of the glass. He's worn down, and I make a mental note to touch base with him. Grab a drink, just the two of us. Let him confide all the hard things Bonnie no longer has the patience for.

My eyes are moving between these people—this disjointed family I've somehow acquired—when Penelope slides into the empty space next to me. She doesn't belong here, but something in me knows I'll never rid myself of her, so her appearance isn't a surprise. Just a disappointment.

"You never showed us much of your own work when you were our teacher." She looks around. "They're all pieces of Ed, right?"

Of course this girl would see that.

"No," I say. Over her head, I see the Santa Fe woman throw her head back in laughter. Ed has his notes in his hand. He must have told her one of his latest jokes.

"I'm moving," Penelope says. "My boyfriend got a job in Missoula, and the library there has an opening. We're not leaving for a month or so, but . . ."

I turn my full attention to her. Missoula is two hours west, and though I'd prefer more distance—how about California? New York? Florida?—it is still far enough away to create a real absence.

"I'm sorry to show up like this. I didn't know how to get ahold of you, and then I saw a flyer for tonight, and I just wanted you to know in case Ed gets confused."

"Are you going to tell him you're leaving?"

"Yes, but I don't think he'll understand."

"Ed understands leaving."

He forgets the details of my departure. He forgets the time frame. But I know he still feels it, and that feeling fuels behaviors—the excuses he makes up when he's late or not where he's supposed to be. He's lost so many threads, but I know he'll absorb Penelope's absence the same way. It will haunt him, like mine does. And he'll look for us everywhere.

He finds me, again and again, and I envy Penelope's ability to truly disappear.

"Good luck out there, Penelope."

"Laura—"

I walk away, toward Ed and my Santa Fe people. I've given Penelope Gatson enough of my life. Now I will have to take on elements of hers. How will I explain to Tim that I need to add reading time to my Ed responsibilities? Or that I need to hire some sweet young thing to meet with Ed regularly at the library? I find myself wishing the brothel were still open—it'd solve at least one of our problems.

"There she is!" Ed hollers. "Woman of the hour! Woman of the year! Isn't my wife a brilliant artist?"

"Ex-wife, Ed."

The Santa Fe couple do their best not to look shocked.

Penelope slips out the door, and I'm relieved that Ed didn't notice her. I couldn't do that tonight—watch them together.

"I love when everyone's amiable," the Santa Fe woman says. "And yes, my dear, our Laura is a brilliant artist. We've bought nearly half the show." She laughs her wealthy laugh and takes her husband to the wine table.

I'm alone with Ed. I feel his hand on my lower back and his breath at my neck. "See?" he whispers. "My talented girl. I always knew you'd make it."

I could tell him that one show in a small-town gallery is far from making it, but instead I let the compliment stand. Ed was my first benefactor, and he has remained my most loyal. I couldn't see that when we were married, but it's obvious now. Tim respects my work, but he ultimately doesn't care what I do for a profession. Ed, though—he loves me in large part because I'm an artist. He couldn't understand why I'd want to work in a boutique because he believed so strongly that I should be home painting.

He didn't know how to communicate that, though, and I didn't have the patience to dig for it.

His hand moves circles on my back. Like Penelope in this gallery, it doesn't belong there, but I have grown used to this truth as well: Ed may feel my absence, but he will claim me as his own whenever he can.

Chapter 39

There are new headaches, a fluid sort of pain Ed can't quite articulate and so chooses to ignore. They flutter around the scars on his scalp, then plumb below, through his skull. They are fishing lines without hooks, but they aren't too bad. Except when they make him sick.

Vitality replaces them today, though, firing through the bright spots of Ed's brain. He is full—alive, vigorous, robust. The day is rainy and cold, but he is warm and alive, summer inside of winter. Time disappears and then returns, like the creek he takes Benjamin to, up in the Big Belt Mountains where they camp, the water rumbling by, spilling down from its limestone canyon. A mile above the campground, it stops, and most folks turn around there, short-timers, disbelievers, but Ed knows the creek's secret, how it disappears underground for a mile before reappearing, and so he always takes his son farther, and the boy delights in the water's resurrection, just as Ed delights in his arrival, here, now.

The creek's name is the name of a fish, *Trout*.

The automatic doors slide open, all those stacks of books before him, and among them, his sweet girl, Penelope.

She is at the information desk. "Give me one minute to finish this up." She pats a stack of papers, and he walks to their spot: two deep chairs tucked away behind the 900s, theirs alone.

When Penelope appears, he is struck—again, always—by her sexiness, such a stunning young thing, and here in a creamy dress, legs bare below the knee, long thin arms.

"You get prettier every day."

"Flatterer."

Ed laughs. He's always been a flatterer, a charmer. "So smooth," Laura used to say when he complimented her dress or her hair or her perfume, her latest painting. "So smooth." The women after Laura said the same thing. He smiles at the memory of them, twelve or so, beautiful and wicked and not his wife but lovely all the same. Complimenting their beauty was easy, natural, innate, and Laura used it as one of her reasons to leave. "You may love me best, Ed, but that's still not enough."

He does love her best, but here is Pen, sitting down across from him. Her face seems sad, but her words are normal. "How are you enjoying the book?"

The possibility of sadness vanishes as his mind fills. He finished this book in one sitting, an ancient story about a king, two thirds god, one third human, and then he flipped back to the introduction to read it completely, and then he reread the whole thing. It read like the poetry Pen first introduced him to, glowing words that moved on their own, more about sound than meaning, water over rocks, wind in branches—something not said but felt. He couldn't determine what it was he was feeling, all of it a labyrinth in the corridors of his mind, sometimes tactile, sometimes wispy, ethereal, sometimes vicious. *His body lay on her; six days and seven nights Enkidu attacked, fucking the priestess.* Ed read those lines again and again. Like Enkidu, he glutted himself on the richness of the scene.

Longing comes in the form of gaps and holes in Ed's mind. Penelope fills a gap, a need he has for a sexy young ex-patient. The books they read together fill another gap—one for the knowledge he accrued and then applied in Boulder. They're reading the oldest narrative in the world, older than Homer, older than the Bible, older than the God Ed doesn't believe in. But still so relevant to his work. Penelope is teaching Homer to the reading group, isn't she? And Keats wrote those particular lines after he first read Chapman's translation of Homer. Lines that Skinner then quoted in his discussion of *Reporting Things Felt*. Ed knows the words . . . *Then felt I like some watcher of the skies* . . . Yes, that's the first line, and it rhymes with *eyes* later, and a planet in between, a planet discovered, and then later, the Pacific Ocean, new and immense.

He pulls out his notes and reads *Keats, re: Homer* on his list.

. . . *Or like stout Cortez when with eagle eyes / He star'd at the Pacific—*

"Skinner quoted Keats to show the practice of association," he tells Penelope. "We describe how we feel by describing conditions that evoke the same feelings." Sharing this book with her is like lying in bed with a woman. His wife. Laura. He didn't do that enough—lie in bed with his wife.

Penelope smiles. "How do Skinner and Keats relate to *The Sunlight Dialogues*?"

The Sunlight Dialogues. Where were Gilgamesh and Keats, Enkidu and the priestess? Ed tries to trace it back, to light the same bulbs that led him here, but they stay dim. Dark. No sunlight.

He brings his hand to his forehead.

"It's fine," Penelope is already saying, dismissing the slip. She nods toward the paper in his hands. "You have your notes."

"I have my notes!"

The library is eerily quiet, even the regulars missing. Taken away by something, a great flood possibly, cleansing in its destruction. Ea told Utnapishtim to go back to his people with a message. *At dawn bread he will pour down on you—showers of wheat.* "Bread and wheat have dual meanings in Akkadian. The word for *bread* also meant *darkness,* and the word for *wheat* also meant *misfortune.*" Ed says it aloud. He read it somewhere.

"Ed? Your notes?"

He looks at the paper in his hands. " 'The whiteness, the hairlessness, the oversized nose all gave him the look of a philosopher pale from too much reading, or a man who has slept three nights in the belly of a whale.' "

"I love that part, too."

Ed thinks of Jonah, one of his mother's favorite tales, foreboding, threatening. *Be good, Eddy, or you'll be thrown from the ship and gobbled up.* He hears his *babcia: Jak sobie pościelesz, tak sięwyśpisz*. "Right, Eddy? You remember: 'How you make your bed, that is how you sleep.' "

Penelope says, "Let's talk about Clumly's wife."

The wife.

Ed flips the pages in his book, that one spot he underlined, he loved. He reads, "'Clumly's wife was a blind woman with bright glass eyes and small, pinched features and a body as white as his own. Her small shoulders sagged and her neck was long, so that her head seemed to sway above her like a hairy sunflower.'"

"Did the priestess remind you of anything?"

The question makes no sense. There are no priestesses here. He looks at her quizzically.

"From Gilgamesh?" she says.

The word is familiar to him, like the remembered flavor of a food he can no longer taste. *Gilgamesh*. Didn't he just speak of it? A book, a story, a film. Something they discussed. They were talking about Clumly's wife, and before that, Jonah, and before that, wheat and misfortune.

"Never mind," Penelope says. He can feel her hand on his knee. "What were you saying about Clumly's wife?" Ed doesn't know what he was saying. There is this book in his hands, *The Sunlight Dialogues*. He was reading it, he knows, and talking about it, but even the bits he already recalled are eluding him, dipping out of his reach, playful and mean. *Damn it. Just remember*. He knows Penelope, sweet beautiful Pen—she's right there across from him in her own soft chair, and they've been having a conversation, one of their great conversations, and it's about this book that he knows he read. He's losing the story, though, the characters, the place, left with disassociated fragments—a burned face, a war, a beard, noble queens, King James, bakery trucks—none of it makes sense, though it *had*. He knows it. "Edmund?" It was in his hands and his mind and his mouth, more than the dulled taste of cigarettes, all that richness, and Penelope here, his girl. "Edmund, are you all right?"

The rain is heavy and loud. He coughs and tilts his head, those damn fishing lines in his brain, and the nausea comes immediately. He pulls a handkerchief from his pocket to cover his mouth and catch the liquid he can feel in his throat.

Escape. You must escape.

Ed shakes his head and struggles from his chair. He limps toward the restroom, flinging that left leg ahead as quickly as he can, throwing it, pitching. *Move,* he commands. He can vomit in his house, in his bed, all over his floor, in the bathroom, but he can't throw up here, not in the library, not in front of Penelope.

"Edmund! Edmund, are you all right?"

He hears her voice behind him, but he can't stop.

The restroom door is under his hand, and he swings it forward, lurching to the closest stall, not quite making it to the toilet but getting near enough to excuse. His stomach heaves—beer and his lunch from the A&W, some breakfast. Everything his stomach can lay hands on comes out, and Ed holds himself up between the stall walls, braced by his thick arms, bent at the hips, his muck sullying his shoes, spattering his pants, covering the toilet seat he hasn't had time to lift.

When the fit finally stops, Ed rights himself sorely, his back aching from the effort of heaving and the strain of bending. He stands in his own vomit. It's too much, he realizes, too far off target, too unpleasant.

He backs out of the stall and walks to the sinks, disappointed by his reflection. His beard is strewn with the mess, and he ducks his head to try to wash it in the nearest basin.

The bathroom door squeaks open. "Everything okay in here?" One of the librarians. Ed recognizes his voice. "Oh, man. You all right?"

Ed lifts his head. "Guess something didn't agree with me. I'll get this. It's all right."

"All right." The man creeps away.

It can't be too bad, then, if he's able to leave like that. Ed stops working on his face and pulls a handful of paper towels out of the dispenser. He returns to the stall and tries to wipe at the toilet seat. Everything moves without becoming cleaner. He knows he's standing in a mess, and he knows he has to get to the place where the mess is gone, but he doesn't know the steps. These paper towels have to be part of it, but they aren't doing their job. They are making things

worse. He drops them on the ground and starts moving the wad around with his foot. No, that isn't it.

"Edmund?" The voice is a woman's this time, Penelope.

"Everything's fine! This is the men's room!"

"Edmund, I'm coming in."

He tries to squeeze himself past the door of the stall so he can close himself inside, but Penelope is next to him before he can get himself hidden.

"Come out of there. Let me help."

"It's nothing."

"Ed."

He tries to argue her away, but the words dribble to a stop. He tries to think, but thoughts don't rise. Everything in his mind has gone wide and blank—a swatch of fabric or a long roll of paper, stretching out into oblivion. There is a current rippling below the blank swatch, but nothing defined, lines strung, cast out wide.

— —

He is at the sink when the world refocuses. Penelope is beside him, working at his beard, which is woven with scraps of food. "We'll get your face cleaned up, and then we'll throw a coat on you and take you home, get you in the shower. Wash these clothes." She keeps talking. "Remember when Chip came back from the woods that time? All covered in mud and twigs and leaves. And poor Margaret always wandering down to the river. We had to clean her up all the time."

Ed sees Margaret walking away from the yard. He hollers at her to get back here.

Giggling, furtive glances.

"And Janet—that time she came back with all those bruises and scratches. And I know you remember how Jenny always squirreled food away in her bed, bringing in all the ants and mice." Her fingers are combs in Ed's beard, and something in his brain says, *Laura,* but he can't catch hold of it. "I remember braiding Hester's hair," she

says. "Hester had the thickest hair, and she refused to let anyone cut it. Remember?"

Penelope is washing Ed's hands in the sink now. The fingernails are black at their edges, a little long, the skin sallowed by smoke. He doesn't resist, but he doesn't help. He is in the yard at Boulder, chasing after Mary. He's under a building with a deaf-mute boy. They've been there for days.

"Wait here, all right? I'm going to find you a coat."

Ed nods, his left hand pulling at a piece of clean cloth on his pants.

She is back without Ed knowing she was gone. Ed's gaze casts toward the hand dryer, the half-tiled wall. Penelope slides his arms into the sleeves of an oversize trench coat he doesn't remember as his own. He lets her fasten the buttons over his belly and dirty chest, the coat so long it sweeps the floor, covering the soiled cuffs of his pants and most of his shoes. Penelope pulls the collar up around his ears and takes hold of his hand, leading him out of the bathroom, through the foyer, out into the parking lot. She counterbalances Ed's weight as he falls into the passenger seat of her car, a trust fall, the movement controlled for only so long.

"We going on an adventure?" Ed asks. "You and me and the open road?"

"That's right," she says, but they are in Ed's driveway, and she is helping him inside. His breathing is erratic suddenly, and his stomach is clenching.

"Are you going to be sick again?"

He nods.

Penelope pushes a mound of garbage from a chair in the kitchen and hauls the chair to the toilet, leading Ed behind her. He can't move on his own.

She settles Ed onto the chair and leans him forward. "Just call for me when you're done, okay?"

Through his retching, Ed hears the television turn on, loud voices coming to him through the bathroom door. A male voice like Ed's father. He hears him say, *I worry about that beautiful house. Are you keeping it clean for Benjamin? You still have a son to think about, Edmund.*

You must be strong for him. Your mother and I are too old to take care of you, son. You need to take care of yourself. You are the same man inside. The voice becomes written words. A letter from his father he'd been reading. Pete had given him a stack of them. That was it. Letters.

Another bout hits and he leans forward.

The phone rings. Ed hears his own voice pick up on the answering machine. "You've reached Edmund Malinowski. Sorry I missed you. Leave me a message, and I'll get back to you as soon as I can." The beep lasts too long, the machine full of messages. When did he last listen to them?

"Hey, buddy. It's Pete. Just checking in. Wanted to hear how your doctor appointment went yesterday and remind you to get the oil changed in that old clunker of yours. Oh—and you'll love this—you remember that son of a bitch Taylor Dean? Driving that piece-of-shit Pinto? Well, it finally exploded. Rammed from behind the other day. Dean's fine—minor injuries—but how's that for justice, right? Anyway, give me a call when you can."

Good old Pete. They'll go drinking at the Tavern later. Shoot some pool.

Ed hears sobbing from the television. He is sitting on a chair in front of his toilet, unsure how he got there. Through the door, Penelope's voice asks, "Has it passed?"

What is Penelope doing here?

"I'll be right out!" he shouts. *Penelope is in my house.* He will clean himself up and take her to bed, like he has many times before.

But she has pushed into the bathroom against his objections. She wipes the rim of the toilet and flushes its contents, turns on the fan, starts the water warming for a shower. Then she sets to undressing him, talking through every movement.

"Eager little one, aren't you?" he says.

"Shush." She playfully slaps his hand. "I was always helping with the other patients out in Boulder. I helped the women in my cottage get dressed and undressed, helped them in the shower. I fed them, you remember. This is nothing. Sit down on the chair again, there you go." She removes his shirt and pulls his pants down, his boxers with them. He sits naked on the chair, excited. He has wanted this for so long. Here is Penelope. They are in his office. "And I started that reading group you always spied on. I'm pulling your shoes off now, socks. There go the pants. All right, let's check the water temp. You like it on the hot side or cold?"

"Hot."

"Good. That'll get you cleaner."

Penelope adjusts the faucets and holds out her hand to Ed, helping him stand. He pulls her against him, and she returns his embrace for a moment, then guides him toward the shower.

"Good idea." He winks. "It's more fun in the shower."

She holds on to him as he swings his stiff leg up and over the edge of the tub. She slides the curtain closed behind him. "I'm taking your clothes to the washer. I'll be right back."

"The washer's in the basement." He peeks out. "Then you'll join me, right?"

"Wash your hair, Ed. And your beard."

He laughs and settles in under the spray. Showers feel good. The hot water, the steam. He should take them more often. The water hiccups with the start of the washer, then comes back strong. He hums, then sings. *April, come she will / When streams are ripe and swelled with rain / May, she will stay / Resting in my arms again.*

A female voice joins on June: . . . *she'll change her tune / In restless walks she'll prowl the night.*

They sing July and August and September. *The autumn winds blow chilly and cold.* He has always loved Laura's voice.

Penelope's face peeks around the curtain. Her eyes are wide, a blend of every amber thing. She is honey and grass and autumn, wax, wheat, a burning sun. "I love that song," she says.

"One of my favorites!" Ed bellows, covering his surprise. She was supposed to be Laura.

Her face disappears, and her voice says, "I got a new job."

"Great! A reading group at another institution?"

"Yeah," she says. "That's right, Ed. Another reading group."

"We'll have to make a list of what you'll teach."

"That would be great, Ed." Her face returns. "Want me to wash your back?"

"Does a bear shit in the woods?" His regular self is back, this new self, carefree and jovial. He is April, ripe streams filled with rain. He is June, prowling the night. He is July, flying.

"Feeling better?" Penelope rubs soap on a washcloth, works up a lather.

Ed guffaws. "Absolutely! Standing in a hot shower with a pretty girl scrubbing my back—how could I not feel better?"

Penelope passes the washcloth up over his shoulders and along his neck. She scrubs along his hairline. Then she scrubs lower on his back, and lower still, and Ed can feel the cloth on his ass and then between his legs and her other hand coming around, too, and—the touch of a woman!—his palms go to the walls of the shower to keep his balance, and it is over so quickly, rising in a great torrent of spring, a bellow ripping itself from his mouth.

Her hands vanish.

"Finish rinsing off. Your robe is out here."

"Thank you, Pen." It is all he can say, and he doesn't know what has happened or what is real, but he is thankful, so thankful.

Boulder, Montana

—

NOVEMBER 1981

Chapter 40

— *Laura* —

Pete's voice is tired and defeated when he calls. The tone says, *The race is over, and I have lost*. The words say, "Ed is missing."

"What do you mean?"

"He hasn't returned a call in three days, and I went by his house today. The car's there, but he's not. No one's seen him at Dorothy's or out at the truck stop. The library staff say he hasn't been around for a few weeks." He sighs, an old man. "I'm sorry to get you guys involved, but I don't know what to do."

I am the one to file the missing person report.

"Last known whereabouts?"

"His home," I say, though I'm not sure. "Six-oh-five Third Street."

"You sure he didn't just go for a trip?"

"His car is in the driveway. I already told you that."

I don't think I've raised my voice, but the sheriff on the line says, "Calm down, ma'am." He asks me to describe Ed, and I adjust the figures I once knew, guessing his new weight the best I can. He is still six-two and broad-shouldered and mostly gray-haired. He still has a beard, gray now, and thicker, longer. "He walks with a limp," I say, "on the left side. He might be using a cane."

The man tells me they'll let me know if they find him.

I think of his disappearance those days before Ben was born.

We hang signs around town. "Missing: Edmund Malinowski. Please contact Laura Cooke or Pete Pearson with information."

There is a photo of him that Benjy took with his new camera, Ed's big smile through his thick beard.

— —

We're on day ten. Ed has been missing for ten days.

"Are you worried, Mom?"

"Yes, baby." I have to be honest with our son, this boy who's had to grow up so quickly the past few years. There's a new hesitancy in his face, clouds in his eyes, a great hole in him somewhere that Ed has left. I worry about the responsibility Benjy will face in adulthood when he takes over for Pete as Ed's manager, his father's keeper.

"Where would he have gone?"

"I don't know, Benjy."

Pete and Benjy both reported that he acted strange on their last camping trip, loopy, confused. "I think he threw up a couple times," Benjy said.

Pete scheduled him an appointment with his neurologist, but then Ed disappeared.

"Go watch television," I tell Benjy. "Take your mind off it." *Go forget. Escape.*

He slips downstairs and I listen to his show come back to me, canned laughter and false voices, all pretend. I pour myself a small whiskey and light a cigarette.

It's been a month since the reception—the amount of time Penelope told me she'd still be in Helena. I couldn't help myself from going to the library the other day and asking after her at the information desk.

"Penelope Gatson? She's not with us anymore. Is there something I can help you with?"

I didn't quite believe she would leave.

But she is gone. And Ed is, too.

It makes some kind of cruel sense to me that they've disappeared at the same time. I know they're not together—Ed and his girl—but I can't help imagining them fleeing Helena hand in hand.

I put them in my dream cabin on the Pacific coast, a roaring fire in the woodstove, rain and waves outside. Part of me wishes it true for Ed's sake, and the other part resents them both for everything they've done to allow such thoughts to rise at all.

The doorbell rings as I crush out my cigarette in the soil of a potted plant, and I open the door to the Baker girls, barely girls anymore. They are young women. "No," I say before they can speak. They are the same girls who sold Tim all those Girl Scout cookies back when we were hesitant and flirtatious, back when I was still married to Ed. They're always knocking on our door to offer their dog-walking services or to collect money for their college funds or to sell more cookies or stale chocolates. I deeply dislike the Baker girls.

"We found that missing guy," they say in unison. "We'll take you to him."

"Edmund? You found Edmund?"

"The guy on the posters." The younger Baker girl holds up one of our signs, pointing. "This guy."

I don't want to bring Benjy wherever these awful young women are taking me, to whatever I am about to find. It feels ominous, these weaselly girls the harbingers of disaster. I leave them on the porch for a minute, leash up the dog, and shout to Benjy, "Sweetie, I'm taking Beau for a walk. Be right back."

"Who was at the door?"

"The Baker girls."

"Gross." It's our joke. He hates them, too.

The girls shy away from Beau's eager sniffs and licks—so much for their dog-walking abilities. They stride with triumph out in front of me, leading me through the neighborhood and down the hill to Lockey Park, along the gravel paths, iced along the edges, then out into the brown grass around the fenced-off wading pool. Snow clings in patches, but the sun is shining, the temperature in the forties, an odd warmth. The younger Baker girl points while her big sister speaks. "We saw him yesterday and thought he was just another one of the hobos, but they had a barbecue earlier and we could see his face."

"Then you waited a whole day to tell me?"

"Is there a reward?" the oldest asks.

"Are you kidding?"

They both shrug and stare at me.

The chain-link fence around the pool is rusted at its corners. The "No Trespassing" sign on the gate hangs crooked. The city has chosen to keep the pool closed the past four summers. First they said it was a temporary product of the economy—too expensive, paying all those lifeguards to sit in the shade while kids and their parents sat out the heat in a few feet of water—and then they said it was closed for improvements. The latest story from the neighborhood group is that the whole thing is going to be ripped out and replaced with some newfangled concoction of water worms leapfrogging out of holes and buckets on poles filling and spilling on the heads of kids. Whatever it becomes will be better than the empty pool as it stands, its chipped edges, its faded numbers. The shallow end is six inches deep, and I can still make out the "No Diving" warnings, the pitched black body crossed through with red.

Ed's cane hangs from the top of the fence, about halfway down, and he is in the far end of the pool, curled like a boy under a blue tarp strung across one of the corners. His back is to me, but I recognize his shape and the suit he's wearing. He wore it to the reception, and I wonder if he simply got confused and tried to go to the gallery again.

There are holes in the bottom of his shoes.

He must be freezing.

"Edmund," I say over the chain-link fence. "Ed." Beau whines. He hasn't seen his former master in a while.

"I think he's sleeping," the oldest Baker girl says, and then they walk away, their feet crunching gravel, skating ice. A pool length between us, they stop together and turn in tandem for the oldest one to say, "The lock's broken on the gate. Just push it."

I nod and watch them make their way to the playground on the far side of the park. They both sit on swings they're really too big for, and my hatred toward them dries like the stems of my hollyhocks, tall along the side of the house, hollowed out by cold. It feels dirty to hate them right now.

I tie Beau's leash to the fence and tell him to sit, lie down, stay. He whines again but obeys, his original trainer a behaviorist, after all. Beau always obeys.

The gate catches in some crisp weeds. I enter the pool in the shallow end and slide toward Ed. The pool bottom is slick with wet leaves and mud, some patches of ice.

Crouching by his feet, I lift the tarp and say his name. His head rises as if he's waking from an afternoon nap, just catching a little sleep while he waited for me to arrive. He rolls over. "Laura." He grins a gapped smile. He is missing teeth. "I was just about to call you."

"You're in a wading pool, Ed. How would you have called me?" I want to ask where his teeth have gone, his beautiful smile. It's all I want to know right now—not what he's doing in this pool in his suit, or how long he's had holes in the bottom of his shoes. I want to know where his teeth are.

"Just resting, my love, taking a little break. Things have been busy." He pats my knee. "Did I tell you Pen went home? Her folks finally agreed to take her out of the institution. It's going to be so good for her to be out there in the community."

The grime on his hands is far beyond dirt.

"You've been missing for ten days."

Ed scans his surroundings. "A quick rest, sweetheart. I was just getting up."

He struggles to rise, and I help him shuffle his body out from under the tarp, his left leg a dead thing, unwilling to lend support. We take the rising in stages, utilizing the edge of the pool to prop up his elbow, and then his hips, where we stay for several minutes. I massage the muscles of his leg as the physical therapist showed me back at the hospital in Great Falls. Ed's leg juts out thick and straight, rigid as a pole.

"He's going to seem like his old self sometimes, and then like a complete stranger," I hear his neurologist say. "His memory will come and go. It'll seem like he's retained everything, and then it's going to seem like he's retained nothing. You'll have to be patient. It's going to take some time to figure out who this new Edmund is."

I hear Benjy asking, "My dad's a new person?"

"Yes," the doctor said. "And you'll get to know him all over again."

I rub Ed's calf, and he lets out a little moan of pleasure.

"That feels nice." His voice is low and seductive, a dirty old man's.

I slap his knee. "Don't get any ideas."

He guffaws. Such an endearing scoundrel, a delightful bastard. Even now he is charming.

"You've been missing awhile, Ed. We have the police involved. There are signs up around town." He looks over my head, his eyes on something far away. I notice the sweater under his suit coat, the hat on his head, the scarf around his neck. Someone has been taking care of him, at least. He scratches his beard, the hairs full of food and dirt, bits of leaves and lint. His clothes are filthy, his pants soiled in the front and back from bladder and bowels. He's lost weight. The skin of his face hangs off the bones. "Ed, you've been gone for ten days."

Confusion overtakes him. His eyes blink too rapidly. His hand starts to pull and tug at the fabric of his dirty pants, a regular gesture in this new Ed. I can see his mind working, trying to find a reasonable explanation for his current condition. *There was a dog. There was a robbery, very small. There was a flat tire and a Good Samaritan.* He is searching, and it is devastating to watch. He is a man running down a hall banging on doors, begging for help. But the doors remain closed to him. Locked.

"It's all right. Let's just get you home." I stand and help him to his feet. "That leg okay? Put some weight on it. Good. Is that your cane over there?" I point to the cane and he nods. "Can you stand here while I go get it?" Another nod, and I am suddenly afraid that he has lost all his language, that he will never speak again. What were his last words? I want to remember.

I was just getting up.

I was just about to call you.

That feels nice.

I grab the cane and tuck it into his left hand, the fingers curling around the handle on instinct, a baby's grip on a finger. "That'll help things. There's Beau, you see? Your dog. I'm going to have you sit with him on that bench over there while I run up and get the car, all right?" He nods, mute, and we take tiny steps to the shallow end, shuffling through the leaves and ice, delicate and careful. I talk to fill his expansive silence. "Easy does it. That's right. Here we are at the edge. It's going to be a big step up, okay? Can you brace your cane on the outside here and pull? That's the way. Good work, Ed. Here we are." A string of words, unreeling. I am talking to my boys as they learn to walk, or eat, or tie their shoes. *Just like that, love. Good job*. An endless line of positive reinforcement.

We shuffle to the gate and then out. A man appears while I'm untying Beau. I don't know where he's come from, where he was. He is tall and young, dirty and heavily bearded and oddly tan for this time of year, these short days with so little sun.

"You out of here, Ed?" His smile is wide and full and white.

"Have you been with him?" I ask.

"Sure have." The man gently punches Ed's shoulder. "Hell of a guy."

"What has he been doing?"

"Same thing as any of us—living. Ain't that right, Ed?" Ed smiles. "This your old lady? Penelope?" The man sticks his hand out, and I shake it without thinking. "Sang your praises the whole time he was here." He drops my hand and shakes Ed's. "You come on back anytime."

Penelope.

It is disgusting to be jealous, but I am.

I settle Ed on the bench and call Beau. The dog is reluctant, scared, but I coax him close and set one of Ed's hands on his head. "You remember Beau, right? You got him for me as a puppy." Ed's fingers awaken in Beau's thick fur, the dirty nails scratching deep. They reach for Beau's ears next, and Beau's back leg starts kicking, and Ed laughs again, rich and loud.

"Hah! Habituated response! Can't help yourself, can you, boy?"

He can talk! It is all I can do to keep from wrapping my arms around him in celebration.

"All right, Ed. I'm going to leave you here with Beau for a minute while I go get the car, all right? I walked down."

He smiles his new smile at me. "Take your time, love. It's a beautiful day." He turns back to Beau, scratching harder. "Isn't that right, boy?"

"Why did you tell that man Penelope is your wife?" I ask before I know I'm asking, and I regret it immediately, such a selfish, damning question.

"Love of my life," he says. He lifts his filthy hand from Beau's head and holds it against my face. "You're the love of my life, Laura."

"What about Pen?"

"Sweet girl," he says, patting my cheek. "You've done so well for yourself. I told you it was right to leave Boulder."

He is nodding to an unvoiced question, eyes glazy. I take his hand from my face and set it on Beau's head again. "Right back," I say. "I'll be right back."

I run home, winded and panting when I arrive. I should check in with Benjy, tell him we've found his dad. I should call Tim, who has Charlie with him at the office, call Pete and Bonnie, rally the troops, get everyone here, stage an intervention. *It's time, Ed. This has gone too far.* We probably wouldn't even discuss it. We'd probably just take him to a facility, check him in, sign him over. *Goodbye, Ed.*

I go in the side door of the garage, take my spare keys off the hook, open the garage door, back away. I tell myself Benjy is absorbed in his television show. He won't hear the noise of my return and immediate departure. I will be right back. He is fine.

Ed is exactly where I left him, his eyes lighting when I come into view. "Laura!" he says again. "I was just about to call you!"

"Beat you to it. Come on. I have the car." I untie Beau, then help Ed up, holding on to his right arm at the elbow.

I load Beau into the backseat, where he stabs his nose against the far window, begging for it to open. He loves car rides, his head outside, those long ears flapping. *Give me a minute, boy.*

Getting Ed into the car is as difficult as getting him to stand in the pool, and I can feel the frustration rising in him as we negotiate his simultaneous climb and fall. I have to push his left leg over to make room for his right. The depth of his odor comes clear in the confines of the car, even with the door open, and I breathe through my mouth to subdue it—vomit and shit and piss and a deep, deep rot. He smells like death, the decomposing body of a run-over cat, the disintegrating remains of a mouse in a trap.

He pats his shirt pocket for his smokes and brings out an empty package.

"We can stop at the B and B," I tell him, closing the door, coming to the driver's side. "Anything else you need?"

Ed pulls one of his note sheets from the same pocket, still there after these ten days, after all the dirt and mess. I lean over and read: "Radio transistor, television, speaker wires, lead soldiers." On another square, there's a whole paragraph of words I can't decipher, but Ed is already laughing at them, saying, "I remember this one, so good. Listen to this joke: A man kills a deer and takes it home to cook for dinner. He and his wife decide they won't tell the kids what kind of meat it is but will give them a clue and let them guess. The dad says, 'Well, it's what Mommy calls me sometimes.' The little girl screams to her brother, 'Don't eat it. It's asshole!' " Ed slaps his leg and laughs and laughs, so thrilled.

It's a good joke. I give him a smile, a small chuckle. I reach back to roll down Beau's window, then across Ed to roll down his, and then mine. I can't reach the one in the back on the passenger side. The day is bright and fresh. But Ed's scent remains strong, even with the airflow. I am breathing through my mouth, and he is unaware. I drive us to the B&B, a tiny place that sells malt liquor and cheap beer and cigarettes. They keep some boxed and canned food on the shelves, a few dairy products and cheap loaves of bread. I leave Ed staring up the street, at a boy on a bicycle, a truck passing, country-western music on the radio.

I hurry in and out of the store and light us each a cigarette when I return. Ed rests his head against the seat, tapping his fingers on his leg in time to a song I can't hear. He smiles. "Recite me a poem."

"I don't know any poems, Ed."

"Come on, now, Pen. I know you have a whole pack of them memorized."

I close my eyes, open them, shift into gear. "I'm not Pen."

I pull onto the street, signal left, toward the home I share with Tim. There it is on the right, one of my sons inside, my other son with his father on the other end of a phone call I should make.

I drive right past and point the car toward the highway, unsure of our destination until I hit the double lanes. Wind gusts through the car, whips my hair over my head. In the side mirror, I see Beau's sleek head out the window, tongue lolling, ears fluttering. *My dog, a gift from Ed when I least needed it.* I can't imagine our lives without this animal, curled at the foot of Benjy's bed every night, sitting by the door when he leaves for school.

"Adventure!" Ed shouts. "You and me and the open road."

The gorgeous Montana sky is blue above us, and winter is white on the mountains. We pass Montana City, enter the canyon, twist around curves. I look at the cliffs and trees, the boulders crouching in their grasses, a herd of deer flicking their enormous ears. Ed lights another cigarette and passes it to me, then lights another for himself. I ash outside, the smoke at home in my lungs.

"I always loved this drive," Ed says.

"Me, too."

I see us driving those first few times I taught at the institution, both of us so much younger. I remember the feeling of Benjy in my stomach, still a secret. I hear Ed's voice fill the car, rattling on and on about his patients, his staff, his lack of funding, his asshole of a director. I feel myself fading without his notice.

My hands are solid on the steering wheel now, and Ed is quiet, reflective, his eyes exploring the landscape. His cigarette goes to his mouth, then to the window, then back to his mouth. Habit. Routine.

The sun stretches wide over the Boulder Valley when we crest the hill.

I thought I was taking us to the institution, but I stop instead on Boulder's one main street, cozying up to the curb in front of the Tavern. "How about I buy you a drink?"

"My lucky day!"

I roll the windows up to cracks and tell Beau to stay. "We'll be right back, buddy."

I am banking on a friendly bartender, an old pal, and there he is, bellowing Ed's name the second we walk inside. "Malinowski! It's been too long, my man!"

"Toby," Ed says, and I am amazed that he finds this man's name so readily. He puts his hand on my lower back, proprietary, and shepherds me to the bar. "Meet my bride."

"Ah, the famous Laura. Only good things," Toby promises.

I am Laura again, my Penelope self tucked away.

Ed orders two shots of Jameson, two beers, and I excuse myself to the restroom, drawing level with Toby down the bar. Ed's attention is on the pool table.

"Any chance you have a lost-and-found I could raid?" I ask.

The man laughs, unfazed. I can only imagine all he's seen. "Closet past the women's toilet. Help yourself. He okay?"

"No."

Toby nods. He already knew that.

I find an enormous red tracksuit, white and navy stripes down its legs and arms, inexplicable. I find an XL T-shirt advertising Glacier National Park. A giant mountain goat peers off a rocky cliff below the park's name. Ed will have to make do with his holey shoes and dirty socks. No underwear.

"Come with me," I whisper in his ear when I return. There's beer in his mustache, a third of the pint already gone. He hasn't touched the shot, though; as with that half a Reuben sandwich, he's saving it for me.

"My pleasure," he says.

The Tavern is sparsely populated, only a few people here and there taking in an afternoon of drinking. No one looks at us as we make our way to the men's bathroom. No one cares what might be happening, what circumstances have driven this fine-dressed woman into this bar with this slovenly, crippled man. Who are they to judge?

I lock us inside.

"Whoa, there."

"Nothing like that, Ed. We're just going to clean you up a bit."

Ed looks down, and I see him recognize the state of his dress for the first time. "Oh," he says. "Damn it." I am unwrapping the scarf, removing his suit coat, pulling the sweater over his head. "I was tracking down a patient, my damn orderlies so few and far between and mostly morons, you know." I am helping him balance as he steps out of his filthy pants. "I had to walk through the goddamned mud along the river for miles, hollering for George, that poor boy. You remember George, don't you? He had that chair over his head."

He stands naked before me, and I pull paper towels from the dispenser, wet them in the sink, run them over his body.

"We're still so understaffed," he says.

"I know, love."

I pat him dry with new towels and start to dress him—Glacier shirt over his head, tracksuit jacket, pants pulled up his legs one at a time as he balances against the sink. I slide his dirty shoes back onto his dirty feet, his long and craggy toenails. I wet his hair and flatten it down, straighten out his beard.

"There," I say, turning him to the mirror. "Good as new."

"Hah!"

"Let's go drink."

I stuff Ed's suit and all the other soiled pieces in the garbage. Toby smiles at us as we emerge. A fellow at the bar winks. I imagine his imaginings. A quickie in the men's room between whom—a woman and her husband? A prostitute and her customer?

I raise my shot of whiskey, knock it against Ed's.

"To you," he says.

"And you."

We drink and then chase the burn with beer. The people at the pool table pay their tab and leave, and Ed challenges me to a game. "Remember when we played back in Michigan? You were so good."

I haven't played pool since then. We married so quickly—only six months after we met—and we lived for each other, deeply, furiously embedded. I remember Ed's voice commanding the bar, all his grad-school friends, all the jealous women, everyone enthralled with my husband. *He was mine*—I'd won him, a prize.

Ed lets me break, and I sink the two and six, which I call luck, but then the three and four, too—talent. I forgot that I used to be good at this.

"Give a man a chance!" Ed bellows.

I miss, and Ed takes over. Even with the limp and stitch of his new diminished body, he twists himself into position, pocketing the nine, twelve, and thirteen. A near-miss on the ten.

I order us another round. "What are we playing for?" I eye the cue ball, calculate the necessary angle to set the seven into the far corner. We played for blow jobs in the past, public nudity, pantsless car rides, Sundays without clothes, Chinese food, burgers, a trip to the drive-in, not answering the phone. I lived a whole life with this man.

"The tab," he says. "Loser buys drinks."

He wears lost clothes. He doesn't have a wallet.

"Deal."

The seven hits wide, and I can't get the five in, no matter how hard I try. Ed sinks his stripes, one after another, smooth as he's always been, masterful. He leaves the cue ball perfectly positioned in front of the eight after dropping the fourteen, an effortless finish.

"Damn it," I say, genuinely disappointed. I could've won.

But this version of Edmund Malinowski has no money, and I was destined to lose.

I pay our bar tab, and we walk to the car. Beau stands up in the backseat, his tail thumping, eager to see his people.

I still haven't called home.

"I need to make a quick phone call, all right? Give me just a minute."

Ed is lighting another cigarette. "Take your time," he says again, like he did outside the B&B, calm and content. *I have all the time in the world.*

Toby gladly lets me use the bar phone. "Any friend of Ed's . . ."

I take in the dark woods of the place, the dim light, the neon signs. The phone rings into my ear, and I can feel Ed here on this same stool, his boys around him, Toby serving his whiskeys and beers. I can see why he came all those evenings after all those hard days. There is a comfort here I never could have provided, an acceptance and a tolerance I refused.

"Hello?" Tim's voice is anxious, terrified, and I'm ashamed of myself for hoping he might finally be angry with me.

"It's me."

"Jesus, Laura. Thank God. Do you know how worried we are? Benjy said you took Beau for a walk four hours ago, and then you just disappeared. He called me at the office in tears. You realize his father is gone, right? And now his mother, too? Where the hell are you?"

"I found Ed." I haven't thought past this line.

"Oh, okay. Good. How's—?"

"He's all right. He needed to run some errands."

The signs in the windows buzz. The man down the bar winks again. Maybe he is hoping I take all the men to the restroom with me.

"Errands? What the hell does that mean? Ed goes missing for nearly two weeks and then you take off with the dog, and now you're telling me you've been running errands this whole time? What's wrong with you?"

It's a fair question.

"Tim, he's really sick. There's no way he's going to be able to go back to living on his own. He wanted me to drive him to Boulder, and I couldn't say no, all right?" It is not completely untrue. "We'll be back in an hour."

Tim is quiet, and I know his anger is waning, drifting away. His love for me rolls over it, his kindness. I can feel the shift, a whole town away, all those mountains between us, boulders and water. He cannot stay angry. He cannot begrudge a sick man who is losing his independence. He can't blame me for giving Ed one more afternoon of his choosing.

I will never tell him I chose to take us here.

"I'm sorry I yelled." Too nice, too kind.

"It's all right. Will you call Bonnie and Pete? Let them know Ed's with me. And tell Benjy I'm sorry I scared him."

"Of course, baby. Be careful driving. It's getting dark, and you know those roads ice quick. I love you."

I tell him I love him, too, and I do. It's not the way I loved Ed all those years ago, not the way I love Ed now. It has none of the gutted need, but it is love all the same.

I thank Toby for the use of his phone, look once more around the bar, memorizing the details, writing them down like Ed's words. *This place was Ed's.* He will probably never see it again.

There are stars overhead when I step back outside, the sliver of a waning moon. A breeze rises, cold and ice-edged, reminding us all that winter is settling in, its breath pinking our cheeks, chapping our hands. A streetlight reflects off the windows of the car, and the Tavern's neon sign. I imagine Ed behind the lights, head back, cigarette in his hand, calm and happy and tired. I will take him home. We will put him in the shower and loan him some pajamas and tuck him into the guest bed, and tomorrow we will take him to one of the facilities Pete has recommended.

I'm so sorry, Ed.

Goodbye, my love.

I open the driver's-side door, and the dome light blazes on, brilliant and blinding. It takes too long to register what I'm seeing. There is the seat. There are the cigarettes. There is the lighter. The smells are here, ripe and fetid, but that is all—stains and cigarettes and smells. There is no dog in the backseat, no tail moving, no excited whining.

Ed is gone, and he has taken Beau.

I know I will think about this moment often throughout my life. I will wonder about the impulse that drove me to sit down behind the steering wheel of my car and reach for the cigarettes Ed left behind, the lighter. I will play it over and over, seeing myself from a distance, a woman alone in her car smoking, the red tip of the cigarette rising to the cracked window, the ash dusting away in the breeze. I smoked two cigarettes before I got out and went back inside the Tavern.

"Everything all right, Laura?" Toby was still there, smiling at me.

"He's gone," I said. I can hear the monotone of my voice. It is not mine. It comes from somewhere else, a ghosted place, the halls of Boulder.

I know I followed Toby out into the cold night. I know the man at the bar came, too, no longer winking, another guy from a back table. I know we formed a motley little search party, setting off in different directions. I know I headed toward the institution. I know I was cold. I don't know how long I walked before a truck came up behind me, flashing its headlights. I'd been walking for minutes, hours, days. I'd been walking for years, long enough to grow old, my hair gray, my back hunched, withered spotty hands. I hear the rumble of an engine. I hear a familiar voice, Toby, from the bar. He is saying my name, and my dog is in the bed of his truck. "Laura," Toby says, his voice raw. "We found him."

On the other side of Toby, the bench seat stretches long and empty.

Take your time. I hear them over and over, these last words of Ed's. *Take your time.*

Chapter 41

Ed walks. He doesn't know where he is walking.

He beat Laura at pool. *Hah!*

He needs to see Pen. She is still his girl. He'll see her soon.

But, Laura?

He will read a new book with Pen. He will—the words in his head swim, billowy and loose. Their meaning slips. The words become debris, floating on white. Twisted shapes, driftwood.

Ed blinks in confusion.

He reaches down for his dog, and he feels Beau's soft head under his hand. *Good dog.*

The pain is familiar, but he doesn't recall it, that long-ago day in some long-ago spring fogged out by blood and surgery. It exists in another life, that one from before, when he was a behaviorist deinstitutionalizing the state, some success, some failure, a broken marriage. *Where is Laura? And Ben?*

He pats his leg. *Come, Beau.*

The pain comes for his temple, just as it did before.

He'll take the dog outside. "Come on, Beau." They are not words. He can barely hear Beau's whining.

Night has come, suddenly dropping out of the sky, and now there is ice at his feet, cracking and busting loose, and there is water, a quiet rumbling. Laura is teaching an art class. Pen is reading poems. Ben is a growing boy. They will build a tree house together, with a drawbridge to keep out danger.

His head hurts. There's a churning sound.

It is wet and cold and warm and bright. It is spring, and it is winter. Cold and frozen, but nearly blooming, soon.

His son is a strong boy, and they will fish together with his friend Pete and Pete's own sons. Laura is a painter, his wife. He sees her disappear, a ghost. Little Ben raises the rope ladder to his tree house, barring Ed's entrance. Penelope presses against him. He holds her face in his hands.

Ed stands in every place, all those doors in his head thrown wide open. He stands with Watson and Skinner, Pete and Penelope, Laura and Ben and Beau. They are all risen, resurrected. The Sunlight Man. Gilgamesh. *Let us all be kings.* The pain blazes, whittling, chipping. A beautiful girl touches him in a shower. His wife dresses him in a bathroom. He closes his book, rises from his chair. Water rises to his knees. Black dog, come here. A door. A library. A deck where he'll fall, a river where he'll wade and kneel and lie, eyes on the star-flamed sky, feet in broken shoes, a tug and a whine behind him. The stars blossom overhead. The dog comes, again and again, and Ed curls against his warm back, protected from the cold.

Acknowledgments

The idea for this book was born during a long conversation with my husband on a cross-country road trip from Austin, Texas, to Helena, Montana. It's impossible to number all we've worked through on those long drives, and I am thankful for the time.

As ever, I'm grateful to my parents, John and Debbie Reeves, my aunt Terrie Reeves and my uncle Wil Radding, my grandmother Therese Reeves, and my sister, Anne. Additionally, I'm thankful for the extended family I've found in the Comptons and Swensons. Their love and generosity are deeply embedded in this story.

Though they have very few things in common in the final draft of this novel, my late father-in-law, Mike Muszkiewicz, was the original inspiration for Edmund Malinowski. Mike was a behavioral psychologist, and like Ed, he suffered an aneurysm in the prime of his life, and then a stroke during the subsequent surgery. I never knew Mike before that event, and I often envied the people who did, which—I realize now—was an affront to the man he'd become. That man—the only Mike I knew—was the one to show me the heart of this book, the one to teach me about unbreakable bonds and the lengths we go for love. He also taught me about joy. Give that man a full tank of gas, a pack of smokes, a cup of coffee with his son, and a wide-open Montana day, and he was the happiest man alive. He had the most incredible laugh. He made an amazing pot roast with equally amazing mashed potatoes. I miss him greatly, and I am honored to have known him exactly as I did.

I'm indebted to the fathers of behaviorism, specifically John B. Watson and B. F. Skinner. Watson's *Behaviorism* and Skinner's *About*

Behaviorism were critical texts in the research of this book. I'm immensely grateful to the Montana Historical Society for their digital archives. MHS made it possible for me to read copies of *The Boulder Behaviorist*, decades of the institution's annual reports, and the full description and history of the Boulder River School and Hospital. Though that location becomes fictional in the context of this novel, the historical record proved invaluable to its creation.

My thanks go to my agent, Peter Straus, who remains an unflagging advocate. My editor at Scribner, Daniel Loedel, remained eternally patient with the (seemingly) unending revisions this book required—thank you for sticking with it and me.

I'd like to thank all the incredible friends who continue to support me in this mad pursuit. Special thanks go to Fiona McFarlane, Maggie McCall, Bethany Flint, Melissa Case, Jill Roberts, Loren Graham, Jaclyn and Eric Mann, Kelley and Nate Janes, and Cristina Mauro.

I'm honored to get to work with the incredible students, staff, and faculty of Helena College.

And lastly, as ever, I must thank my family. Margot, you continue to inspire me with your unflinching discipline and staunch loyalty. Those who have earned your love are lucky indeed. Hannah, the breadth of your compassion for others astounds me, and your passion for the things you care about motivates me to follow your lead. Luke—what can I say? This book wouldn't exist without you, and I certainly wouldn't have been able to write (and rewrite and rewrite) it without your continued love and support. Thank you, for everything.